## Sons of Sigurd

*Driven by revenge, redeemed by love*

When Sigurd, King of Maerr on Norway's west coast, was assassinated and his lands stolen, his five sons, Alarr, Rurik, Sandulf, Danr and Brandt, were forced to flee for their lives.

The brothers swore to avenge their father's death, and now the time has come to fulfill their oath. They will endure battles, uncover secrets and find unexpected love in their quest to reclaim their lands and restore their family's honor!

Join the brothers on their quest in

*Stolen by the Viking* by Michelle Willingham
*Falling for Her Viking Captive* by Harper St. George

And the story continues with:

*Conveniently Wed to the Viking* by Michelle Styles
*Redeeming Her Viking Warrior* by Jenni Fletcher
*Tempted by Her Viking Enemy* by Terri Brisbin

Coming soon!

## Author Note

This story is set in what is today known as Ravenglass in the Lake District. Originally a Roman settlement, this area has been known by a handful of names throughout the centuries, including Clanoventa, Glannibanta, Tunnocellum and Cantiventi. I chose to use Glannoventa, because it is the widely accepted Latin name.

I hope you enjoy reading about Annis and Rurik. If you would like to know how the mystery of King Sigurd's betrayal and death is finally solved, please make sure you pick up all five books in the Sons of Sigurd continuity. Find me on Facebook (www.Facebook.com/harperstgeorge) or go to my website to keep up with what I'm working on now (www.harperstgeorge.com). Thank you so much for reading.

# HARPER
# ST. GEORGE

—

## Falling for Her
## Viking Captive

**HARLEQUIN**®
**HISTORICAL**™

Recycling programs
for this product may
not exist in your area.

ISBN-13: 978-1-335-50547-7

Falling for Her Viking Captive

Copyright © 2020 by Harper St. George

This edition published by arrangement with Harlequin Books S.A.

For questions and comments about the quality of this book, please contact us at CustomerService@Harlequin.com.

Harlequin Enterprises ULC
22 Adelaide St. West, 40th Floor
Toronto, Ontario M5H 4E3, Canada
www.Harlequin.com

**Printed in U.S.A.**

**Harper St. George** was raised in rural Alabama and along the tranquil coast of northwest Florida. It was these settings, filled with stories of the old days, that instilled in her a love of history, romance and adventure. In high school she discovered the romance novel, which combined all those elements into one perfect package. She lives in Atlanta, Georgia, with her husband and two young children. Visit her website, harperstgeorge.com.

## Books by Harper St. George

### Harlequin Historical

#### *To Wed a Viking*

*Marrying Her Viking Enemy*
*Longing for Her Forbidden Viking*

#### *Outlaws of the Wild West*

*The Innocent and the Outlaw*
*A Marriage Deal with the Outlaw*
*An Outlaw to Protect Her*

#### *Viking Warriors*

*Enslaved by the Viking*
*One Night with the Viking*
*In Bed with the Viking Warrior*
*The Viking Warrior's Bride*

#### *Sons of Sigurd*

*Falling for Her Viking Captive*

Visit the Author Profile page
at Harlequin.com for more titles.

For Michelle Willingham, Michelle Styles,
Jenni Fletcher and Terri Brisbin.
It was a pleasure creating the characters
in Sons of Sigurd with you.

# Prologue

*The Kingdom of Maerr, Norway*
*AD 874*

They were meant to have arrived at a wedding, but they were greeted by the remnants of a massacre. The smell of smoke had been heavy in the air long before Rurik drew his horse up at the highest point of the rise and stared in disbelief at the valley below. Maerr was in chaos. It was as if a *volva* had spread her dark magic, transforming his home from a place of beauty and celebration to a scene of death and agony in the mere hours since they had left.

His oldest half-brother, Brandt, drew to a stop beside him. 'What madness is this?' he whispered with a stunned reverence that could only be summoned when the horror of a situation eclipsed belief.

The air in the valley was filled with smoke and ash. From this distance, only the sounds of wailing reached them. Bodies lay scattered across the clearing, but Rurik could not tell whether they were living or dead. Weak afternoon sunlight reflected off the blue-grey waters of the fjord, drawing his attention to the stark emptiness. The murderers had fled, leaving his brother Alarr's wedding a bloodbath.

Were his brothers alive? Alarr, Sandulf and Danr had been left behind while Rurik rode north with Brandt to quell a disturbance in a neighbouring village. Had they been left to face their deaths alone or were they among the living?

As his heart resumed its beating, pumping his blood in a fierce rhythm, Rurik roared his outrage and fear as he followed Brandt towards Maerr, their handful of warriors trailing behind them. A rush of anger prickled over his skin and, with no other adversary in sight, it focused on their father. Advisors had warned him against the recklessness of inviting so many warriors, some of them old enemies turned new allies, to the wedding. Having that many strangers about, many of them unknown to their family, invited danger.

King Sigurd had not listened. He had been too caught up in his grand scheme for power to take well-meaning advice from his trusted men. If he could organise co-operation between the diverse group, he could elevate himself from a minor king to someone whose influence would rival that of King Harald Fine-hair himself, or so he had reasoned.

Father was nothing if not ambitious and it might have killed him.

The need to fight coursed through Rurik's blood like a second heartbeat, urging him to take action. He had inherited that impetuous need for action from Sigurd and it was not easily tamed. Gritting his teeth, he urged his horse faster and made it into the clearing at the same time as Brandt. His gaze immediately sought out his brothers among the chaos.

'Where is Ingrid?' Brandt shouted for his wife as their youngest brother Sandulf ran to meet them. The boy who was barely out of adolescence had blood on his clothing, but Rurik could not tell if it was his own or if it belonged to someone else.

Vaulting down from his horse, he made it over to them in time to hear Sandulf whisper, 'Brandt, there's something you must know.' His voice held a slight waver.

Their older brother was not listening. His eyes were wide and on something in the distance. Rurik turned to see several bodies lined up on the ground. His gaze skimmed over them, unwilling to linger on a face, afraid that he might see one precious to him. On the end, a cascade of golden hair spread across the dirt, somehow saved from the dark red blood that marred the wearer's gown and puddled next to her. Rurik did not have to see her face to know that his brother's pregnant wife lay dead. Nausea turned his stomach as Brandt let out a howl of pain so terrifying in its sorrow that Rurik's limbs went cold.

In his mind's eye, he saw Ingrid's smiling face and gentle eyes as she had been mere hours ago. He saw Brandt lean over her, pressing her back to the wall as he grinned and stole a kiss… Their final kiss. Her voice had been high and clear like music as she had called out to them to be safe. No one had thought to repeat the warning back to her. She had been home, surrounded by their father's warriors. She was supposed to have been safe.

Sandulf made to go after Brandt when he went to

her, so Rurik put a hand on his shoulder. 'Leave him.' His voice sounded raw and jagged. He existed in a void where numbness and rage struggled for control.

Sandulf paused and up close Rurik could tell that he had minor wounds. He favoured one shoulder while blood and soot crusted over a gash on his head. Though he was young, Sandulf had seen battle before. Rurik could not help but wonder how his wounds were not worse if he had been involved in this battle. 'What happened?' he asked.

Sandulf was pale and visibly shaken. 'They went into the hall and locked the doors. I tried to…' He swallowed as if the very telling of it was trying. 'Father is dead, Rurik.'

Rurik's gaze jerked back to the line of bodies at the edge of the clearing, searching for their father. If Sigurd was dead, then Rurik had no chance of ever reconciling with him. The man had never been easy and Rurik had always felt at odds with him, but never had he thought there would not be enough time. The bulk of a man lying at the other end, opposite Ingrid, drew his gaze. There was a familiarity in the breadth of the man's shoulders. Pain swelled in Rurik's chest, drawing his lungs tight as it forced its way up through the numbness.

Sandulf grabbed his arm in a near-desperate grip. 'I tried to stop this. I marked one of them.'

*Rurik* should have been here, but instead he had been sent north. He should have stopped this. Instead, Ingrid's life had been entrusted to this boy. It was unfair, but Rurik could not stop the words that tore out of him. 'Only marked? Were you not able to kill one of them?'

He left before Sandulf could answer him. Rurik needed to find his twin Danr, and Alarr. They were the only real family he had left. The only ones who mattered to him. He found Alarr lying in his own blood.

Rurik hurried to his side and knelt beside him. 'Where are you wounded, Brother?'

'Gilla.' Alarr's voice was a harsh rasp as if his throat was raw from yelling for his bride. He seemed only half-aware of what was going on around them, his eyes unfocused and wary. Someone had already tied cloths around both of Alarr's calves to stem the flow of blood from his wounds. There was so much of it, Rurik could only guess if his brother would ever walk again.

'Who did this to you? Tell me and I swear to you that I will hunt the coward and cut him down.' He did not know if Gilla was alive or dead, but the fact that he had not seen her among the living did not bode well for her.

'Feann,' Alarr whispered. 'Feann and his men.' He closed his eyes as Hilda, Alarr's mother, brought a cool cloth to his face. She deftly ignored Rurik, much as she had for all his life, unwilling to acknowledge the living proof of her husband's unfaithfulness.

It was no surprise the Irish King had turned on them. Rurik had been suspicious of the man's cunning eyes and arrogant smiles from the start. Feann would be taken care of. 'I will find him. I promise you.'

But now he had to find out if Danr lived. Rurik was close to all his brothers, but Danr was his twin. The only full-blooded brother he had. The only connection left to his mother. If Danr had died… He forced himself to swallow the ache in his throat and stared at Hilda.

Her hands were eerily calm in the face of what had happened. That had always been her way. She faced all that Sigurd and life had thrown at her with a calm efficiency that might have brooked respect in Rurik if she had bothered to offer him a tiny scrap of the affection she held for her own children. Hilda had never liked him and Danr, for they represented a time when she had lost Sigurd's affection to the twins' mother.

'Have you seen Danr?' he forced himself to ask Hilda. 'Does he live?'

Her shoulders tightened and she did not look at him, but she did answer. 'I do not know.'

His breath rushed out in frustration as he raised his gaze to the devastation. The living rushed around them, hurrying to put out errant flames and to tend the wounded. He wanted to scream out the rage and sorrow building within him. Danr had to be alive. He wouldn't allow himself to believe otherwise. Finally, his gaze dropped to a lone man standing near the line of fallen bodies, near the bulk of the warrior he knew was their father.

'He's dead,' Danr whispered when Rurik hurried up to him.

Rurik drew his brother into an embrace and thanked the gods he was alive. 'Are you injured?' He could see no wound, but Danr was covered with soot as if he had been helping with the fires.

Danr shook his head and faced him. His eyes were stricken and filled with pain. Though they were similar in build, his twin's hair was blond instead of dark like Rurik's. In many ways Danr was light to Rurik's dark. He was often quick with a jest when the moment called for levity, while Rurik would rather brood in his thoughts. Nevertheless, the bond between them was unbreakable.

'I wasn't here,' Danr said with disgust in his voice.

'Why? Where were you?'

'I… I meant to come later.' He took in a long wavering breath. 'There was a woman.'

Rurik turned as a sharp ache seized his throat. There was always a woman when it came to Danr.

'Alarr says it was King Feann,' Rurik said.

'There were others. I do not know who they were, but the whole place burst open with violence,' said Danr.

Rurik finally allowed his gaze to come to rest on the bodies at their feet. Their father, Alarr's bride and her parents, with Ingrid on the end. So much senseless death. He might have understood their father's murder, but why the others? Why did Ingrid and her unborn child have to die? He stared down at the face of Sigurd, his father. He looked strangely peaceful, yet no less severe for the fact that death had claimed him. His arms were crossed over his chest and his formidable brow was as intimidating as ever.

A swell of tenderness and fury for the man rose in his chest. As a bastard, Rurik had always felt as if a void existed between him and his father. The man had claimed him and Danr, but there had lingered a resentment in Rurik that his own mother had never belonged here. She had been treated as little better than a slave. Now that void would always be there.

His gaze sought the fjord, now empty of ships except the burned-out hulls that had been left behind.

Sandulf and Alarr had been the only ones here to face those murderers. With Rurik and Brandt sent north and Danr off with a woman, the attack could not have been planned any better. It was almost as if someone had known they would be caught unawares.

'No one regrets that I wasn't here more than I,' Danr said into the silence.

There was a solemnity in his eyes that Rurik had never seen there before. This day had likely changed them all in ways they could not yet determine. In that moment, the rage burst through, overshadowing the sadness and pain.

How dare anyone come here and destroy them? His gaze moved from Sigurd to Alarr's bride. She should be preparing to dance on her wedding night. Then he looked at Ingrid. She should have been a mother in only a few weeks. Brandt should be looking forward to welcoming his child into the world. Whatever Sigurd had done to deserve his death, these innocents should not have suffered his fate.

Revenge became more important than his own life. It was the only tangible way to deal with the well of anger opening up inside him.

'We will find who did this,' he said to Danr. 'All of them.'

# *Chapter One*

Glannoventa, Northumbria
Two years later

Sins of the past were never forgotten. Father Cuthbert had spent the greater part of Annis's early childhood trying to make her understand that. To her eternal shame, Annis of Glannoventa had never paid the old man much attention. He had lectured and made her stand primly against the wall of the abbey to listen. Her legs had gone stiff and her back had ached, but none of his efforts had made her truly understand. She had happily continued to wreak havoc on his sense of order and decorum at each lecture's conclusion.

It was not until this very night, standing in the shadows of a seedy tavern near the sea, that Annis finally appreciated the sentiment. With a dagger she was prepared to use sitting heavy in the belt at her waist, she wasn't in any position to ask for divine guidance. Nevertheless, Annis sent up a prayer as she checked one last time to make certain the blade was hidden in the folds of her cloak. The cool metal greeted her hand, the filigree work on the hilt threatening to cut into the soft flesh of her palm if she squeezed it too hard. Though it was a beautiful piece of craftsmanship, it was meant for protection. It had proven its worth many times over, most recently two years past.

She closed her eyes against the memory of that long-ago day in Maerr. There had been more blood than she had ever seen in her life. So much blood that the smell had haunted her for months and she had locked the dagger away in the armoury, never to be seen again.

Until tonight.

Tonight, she had taken it out in the hope she would not be forced to use it. If only her target would cooperate. The Norseman stood ten paces across the tavern from her. A tankard of ale sat before him on the table as he looked out across the crowded room. The fur cloak fastened at his shoulders was thrown back, intentionally revealing a malicious-looking pair of blades at his hips. She had no doubt that a longer blade would be found strapped to his back. They were harsh reminders of her fate should she fail.

The tavern was filled to overflowing with men from the ship that had arrived earlier. The same ship that had brought the Norseman to their shore. She was forced to brush against a few as she went past. This garnered her looks, because she clearly was not a serving girl. Biting the inside of her lip to keep her nerves at bay, she kept her eyes on the man.

His profile was strong, showing a straight nose and moderately square jaw. He was broad shouldered with dark hair that shimmered gold where the firelight touched it. Up close, he was larger than she had originally believed him to be. It wasn't a burly strength as much as one forged in battle, with lean muscle and solid brawn, which made it all the more dangerous. This was a man who knew how to fight.

She was a few steps away from him when she caught his eye and he turned his head to look at her, stopping her on the spot. His eyes were blue with a quiet intensity that seemed to see her for what she was: a wolf in sheep's clothing. A deep groove formed between his brows in a way that made her think he did not smile very often. Thank goodness there was no cruelty lurking in his features, only a solemnity that said he was not one to suffer fools. She might have liked him for it had she not been there to imprison him.

His rugged handsomeness made it easier than she had expected to give him a smile she hoped was sensual and inviting, her ruse to get close to him. Fighting to control the trembling in her hands, Annis pushed her hood back far enough that he could clearly see her features while hoping to keep the rest of her hidden from the crowd. There was always the chance that someone would recognise the auburn of her hair.

'Good evening,' she said, and pushed her way to his side, her hip brushing his as she rested an elbow on the time-worn wood of the high table. The Norseman shifted backwards, but not far enough to put any real space between them.

His movement made his scent waft over to her and she was surprised at how appealing she found it. It was a combination of clean male sweat laced with woodsmoke and an undercurrent she couldn't quite name. Soap of some kind, she would guess. A quick glance confirmed that the short hairs at the nape of his neck curled with dampness from a recent bath. Catching his eye again, she gave him a small smile and tried to think of something witty to say.

Now that she was here and this was happening, she found herself faltering. He was staring at her profile and she could *feel* his gaze on her. It was like standing before a serpent and waiting to see if it would strike. Her breath threatened to lodge in her throat, but she pushed it out and took another one in. All the while she reminded herself that the Norseman did not know that she was his enemy. She could not appear meek or he would never follow her outside.

With that in mind, she forced her hand to move to his forearm as she leaned closer to him to be heard over the din of the conversations going on around them. The solid strength under her palm caused a flicker of unease in her belly.

'The road was quite dusty and I am parched. I would be ever so grateful for an ale.' She grimaced internally at the words. They came across as needy. He would never follow that sort of woman outside.

His frown didn't ease, but he raised a hand and signalled to the barmaid. The girl had been awaiting the signal, perhaps a bit too obviously for Annis's comfort, and hurried over to place a tankard down with a murmured reply. Annis drew a coin from her drawstring purse, but the Norseman was faster and tossed a coin on to the counter.

'Thank you.' She smiled up at him as she wrapped a hand around the tankard, letting her gaze linger on his eyes before dropping to his lips in a rehearsed move. She was surprised to find them well formed and lush, neither too thick nor too thin for her liking.

They made a perfect bow. Strange how she had never noticed male lips before. Had Grim's mouth been thin or wide? She was ashamed that she didn't know. Certainly, a few years should not be enough to make her forget her own husband?

'I have a seat for you if you want it,' said one particularly crude man from a nearby table as he gestured to his lap. The salt encrusting his patchy beard and thinning hair marked him as a sailor, but his wiry frame had her wondering how the first strong gale did not send him hurtling into the sea.

'You are too kind, but I prefer my seats to have more brawn.' She turned her back on the table as the men broke out into a roar of inebriated laughter.

The Norseman's lips twitched as he brought his ale up for a drink. She found herself relaxing the tiniest bit at his approval. Giving him an amused look, she said, 'You can understand why I chose a place at your side.' To be fair, at his side was the only place she could have gone had she truly been a traveller passing through. He gave off such a feeling of danger that the crowd naturally gave him a wider berth, leaving the space next to him free.

'Are you travelling alone?' he asked. His voice was pleasantly low and smooth for someone who was supposed to be her enemy.

She pretended to take a drink of her ale, letting a little of the bitterness touch her tongue. The ale had been laced with poppy and valerian, as had his ale which he had nearly finished. Her plan had been to press him to drink hers after he had finished his own. To her chagrin, he didn't seem to be particularly affected by the combination of herbs, yet.

'If you mean to ask if I am with a man, I am a widow.' She had decided she would do better with lying if she could stay as close to the truth as possible. 'I do have servants with me.'

He glanced at the door, then back at her. 'Perhaps you should have sent one in here in your stead.'

Her natural indignation made her bristle. 'I can take care of myself.'

It was the wrong thing to say. She had come in here expecting to play a ruse, to pretend to be a seductress to lure him outside into an assignation. Barring that, she would play the helpless widow in need of his help. Antagonising him would not get her far. She smiled at him to soften the words.

'That is obvious.' He glanced over his shoulder at the man she had offended. The sailor had made a move to rise, but one of his friends had pulled him back into his seat. Whether he meant to come over and make her sorry for embarrassing him in front of his friends, or if he was simply attempting to totter off into the night, she did not know.

Turning his attention back to her, the Norseman asked, 'Do you often travel alone, taking care of yourself?'

'You ask many questions for a man whose name I do not know. Do you travel alone?'

His gaze touched her face, stroking over her brow and then down to her mouth before settling on her eyes again. It was reminiscent of the seductive way she had looked at him just moments before and it made something exciting flicker to life in her belly.

'Sometimes,' he said and it was a moment more before she realised he was answering her question.

How was she so terrible at this? Before she could gather her thoughts, he threw back the last of his ale and said, 'Be careful who you allow to purchase your ale. He might expect some sort of repayment.' The tankard echoed with a hollow thump when he set it down.

She tensed, certain that he was about to walk away and she would miss her opportunity. They had failed in their attempt to find out where he had secured lodgings. It was entirely possible he would go upstairs or bed down in the common room and she would not get him alone. Her mind swirling with the possibility of failure, she placed her hand on his arm again. 'Were my answers repayment enough or were you expecting more?'

Annis had never played the seductress in her life, not even with her husband, but she had to do it. Her thumb stroked against the inside of his wrist. She allowed her gaze to trace lazily across his features, as if she were anticipating him asking for more.

Leaning down to be closer to her, the Norseman spoke and his breath brushed across her cheek. 'Finish your ale, woman, before you take on more than you can handle.'

'You never answered my question.' When he raised a brow, she asked again. 'Are you alone?' It was a valid question. She needed to know if anyone would miss him. Cedric and his men hadn't yet been able to figure out if he was travelling with companions.

'Am I with a woman?' He tossed her response back at her with a teasing gleam in his eyes. 'There is no woman.'

'Not even at home?'

The glimmer of dark humour flickered out. 'I have no home.'

'Then you've come to Glannoventa to stay?'

He shook his head and glanced to the table where the men's voices had grown louder. 'Passing through.'

Before she could respond to that, someone dragged the hood down off her head. She turned to face a man she did not recognise. He was likely a fisherman. The stench of fish rose off him and a few scales clung to his shirt sleeve. Instead of letting her go, he twisted the fabric of the hood in his fist. Her palm itched to grab the dagger at her hip, but she didn't want to reveal its presence.

Towering over her while giving her a lascivious grin, he asked, 'You alone, wench?'

'Release my cloak.' Her words came out with the full authority she had accumulated over her years as the Lady of Mulcasterhas.

Both the fisherman and the Norseman paused in obvious shock. Her assailant recovered quickly and gave her a crude grin as he realised she must be alone since no one had stood up to challenge him. He opened his mouth to speak, but that was as far as he got before the Norseman stepped forward and grabbed him by his throat. A choking sound was the only thing she heard. She gasped at how quickly the Norseman had moved and she jumped back, dropping her ale on to the straw-covered floor.

Across the room, Alder, her most trusted warrior, stood, but she quickly shook her head to warn him away. The Norseman had things under control. The fisherman had released her and was now grabbing the Norseman's arm with both hands to loosen his grip.

The tips of his toes worked for purchase on the floor, but it was clearly a fight he was losing.

'Leave here.' The Norseman spoke with a calmness that belied the fact that he was in the process of strangling a man.

The man gave a jerky nod as well as he was able and found himself immediately released. He sank to the floor, gasping for breath, before finding his feet and disappearing through the crowd.

'We need to go, too.' The Norseman's gaze took in the room, as if expecting the man's friends to make themselves known.

She nodded and stepped over her fallen tankard as he took her arm to lead her outside. This was not how she had planned to get him to leave with her, but she would not argue if it got him out the door.

'Where are you staying the night?' he asked once they were outside. The tavern's door closed behind them with a hearty thud, muffling the voices inside. He showed no intention of releasing her and she didn't care. This was playing right into her plans of getting him alone.

The cold air caressing her face was a welcome change from the almost stifling heat inside. Her breath made a cloud of mist as she said, 'I am not certain I should tell you.'

Tilting his head down, he asked, 'Do you think I would save you inside the tavern only to ravish you now?'

'Perhaps you simply do not like to share.' Despite her words, she started walking down the cobblestone path that led through the village and past the docks and shops. A few of her men were waiting there where it was darker and no one could see them overtake him. A twinge of guilt pulled at the edge of her mind. It didn't help that she was starting to like him a little.

'Besides,' she added with a smirk when he fell into step beside her, 'you did not save me. I told you I was perfectly capable of handling myself.'

'Yes, I heard your strongly worded request. It was terrifying.'

Despite herself, she laughed out loud at his dry tone. He spoke as if he was in on their game and more than happy to spar with her. 'It was an order and a warning. Had he not listened, I would have followed up with a well-placed knee to his groin.'

'He would have blocked you,' he said as his gaze moved from one shadow to the next, alert to the possibility of an attacker. This man was a seasoned warrior and she would do well to not underestimate him.

To keep him talking and hopefully distract him from the fact that Alder almost certainly followed them, she asked, 'Why do you think so?'

His hand tightened gently on her arm, careful not to hurt her, and he gestured to her clothing with his other one. 'The wool of your skirts. They're too heavy. He would have likely brought his own knee up faster than yours and, on the chance he could not due to his inebriated state, the blow would have been far less effective than you intended.'

Annis had lived in the household of her father-in-law since the age of eight. Having no surviving daughters of his own and a wife who had died soon after Annis's arrival, Wilfrid had been at a loss as to how to raise a girl. But he was not a man given to defeat or neglect, so he had more or less raised her as one of his own sons. She had been allowed lessons in combat which had included blade skills and fighting. She had grown up confident in her ability to protect herself. Perhaps too confident, because she had never once considered that her heavier winter wool might be a hindrance.

'I really do not think—' Her words broke off as he grabbed her about the waist and whirled. She ended up with her back against the plaster wall of a shop that had long been closed for the night with him towering over her.

'Try it.' One corner of his mouth tilted in a dare.

She was suddenly very glad for the full moon above him. Though there was some cloud cover, the light that did break through was enough to allow her to see him. Her stomach gave a little flip of excitement at the way he looked at her. His gaze was hot and alive with excitement. Whether it was from his game or his interest in her, she didn't know. 'I cannot.'

'Do it.'

'I could hurt you.'

He gave a quick shake of his head and said with an infuriating grin, 'You could never hurt me.'

It was a taunt, plain and simple, said to spur her into action. Part of her despised how easily she rose to the bait, while the other part of her simply wanted to prove him wrong. That turned out to be the stronger part, because she reared back and brought her knee up. He blocked her and twisted her so that her back was against his front, her hands pressed against the wall.

'Do you see?' he said against her ear.

A pleasant shiver ran down her neck. 'I see.' She gave a jerky nod as much to dislodge the unfamiliar feeling as to acknowledge him.

'You would do much better to use your weapon straight away in situations like those.'

'What if I don't carry a weapon?'

She swallowed a gasp when his hand moved over her hip and to her waist. 'But you do,' he said, his fingers touching the hilt of the dagger.

Despite her misstep tonight, she was still confident that she could have levelled that man had she been pressed to do so. Instead of saying that, she turned in his arms to face him. A little surprised when he didn't immediately release her, her words came out slightly breathlessly. 'Why do you care?'

He stared down at her. 'I don't.'

She smiled as he was obviously lying. 'I think you do.'

Her smile faded when his gaze slipped down to her mouth. The air between them changed immediately, as if even it was aware of what was happening between them and had slowed down to take notice, thickening and pressing in close. His grip had somehow softened at her waist even though he still held her quite firmly. And while his eyes were alert, there was a slumberous quality about them now as if he were thinking of what it would be like to kiss her.

Her lips parted as his head tilted the tiniest bit. Somewhere in the back of her mind she was aware of the echo of boots on cobblestone, but it hardly signified. Her mind went dim as he leaned closer, easily consuming her attention, unexpectedly wanting his kiss more than she had wanted anything in a very long time. Except at that moment, the clatter of swords and boots became too loud to ignore.

The Norseman whirled, keeping her at his back to face the men. A small part of her sighed in relief when she saw Alder and his men spread out before them in a half circle. A larger part of her bemoaned the fact that they had come at precisely the wrong time. A moment sooner and that almost kiss would not have happened. A moment later and she would at least know the pressure of his lips on hers.

'Draw your dagger,' the Norseman commanded without looking back at her. The whisper of his own twin blades being pulled from their leather sheaths accompanied his words.

She drew it slowly, as guilt once more made itself known. He didn't know. He was bent on protecting her still, not even realising that she was about to betray him.

'These men are not friends of that man at the tavern,' she said.

He turned his head partially towards her while keeping them in his sight. 'Thieves, then?'

She slipped away before he could react, moving towards the group. 'Not thieves,' she said, turning to face him.

He understood then. For one moment before the fury took over, the hurt of betrayal flashed in his eyes.

Alder took advantage of his distraction and cracked him across the back of his skull with the hilt of his blade. The Norseman crumbled to a heap on the stones.

Despite the fact that she told herself she did this to protect them all from him, watching him fall very nearly broke her heart.

## Chapter Two

Rurik opened his eyes to blackness. The complete absence of light was like waking up in the dark, rank depths of the earth. He blinked, wondering briefly if he had gone blind, but it did not help. The air was heavy and still, the silence so complete that it gave rise to a roaring in his ears. Had he died and been condemned to this fate of nothing? The idea brought with it a swell of panic that tightened his lungs and made the air too heavy to breathe.

He tightened his fists and the tips of his short fingernails bit into the heel of his hand, the pain bringing back rational thought. No, he was not dead. Captured, but not dead. He had awakened several times in the back of a wagon, but had almost immediately fallen back into unconsciousness. Anger at the turn of events threatened to overtake him, but he managed to keep a hold on it. Fear and rash impulses would not help him. His father's blood ran strong in his veins and it often urged him to act on his fury. He'd had years to practise keeping it contained and he would continue to control it in death if need be.

Taking several deep breaths, he dared not move until he knew exactly what he was up against. Subtle shapes and shadows incrementally revealed themselves to him as he lay still. The sweet scent of fresh straw met his nose while he became aware of a few pieces poking him in his back. The pleasing smell could not, however, cover up the rank and stagnant air of the mysterious place. There was no way to be certain of how long he had lain there, but already a chill had settled deep into his bones. Now that the panic and roaring had subsided somewhat, he could hear that there was a constant dripping of water in the near distance. He must be underground.

Had the Saxons buried him alive in the depths of a crypt?

As his eyes slowly adjusted to the near absence of light, the craggy nooks and jagged points of the stone wall at his side came into focus and he knew that he was right. This was not one of the wattle-and-daub buildings he had seen in the village. He was underground.

He sat up and lifted a hand to the pounding at the back of his head. The clanging of the chain registered almost as quickly as the weight of the cuff pulling at his wrist. Letting out a low curse that seemed overly loud in the deathly silence of the chamber, he switched to his other hand. The place where he had been struck on his head was tender, but thank the gods his fingers did not come back sticky with blood. There was no open wound to contend with.

Reasonably certain that he would live, though for how long he had no idea, Rurik rose. His bare feet encountered the cold floor as a wave of dizziness overcame him, so he put a hand out to the slimy wall to keep himself upright. His stomach churned and his mouth tasted bitter. In the moments before he had been attacked, he had felt off balance and nearly giddy. Some part of him had worried that those reactions had been because of the woman. Now he understood that he had been poisoned. The sweet and bitter taste of the ale had included an elixir meant to unsettle him.

It had made him lower his guard so well that he had nearly kissed the wench against the wall where anyone could have overtaken him—and had. It was a relief to know that it wasn't she who had made him forget himself, but the potion. The knowledge still rankled, but it was better than the alternative. Rurik was not Danr, who had a habit of forgetting himself where women were concerned.

There came a scraping sound, like iron being dragged over stone, followed by the brisk scrape of a boot. He immediately reached for his knife, habit overcoming the knowledge that it had been taken from him. He cursed inwardly at its absence. The bone-handled knife had been handed down to him from his mother, the only remnant of his Irish heritage he had. Drawing himself up, Rurik waited for his jailer to approach, even his toes tensed in anticipation against the cold floor. Though the large clasps holding his fur to his tunic at the shoulders were missing, his fur had been left for him. He soundlessly dropped it to the ground, wanting his arms and hands free should he need to defend himself.

The flickering glow from an oil lamp revealed the vertical bars keeping him inside moments before the woman appeared. He recognised the wench from the tavern immediately. She wore the same violet cloak as before, only the hood was pushed down so it lay on her back. The tavern's light had been dim at best, revealing what he had thought to be highlights of russet in her hair, but with the full light of the lamp upon it, he could see that she was auburn haired. The tresses were nearly as bright as the flame.

The moments before he had been hit were a blur and he hadn't been certain if the memory of her walking to join the men had been a true one. He had a particular dislike of liars. He had been surrounded by liars his entire life. His own father was one of the best he had ever known, never telling his twin sons the truth of their birthright, that King Feann was indeed their uncle. He'd had to learn that bit of information from King Feann himself after confronting him about the massacre. In the years since the wedding, Rurik had added betrayers to his list of dislikes. To arrive as a friend only to wreak destruction was a cowardly act.

This woman was both a liar and a betrayer. She had pretended to be a seductress to lure him outside all while she had been plotting his destruction. She had known his attackers. She had moved to join their ranks just before their leader had delivered the blow that had sent him hurtling into darkness.

'I am glad to see you awake,' the woman said, with no hint of her earlier friendliness.

'You might have ordered your men not to bash my head if you wanted me awake.' His voice was low and hardly able to contain his anger. She gave a slight wince at his words, but it might just as easily have been an effect of the flickering light.

'It was necessary to get you here,' she said.

A quick survey revealed that he was surrounded by stones on three sides. The width was barely enough to allow him to lie down. The iron bars made up the fourth side and they were placed close together so he had no hope of ever squeezing through them. The ceiling was so low that had he been any taller he would have had to stoop to stand upright. It was a cage for an animal and he was the animal trapped inside.

'How long have I been here?' Low-burning fury gave his voice a smoky rasp that fairly trembled with his effort to keep it under control.

'Not very long. It's not yet morning.' Her voice was strong as her gaze held his. She seemed unaffected by the anger in his.

He hoped the fact that he was nearly recovered meant his head injury was not severe. 'You would do well to let me go.'

'If you answer my questions truthfully, then perhaps I will have no reason to keep you.'

He stalked closer to the bars, hoping to intimidate her by his larger size. 'You don't think I've come alone, do you? My men will know that you have taken me. They will come for me.'

It was not even remotely true. His misguided pride had sent him out on this quest alone and now he was paying the price for such a brash decision. King Feann had offered to send men with him in an effort to assuage his own guilt for his part in the massacre. Rurik had not been prepared to accept his help. The sting of Sigurd's impulsiveness running in his blood had never been felt as strongly as it did now.

She shrugged, appearing unconcerned. 'Your men are not a problem.'

Changing tactics, he asked, 'Where am I?'

'Mulcasterhas.' Giving him a little smile, she added, 'Isn't that where you wanted to be? I'm told you were asking many questions about my home.'

Mulcasterhas was the home of Wilfrid, the Lord of Glannoventa. Rurik and Alarr had spent the past months in Éireann, getting close to King Feann of Killcobar to question him about leading the attack on their family. While the King had admitted his part—that he had gone to Maerr to avenge his sister who had been taken years ago by Sigurd—he had not been the one to deliver the death blow to their father. His confession had revealed that this man named Wilfrid had been involved. Alarr had stayed behind in Éireann with his new wife, Feann's foster daughter, while Rurik had come alone to seek vengeance against Wilfrid, a man he did not know but already despised immensely.

'You are Annis.' Since arriving earlier that day, he had learned from the villagers that Wilfrid's only son had long been dead, but that he had a daughter.

'*Lady* Annis.'

It might have been unintentional, but her chin moved up a notch and her eyes flashed with indignation. Her eyes were dark and striking against her pale skin. With finely arched cheekbones and a delicate chin, she was as lovely as he had thought her to be at the tavern, but now she seemed to have a thread of iron running through her, where before she had been more yielding. A ruse, no doubt, to lure him in for her scheme. She was anything but yielding.

Anger simmered to the surface at the look she gave him. How dare she appear so arrogant when her own father had likely been the one to kill his father? 'I have no trouble with you, *Lady* Annis. My trouble is with your father. Send him to me!' It was impossible to keep his voice from rising on that last demand.

'Wilfrid is my father-in-law and I will not simply turn him over to you. You are a prisoner and are in no position to make demands, Norseman.' Her voice cracked like a whip through the heavy air.

The chain bound to his right arm stopped him from reaching the bars, but if he angled his body just right he could reach them with his left. So that was what he did. His fist curved around the cold bar and he pulled himself as close to her as he could get. To her credit, she didn't back away. Whether she had done this standoff a number of times with other prisoners, or if she simply knew he had no hope of reaching her no matter how hard he tried, he didn't know. But his grudging respect for her moved up a notch. There were many men who had crumpled beneath the withering heat of his anger. It was the one trick he had learned from his father that he found useful.

'Any man who would send a woman to fight his battles for him is no man at all. I demand to see Wilfrid. Send him to me or kill me now, because I will not resort to using a woman as my messenger.'

If it was possible, the fire in her eyes turned into a full blaze. 'Then you are free to rot down here as long as it takes for you to lower yourself to speak to a woman. There is a bucket of water and a bucket for your necessaries. Enjoy the rest of your day.'

To his utter astonishment, she set the lamp down on the ground and left, her footsteps echoing down the walkway. He counted ten footfalls before she made her way up the steps leading out of the cellar. There were twelve of those. The door scraped across the stone step as it clanged shut behind her.

Letting out a curse, he banged the heel of his hand against the bars until pain vibrated up his arm. His gaze fell on to the buckets she had mentioned that he had not noticed before. Indeed, one was filled with water and the other was empty. Gingerly picking up the one with water, he moved it across the cell and sat down on the straw to take a long drink and cure his parched throat. It tasted of oak, but was otherwise clean.

The only good thing to come of the exchange was that he was fairly certain Wilfrid was here. His initial questions for the villagers in Glannoventa had produced troubling answers. It seemed that no one had seen Wilfrid for quite some time. One shopkeeper had told him that he was off travelling and spent most of his time in the company of the Northumbrian King. Another had told him that Wilfrid was visiting the Dane, Jarl Eirik, in the east. A fisherman's wife had overheard and laughed, saying that he was chasing a ghost. Wilfrid had not been seen since early summer. There were rumours that he had died. It seemed that no one knew the whereabouts of their lord.

At least now Rurik knew he was close. Annis had not said he was not here, only that Rurik should send his message through her. But then, she had not said Wilfrid was here either. Rurik had allowed his anger to take control, knowing that anger would not serve him well in this. Perhaps he had used the wrong tactic to deal with her. She was obviously proud and given to righteous indignation. It would have been better to attempt to charm her and remind her of how easy things had been between them earlier in the tavern than to attack her with his words.

The problem was that he did not know how to go about it. He had never worried about charming a woman. The women in his past had made it known that they were interested in a quick tumble and he had obliged them. He had no immediate interest in marriage so he had never had the need to speak pretty words. He cursed again and fell back on his straw bed. If only Danr were here, he would have already found a way to charm her into the cell.

The scrape of the door above the steps woke him. Rurik sat up, surprised to find he had slept. The herbs must have lingered in his blood, luring him to sleep as he had lain on his bed of straw wondering how to proceed. He felt much better this morning. There was still an ache in his head, but it no longer throbbed. Whatever had been put into his ale had passed so he felt like himself again. The steady scrape of boots on stone told him Annis returned even before the light from the oil lamp lit up her hair.

She stood before him in a finely made gown of blue wool, embroidered with amber-coloured thread at the sleeves. A cloak in a deeper shade of blue clung to her shoulders, this one without a hood. She looked every bit the Lady of Glannoventa and he wondered how he could ever have mistaken her for a common wench at the tavern. It wasn't simply her clothing or the way she held herself that made her appear noble. There was something in her face, her eyes as she gave him a cool, superior look, that placed her in that class.

Something akin to attraction swirled in his belly. Akin, because had it been mere attraction, he could have identified it as such. Last night he would have called it something as base as desire. This was more. It was admiration and awe mixed with temptation. The effect was staggering. He could see himself clearly for the fool he had been at their previous meeting. Matching words with her would not get him what he wanted.

'Lady Annis.' He was sure to keep his tone even, though fury still burned through his veins.

The quirk of one eyebrow was the only acknowledgement of her surprise. 'Norseman.'

Hoping that he adequately disguised his anger, he asked, 'Are you here because you've reconsidered letting me out? Because if so, I accept your offering of peace.' It was a horrible jest, but it seemed to work.

Her lips twitched in the beginnings of a smile and he breathed a little easier. This would go much faster if he could rekindle their ease from the tavern.

'I am sorry to say that I cannot.' She looked down at the food she had brought, a bowl of some sort of stew in a thin broth. 'Here. I do not intend for you to go hungry.'

The bowl was just small enough to fit between the bars. She did not seem to worry that he might grab her hand or otherwise harm her. Whether that was from sheer arrogance, or inexperience, he did not know. Though harming her while still being locked inside would hardly get him anywhere, so perhaps she merely took him for a reasonable man.

A memory came to him from several years ago, long before the massacre. He and his twin had been sent on a mission by their father to a kingdom in the south. The purpose of the voyage had been so minor that Rurik could not recall the specific details, but one of their stops along the way had been at a farm where they had spent the night. The home had been crowded with several families living there and several of the various daughters had taken a liking to them. Danr, however, had only wanted the haughty one who also happened to be the most beautiful. Likely because of her disinterest, she had been sent to serve them their meal and Danr had set about charming her. The girl had stood little chance and, before the night was over, she had figured out a way to disappear with him outside.

Rurik stared into Annis's eyes and, when he reached forward, he allowed his fingertips to brush over the tender inside of her wrist. It was a gentle touch, but it was enough. Just as the haughty daughter had reacted to Danr's touch, so Annis did to his. Her lips parted silently and she dropped her gaze to his touch. Most tellingly, she stepped back as he took the bowl from her. Rurik found himself swallowing the tiny flame of awareness that warmed his own hand. Disgust at himself mingled with that attraction and he did not know what to do with the competing notions.

'I need you to tell me why you demand to see Wilfrid.' She spoke as if the moment had not happened.

Shaking his head, he said, 'I must talk to him myself. I misspoke last night. It has nothing to do with you being a woman and more to do with the fact that the matter is private. I would determine whether he is the Wilfrid I seek before casting public accusations.' He did intend to verify the man had been at the wedding before killing him. He had resolved not to involve any more innocents if it could be avoided.

'I am his only relation and a trusted advisor. You can tell me and I can assure you it will not become public.'

Rurik shook his head. 'I will not speak to anyone but Wilfrid.'

If he spoke about the massacre to anyone, Rurik was certain he wouldn't live to draw his next breath. His only hope was to try to talk himself out of this somehow.

'As you will. Enjoy your day.' She turned on her heel and stormed out, much as she had before.

Rurik lingered at the bars, gratified the touch had worked. It would be like chipping away at the stone of a mountain to make a path through, but she would soften towards him. He need not seduce her. Merely making her see him as a man and not an enemy would be enough to assure his survival…for a while.

The difficult part would be not falling under her spell as he did so. She was beautiful and there was something in her eyes that he had never seen before. It called to him to match wits with her. However, that was a dangerous proposition. He did not believe that she had knowledge of the events in Maerr and Wilfrid's hand in them—he hoped she was not involved— but the fact that she was a relation of Wilfrid's was enough. His sham of a flirtation could not lead to more.

Letting out a curse that was absorbed into the damp stone walls, Rurik evaluated his options. Unfortunately, he was left with the same conclusion he had already come to. He had to befriend the woman.

It was the only way he could think to get himself out of this. The very idea of befriending anyone related to Wilfrid set his teeth on edge. The bastard had led men into Maerr with the intention of killing Sigurd, or so Rurik was left to assume, except Ingrid and Gilla and many other innocents had died alongside his father. They had done nothing to deserve their fate and yet Wilfrid had delivered it to them regardless.

Many would say he would be justified in visiting vengeance upon Wilfrid in kind. If his father had lived, he would have led men to Glannoventa's shores and burned the whole village, slaughtering all who stood between him and revenge. Rurik could not condone the slaughter of innocents, so he would use Annis and whomever else he needed to get to the men who had committed the unforgivable crimes.

# Chapter Three

'Annis?'

The sharp sound of her name caught her off guard as she locked the door to the cellar behind her. Letting the key fall back in place on the ring at her waist, she took in a breath and turned to face Cedric, the man in charge of Wilfrid's warriors. His old and dear face was lined with concern as he approached her.

Her parents had sent her to be raised by Wilfrid at the age of eight after their home had been invaded by Danes. They had deemed it safer in the west and, since she had been betrothed to Wilfrid's son, Grim, moving here had been a logical measure. As a result, Cedric had been a great source of comfort and support to her for more than half of her life. Even more so when Wilfrid's health had begun to decline in recent years after Grim's death, leaving the weight of Glannoventa to land on her capable shoulders.

Cedric was a dear friend and advisor and she longed to have his guidance in this. Yet, however much she trusted him, it would be best if he kept away from the Norseman. He was the only one who was truly innocent in this entire tragedy, and she hoped that it would stay that way.

'So it is true. You took the Norseman.' His brow was furrowed in both anger and concern as he closed the distance between them.

'Alder told you?' While she had not expected the events of the previous night to stay secret, she had hoped to break the news to Cedric herself.

'Is it true?'

Nodding, she said, 'I took him his morning meal. He's fine.' Ready to spit fire because he was so angry, but otherwise fine.

'You should allow someone else to deal with him.'

It would suit her if no one knew that the Norseman was down there, but, unfortunately, that was impossible. While no one had seen them load him into the cart and they had kept him covered on the short drive from the village, she had no doubt that a vigilant servant would have seen them taking him downstairs and she could not hide the fact that she took him food. Servants would eventually begin to talk.

'He is my responsibility,' she said.

Losing her unborn child so soon after her husband's death had left Annis with a well of grief so deep it seemed she would never be whole again. The need for revenge had filled the empty spaces they had left behind in her heart. This was her mission. She wanted to limit the involvement of the others as much as possible.

Cedric's scowl deepened. Something in his face had always reminded her of a handsome falcon. His nose was prominent and blade straight with well-shaped nostrils. That, combined with a lean face and high cheekbones, would have been enough. But his eyes completed the impression, since they were dark and observant, always taking in what was happening. In her childhood, he was often the one who would catch her in some mischief before she had scarcely started it.

'The danger to you is too great to allow—' He abruptly broke off at the sound of footfalls. Gently taking hold of her arm, he led her down the wide corridor.

Their home occupied the ruins of the praetorium in the old Roman fort. Wilfrid and his ancestors had prided themselves on caring for the structure. Most of the walls had been maintained with new stone and plaster over the centuries, as had the roof. As the original commander's home, it was built in the Roman style with rooms surrounding an atrium and a courtyard. This was where Cedric led her now. It was the one place no one would disturb them and had been the setting for many of her childhood lectures. Once she had come to live with Wilfrid, Cedric had wasted no time in picking up those lectures where Father Cuthbert had left off. She nearly rolled her eyes as she might have years ago.

Closing the great wooden double doors behind them, Cedric turned to face her. 'You must not see to the prisoner, Annis. Let someone else do it.'

'You do not understand. I *must* do it myself.'

'*I* do not understand?' He waved his hands in agitation before settling them on his hips. 'If he were to escape, he would harm you.'

She inclined her head in acknowledgement of his concern for her. 'Please trust that you and Grim taught me well. I can use the dagger at my hip and am fast when speed is needed.'

His sharp gaze caught on the dagger at her hip. 'It's not your skill that I question, child, but your experience with this particular type of beast. You have never faced an opponent with nothing to lose. He is trapped down there and would harm even himself if it meant any hope of escape.'

Suddenly, things did not seem quite so clear to her. Even though there was a peal of truth to his words, she said, 'That is a bit of an exaggeration. He's hardly a beast.'

'He is,' Cedric said without hesitation. 'For all that he is a man, he is chained and kept in a cage. Soon the animal will win out and he'll be acting on instinct. He is a heathen Norse. They cannot be trusted to take into account refinements.'

'What refinements?'

'That you are a woman. That you are the lady of this household.'

Her heart pounded in response to the vision that brought to mind, causing her to place a hand on her breast to attempt to settle it. She did not particularly like it that she might be the one responsible for turning a man into an animal. She also did not think that any man, Norse or otherwise, would take into account that she was a woman if he escaped. She had learned to fight because she would be treated as a warrior.

Deciding to ignore that, she said, 'He is being cared for. He is chained, but he can move about freely. He has food and water.'

'Food and water, but the threat of death hangs over his head.'

Pain beat behind her temple. Cedric was right. The scene he described was very accurate. She had put that man in a cage and he would soon turn into a raving beast. Guilt and self-loathing ate at her from the inside. She had taken a terrible turn of events—the fact that he had come here seeking vengeance—and made them even worse. If anyone should be in a cage it should be her and that Gael assassin who had gone to Maerr and killed with Wilfrid's coin in his purse.

But what could she have done differently? She could not allow the Norseman to wander free, not when he wanted them dead. Not when the pain of her own loss was sometimes so keen it still had the power to take her breath away.

'Annis?' She did not realise that she had been pacing until Cedric touched her shoulder to stop her. His eyes were kind with concern as he said, 'Tell me who this man is.'

'I—I am not certain.' She regretted the lie as soon as it was spoken. It sat like ash on her tongue.

His knowing gaze combined with her guilt stripped away the layers of her reluctance. 'Then tell me who you suspect him to be. I cannot help you if I do not understand what we might be up against.'

He was right. Again. He was nearly always right, yet she could not bear to tell him. Or perhaps it was more that she could not bear him to know what she had done. She could hardly face the truth these last two years, much less confess her crime to him.

Stifling a groan of protest, she turned away and sat down on one of the many benches that lined the courtyard. In spring and summer, she planted flowers in the beds that filled the gaps between them, but they were dormant now with winter upon them. She had been too caught up in her own anguish to notice the cold, but she felt it now as it seeped from the wood of the bench through her clothing. As if her cloak were a bandage that could bind her hidden pain, she pulled it tight around her.

Cedric sat quietly beside her, his strong presence as calm and reassuring as always. Annis knew she had to tell him what she had done. If this Norseman was from Maerr as she suspected, then more would follow. Cedric deserved to know why.

Despite how strong she claimed to be, Annis had always suspected that she was very weak on the inside where it counted. After her Aunt Merewyn had been kidnapped by Danes, her parents had not wanted to chance another raid, so they had sent her to Wilfrid's home. Annis had pretended to be glad. Without Merewyn there to care for her, she had not wanted to stay with them anyway. Her father was so busy she wondered sometimes if he even remembered her name, while her mother had never shown much interest in her. It had been easier to believe that she welcomed the move than to acknowledge the pain she harboured from their ease at ridding themselves of her. It did not mean the pain did not exist, it simply meant that she could not face it.

It was the same now. She had been sent to Wilfrid's household with the understanding that she would marry Grim when she was old enough. She had not chosen Grim, but she had loved him. At first like a much older, distant cousin, but that had slowly begun to deepen after their marriage. It had hurt her when he had been killed and even more so when the babe in her womb had soon followed. While she had acknowledged that pain to an extent, it had been easier to plan revenge. When Wilfrid had nurtured that anger, it had been no problem at all to watch it grow until it had been all-consuming, driving out any thoughts of pain, of vulnerability.

She was not strong at all. Pain was something she carried around with her constantly. If she were a strong person, that pain would not hurt nearly as bad as it did. Perhaps if she wasn't fighting against that pain, she might have made better choices.

'Annis.' Cedric took her hand in his and gave it a squeeze in silent encouragement.

She could not meet his eyes as she spoke, so she set her gaze to the silver and black hair at his temple. 'Do you remember when I left two summers ago to go to Merewyn's bedside?'

Merewyn had returned from the Norse lands with her Dane husband years ago and had taken up residence on the eastern coast. Her husband, Jarl Eirik, oversaw the Dane relations in the area Annis had called home as a small child. Annis had a fondness for her aunt and had spent time with her over the years, even if it did mean spending time with the Danes as well. 'She was bedridden during the final months of carrying her last child?'

Cedric nodded. 'I remember.'

'Going to her bedside was merely an excuse to get away. I never saw her. Instead, I went to Maerr.'

'Where the devil is Maerr?'

'The Norse lands to the east. The home of Sigurd, the King of Maerr.'

Recognition dawned in his eyes at that name. Several years ago, before the killing in Maerr, Wilfrid had been part of a plan to assassinate Sigurd. Since Danes were scarce in the area, the Norse had come with the intent of staying. The Danes were already squeezing Glannoventa from the east, so Wilfrid wanted to stop this potential invasion by more outsiders. He had recruited Grim in his failed plan to kill Sigurd. Not only had they not assassinated Sigurd, but they had both received extensive injuries from the attack. It had taken many weeks, but Grim had died a gruesome, agonising death. Annis had tended him faithfully, but she hadn't been able to help him. Unfortunately, she had lost the child she had been carrying soon after Grim's death. The boy would have been their first child.

'Sigurd…the one who wanted to take over Glannoventa,' he said.

She nodded. 'The same man. After he caused Grim's death, Wilfrid became more determined than ever to kill him. Around two years ago, the hired men Wilfrid and Grim had used in their first attempt came for a visit. They had heard about an upcoming wedding in Maerr for one of Sigurd's sons. It was an excellent opportunity to get close to the King, as many guests had been invited from all over. They wanted to know if Wilfrid wanted to be a part of another attempt.'

'And of course Wilfrid wanted a part.' The bitterness in Cedric's tone was not lost on her. Wilfrid had not shared this with even his most trusted man.

Squeezing his hand gently, she said, 'He did, but was too ill to go.' A huff of air escaped Cedric, so she touched his shoulder to offer him some solace. 'Wilfrid did not want you to know, because he knew you would not approve. He did not want you to be a part of it in case it went badly again.'

'But you were a part of it? You went in Wilfrid's place?' He could not keep his disbelief from his voice.

Shaking her head, she said, 'Wilfrid does not know that I went. I overheard a bit of their conversation, so I knew he paid them some up front. I approached the assassins secretly and demanded to be a part of it. I did not trust them not to run off with the coin and never set foot in Maerr.' She looked down at her lap. Her voice lowered when she added, 'The truth is that I also wanted revenge for Grim and our child. I wanted to see Sigurd dead myself to know that he was punished for their deaths.' She also felt that by losing her babe, she had failed to give Wilfrid the only part of his beloved son that was left. It was only right that she participate to help bring some sort of justice for their family's losses.

Cedric rose to his feet as the implications of her words settled over him. 'Then this Norseman—the one who arrived yesterday—is from Maerr?'

'I believe that he may be.'

'Do you recognise him? Does he recognise you?'

She shook her head and rose to stand before him, hurrying to explain. 'We have learned that his name is Rurik and he arrived yesterday on a ship looking for Wilfrid. I believe that he might be one of Sigurd's many sons. As we were waiting for the wedding to begin, I learned all their names in case something like this came to pass. However, I never saw the one named Rurik. He was away.'

Though she had met one of them up close. Sandulf. He had been barely more than a boy, but he had marked her. The scar he had left on her lower back throbbed with her guilt.

'And your mission was a success. Sigurd was killed,' Cedric concluded. Word had reached them of Sigurd's death months later.

'He was killed, but not because of me or the assassins.' When she closed her eyes, she could relive the mad fury that had broken out in the hall. The whole place had erupted into a battle. 'We did not know it, but there were others there who had come with the same intentions. Someone else killed Sigurd.'

And the others. So many others had died when it was only supposed to be Sigurd. The men Wilfrid had hired had battled for their lives against the other warriors. The Gael, their leader, was the one who had broken from the plan. He had attacked a pregnant Norse woman, a wife of one of the sons, and brutally killed her. Annis had tried to stop him, but she had been too late to intervene

'Then why has Rurik come?' Cedric asked, breaking up her thoughts.

Annis shrugged. 'The longhouse was chaos. It is possible that no one knows who drew the blade on Sigurd. And there were other deaths that he would want to avenge.' The blonde woman, her belly swollen with child, had met a gruesome end beneath the Gael's sword. The memory of her death was burned into Annis's mind. She had relived it so many times that she could recall the exact pitch of the woman's scream and how she had reached out into the empty air in the end, hoping to be saved.

The memory was too painful to share with anyone. Instead, she said, 'Perhaps he has come to exact vengeance on anyone involved. He would likely think Wilfrid was involved because that idiot Gael insisted

on calling me by that name. It is possible that someone heard it and made the connection.'

She had disguised herself and had even contrived
a new name, but the Gael had surprised her by using
the name Wilfrid. It was as if he had delighted in
using Wilfrid's name in front of others. Perhaps he had
wanted this to happen all along. If someone came for
the group of assassins, they would seek a man named
Wilfrid because he would be easier to find. Had she
been smarter, she would have made certain that everyone knew the Gael's name. She was not smart. She
was not even strong.

'Is it possible that the assassins have been found
and betrayed you?'

'Anything is possible, but the Norseman asks for
Wilfrid.'

Cedric nodded and hung his head in a look that suspiciously resembled defeat. It tore at her heart.

'I am sorry, Cedric. I have led us to this fate and I
will accept responsibility. Wilfrid need never know
that the Norseman is here.'

Cedric stared down at her, all kindness wiped from
his features, but his voice was not harsh when he said,
'Wilfrid paid them and he agreed to be a part of the
first assassination attempt, so he bears the brunt of
the responsibility.'

'It is kind of you to say so, but if anything, we share
responsibility. The Norseman would not be here now
had I not gone to Maerr.'

'He paid the assassin. It is possible the Gael would
have used Wilfrid's name while there.'

Annis inclined her head in acknowledgement. That
was true; there was no telling how the assassin might

have betrayed them. However, it did not relieve her of any responsibility for her own actions. She had chosen to go. She would have to face the consequences of that decision.

'We have to kill him.' Cedric's words were so abrupt and unexpected that Annis jolted with them.

'We will not!'

'We have no choice. He cannot be allowed to let others know where we are.'

Her mind raced with some way to convince Cedric that he was wrong. Killing the Norseman would not be the right course of action. Her heart would not allow her to be responsible for another death. 'They will know already. He claims that he has men out there. That he arrived with some and they will even now be wondering where he is. Perhaps they even know that he was taken.'

'Do you believe his claim?' he asked.

'I have doubts. I have had the men looking all night and they found no one.'

'Good,' he said. 'Then no one is here. Even if men do come later, they can prove nothing without the Norseman's corpse.'

It was Cedric's duty to evaluate threats and snuff them out. Perhaps that was the best thing to do in this case, but she could not allow it to happen.

'Cedric, I cannot have another death on my head. Besides, I am certain he must have told someone—perhaps his brothers—where he was heading. Someone knows he is here.'

Cedric paused. He turned from his pacing where he had possibly been playing out ways to kill the Norseman and dispose of his corpse in secret.

'*Another* death?' he finally asked. She was so concerned with the Norseman's fate that she had not realised what she had said.

She gave him a jerky nod, but found that she could not tell him about the Norsewoman's death. It had been too horrific, too painful. There was no way that she could speak of it. 'It was chaos. We had to fight our way out.'

Cedric raised a brow, but he did not ask again. 'We cannot keep him down there indefinitely.'

'I know.' The words came so softly that she did not know if he had heard her until she felt his warm hand on her back.

'I wish you would have confided in me earlier. I would have forbidden you to go to Maerr and none of this would have happened.'

She forced a smile in an attempt to return to normal. 'You would have forbidden me to go and I would have left anyway.' She had been so determined to avenge Grim, and so lost in grief for the child that was never to be, that nothing could have stopped her.

He gave a mirthless chuckle and put his arm around her shoulders. Warmth spread through her chest. Despite the heartache of her past, she was very lucky to have Cedric and Wilfrid in her life. The men had both filled the role of father for her in very different ways. Cedric was the one who listened and guided, while Wilfrid had always been the playful one. The one who had urged her to learn to fight and hold a dagger.

'Death is the only way to end this, but since this is your mistake, you get to decide. But decide quickly what is to be done,' he said after a moment. 'We do not have much time.'

The thought sobered her instantly. Death was not something she would consider, but what other option was there? The Norseman was here and she did not foresee him leaving until his vengeance was satisfied. What could she offer him instead that would gratify him?

## Chapter Four

Rurik had been a captive for almost a full day. His major discovery during that time was that if he craned his neck a certain way and looked towards the end of the corridor, he could make out a sliver of sunlight sneaking in through a gap between the stones. That light was fading now as the sun set, meaning he was no closer to getting himself free than he had been when they had carried him in. At least he was conscious and had suffered no ill effects from being captured. It was a minor detail for which he was grateful as it might mean the difference between life and death.

A thorough search of his cage had taken most of the day. He had explored every crevice and crack in the stone, only to discover there was no easy way out. The rocks were beginning to crumble in several areas and he had managed to use his chain to scrape away bits and pieces of old mortar. The stones were only a single barrier to the soil. Once a few were removed, it would be simply a matter of digging himself out, which meant that the cell would not hold him indefinitely. However, he did not have the weeks it would take for that particular escape route. Every day he stayed down here was a day closer to his eventual execution. He did not know why he was being kept alive. Perhaps they meant to ransom him to anyone who happened to come looking for him. One day soon, they would realise it would be easier to kill him and pretend that he had never arrived on their shores.

He paced his cell, unwilling to accept that he had failed. This could not be the end. He had not failed his brothers in bringing this murderer to justice. He would return to them with this triumph so that he would finally belong. Escape would simply have to come by some other, quicker means. Since the woman was the only person he interacted with, it would have to come through her.

He had no choice but to get her into the cage with him. If he could bind her in some way, then he could take the key from her. From there it would be a matter of locking her in—killing women, even those who took him captive, held no appeal to him—and then finding his way to wherever that coward Wilfrid was hiding. He briefly considered taking her along with him and using her as leverage, but decided that she would be too much work. She had proven herself to be feisty and not the least bit biddable. He could not imagine that kidnapping her would improve her disposition.

The rusty hinges of the door at the top of the stairs creaked and squealed in protest as the door opened. He straightened, his mind racing with how to entice her into his cage. It would have to be something believable, something that would make her disregard her own safety to enter. There came her even footfalls on the steps. One…two…three…

He moved as silently as possible with the old chain attached to his wrist. Holding it against the stone, he debated on pretending to have got it stuck on one of the rocks. If she had brought food, he would not be able to reach it and she would be forced to come in. He disregarded the idea just as quickly. Anyone with any sense would suspect it for the ruse it was, and she did seem intelligent. She would likely seek help before coming inside and he would have lost his advantage in having her alone.

The only thing to do was to pretend to be injured. Despite the fact that she had kidnapped him, he had seen a reluctance in her eyes to bring him harm. His only chance to get her inside would be to pretend to have some lingering head injury from the assault. If she believed him and reacted as he hoped, she would come inside. If she went to get help first, then it would have been a failed attempt that cost him nothing, because they could not prove he had no ill effects and thus he wouldn't be punished. It was his only hope.

The moment her boots touched the floor, he dived for the straw pallet, grimacing at the low clink the chain made as it scraped against the stone. He closed his eyes just as the light from her lantern flickered against the iron bars.

'Norseman!' Her voice was a sharp contrast to the thick silence of the underground chamber.

He forced his breathing to stay shallow and kept his face turned away from her. The scent of roasted meat met his nose, making his stomach rumble in greedy displeasure. He only hoped it was not loud enough for her to hear. His heart pounded in his head every moment she stood there watching him. She stayed still, the weight of her stare a nearly tangible touch as she tried to determine if he was faking an injury.

Finally, her breath exhaled on a sigh and there was a series of soft clips as she set the wooden bowl and the lamp on to the floor. The one from earlier had long since burned itself out. The rattle of keys followed a moment later as she pushed one of them into the lock. It must have been stubborn, because she had to fumble with it for a bit before it gave way with a harsh clang. The creak of old iron told him the door was opening, but he would have known even without the sound. The very air changed around him, becoming thicker with her presence.

'Norseman?' The tip of her boot pushed at his hip. Apparently satisfied that he wasn't pretending, she knelt down at his side and touched the pulse at his neck.

Conscious thought gave way to instinct as he grabbed her wrist with one hand and her hip with the other. He twisted his body and attempted to roll her beneath him before she could make a sound, but he wasn't quite prepared for the ferocity of her response. She struggled with her whole body. Her hips rose to thwart him while her knees did their best to unman him. She struck a blow to the side of his head that had him seeing spots even as he tried to wrestle her into submission. The tables had turned and she was the animal bent on fighting her way out of captivity.

Only his greater weight saw him succeed in the end. They were both breathing heavily by the time he managed to sit on her thighs, his upper body leaned over her as he held her wrists to the straw pallet at her back. Her eyes blazed with her fury. Had they been weapons, he would have been ripped to shreds by their intensity.

'You have made a grave mistake.' Her voice was as hard as that of a queen whose sovereignty had been called into question.

He had expected yelling and more than a little screaming. What he got was a vow of retaliation that was all the more powerful for its unwavering belief that she would prevail before this was over. The proclamation was so jarring that he hesitated, but only for a moment before he renewed his commitment to the path he had set out for himself. He had to escape and the only way to do that was through her.

'It is you who made the mistake, Lady Annis. You believed that you could take me captive with no ill effects. You were wrong.'

Giving a quick shake of her head, she said, 'I never thought that. You left me no choice. When you came here to my home asking questions about Wilfrid, what did you expect would happen? I cannot allow you to bring harm to him.'

It wasn't the first time she had spoken of Wilfrid as if she were responsible for him when it should very well be the other way around. Suspicion had niggled at the back of his mind the day before and now it became full-blown.

'Do you not mean that he cannot allow harm to come to you? Should he not be here himself?' At the look of mutinous righteousness that flared to life in her eyes, he added, 'Not that you are not capable of defending yourself, as we can both plainly see.' He smirked at the flash of rage the remark evoked. Now that she was beneath him and powerless, he could not help but take the time to enjoy her righteous anger.

'Are we back to this again, Norseman? Tease the woman because you are so much bigger and stronger than she?' She sniffed. 'I am disappointed. I thought you would be above such things.'

His smile had broadened before he even became aware of the fact that he was smiling. He couldn't take the time to ponder it now, but one day when he was far away from Glannoventa and its dangers he would sit and wonder how she could affect him so. Settling into the back-and-forth game they were playing, he said, 'As you can see, I am not, but I am above you which does give me something of an upper hand.'

'You are despicable.' She bucked against him to no avail. Well, to no avail but to raise his awareness of the fact that she was indeed beneath him.

Strange as it was, a rush of heat began to simmer deep in his belly and his body tightened in response. The thighs between his were taut and firm, but there was no denying the curve of her hips or the softness of her belly when she bucked up against him. She was strong and lithe, while also being supple. Her beauty rivalled that of any great beauty he had ever known. Only, it was different in a way he could not describe, but could appreciate no less for his inability.

Strong. Feminine. Powerful. It was odd how that particular mix of attributes was appealing to him, but he could not deny her allure. Even chained to the wall of her prison on a bed of straw, he wanted her. Badly.

The night they had met had found them in a similar position to now, him holding her pressed against the wall as he had tried to show her a better way to defend herself. There had been a hitch in her breathing when he had spoken to her softly. In that moment before the attackers had come upon them, Rurik had known that she was attracted to him. The knowledge had been heady then and it was heady now for all that they were in a cage. Thoughts of seduction whirled in his head. If he could get her into his bed and compliant, she might very well give him the freedom he wanted and even the information he needed. Of course, he had a feeling she would also give him far more pleasure than he had ever known, but that was secondary to his real motivation. Wasn't it?

As if she could read his thoughts, she stopped bucking. But the moment her gaze met his he saw that it was because she had noticed the heat between them. The blacks of her eyes had grown larger, which could have been a result of the weak light, but was most likely enhanced by the shift in the mood between them. Her gaze went to his mouth and, whether she realised it or not, her own mouth softened. The pink tip of her tongue laved her full bottom lip before her eyes darted back to his. They were wide in awareness and perhaps a tiny bit of fear.

The fear he could understand. He felt it, too. She was the last woman in the world that he should feel anything for…but that did not seem to matter. Before he could remind himself that he was only doing this to gain the upper hand, he followed his need for her and leaned down to kiss her.

For one tiny moment, Annis went mad. Rurik's intent was clearly written on his face. His eyes fairly lit up with his carnal interest in her. Instead of being appalled or using the seax at her waist to ward him off, she wanted his kiss, welcomed it even.

It had been years since Grim had kissed her and he had only ever kissed her in the darkness of her chamber. Even then his eyes had never gone so deep and intense, as if kissing her were the most important thing in the world to him. He had never once kissed her outside of her bed and never would he have done so at such an inappropriate moment. The need in Rurik's eyes…the way they seemed to eat her up… Annis had never felt so *wanted*. The feeling was so heady that she was drunk on it, dizzy with weighted limbs that would have trembled had he not held her so firmly… *so very firmly*.

As Rurik came closer, his head tilting to the side, his thumb a gentle stroke along the inside of her wrist, she found herself licking her bottom lip in preparation for him. When his breath touched her cheek, hers became shallow in anticipation. There was a flicker deep within her belly. She barely had time to ponder the hows and whys of this ill-advised kiss. One moment they had been struggling for control and the next there was this.

His lips were incredibly soft as they touched hers. She had expected a hard kiss, as rough and terse as the man himself. What she got was so much different. So much more. He took his time. Even as they lay there in the cell on a pile of straw, he kissed her as if they were lying in bed on a morning of leisure. His lips brushed hers once, twice, in a lazy back and forth before pulling away to tilt in the opposite direction as if he could sample her better that way.

She should end it before it became deeper. She

meant to, but some urgency in the back of her mind made her extend what would surely be the only kiss in her foreseeable future. So instead, she touched her tongue to his bottom lip before retreating. She should end this now and was tensing to do just that when his soft groan gave her pause.

The sound vibrated in her, sending a bolt of molten need shooting to her core. She barely had time to register it before he gave chase, plundering her mouth as if it was his for the taking. Perhaps it was, because she only arched beneath him to give him better access. Grim's kisses had never been anything like this. This was nothing short of a pillaging, a stealing of her very soul if only she hadn't meant to hand it over. She was very certain that she might do just that, because so far she was kissing him back. Not passive in accepting him, but her tongue twirling with his as if it were a long-lost lover come back to her.

He pulled back to take in a breath. His callused hand moved gently down her arm on its way to what she thought might be her breast. Or at least her breast seemed very hopeful as it swelled and her back arched even more to push it higher. Opening her eyes a sliver, she looked at him through a glossed haze to see the corner of his mouth tick upwards as he watched her response. A grin of triumph. A smirk of conquest.

The excitement building in her crumbled on its shaky foundation. That smile broke the spell he had cast on her far faster than anything else could have. He was using her and why wouldn't he be? She was his captor and a veritable fool to have succumbed to her curiosity. She would be damned if she would allow him to gloat over it.

Using his inflamed opinion of himself against him, she moved quickly, knowing that he would think nothing of it, and drew back as far as she could in the cushion of straw at her back before swinging her head forward so that her forehead caught him on the bridge of his nose. He let out a cry as he released her to bring his hands up to his face. Taking advantage of his momentary incapacitation, she wiggled free and drove her knee into his stomach. He let out a guffaw of air as he crumpled to the straw. His hand shot out to grab her ankle, but he was too late, grabbing only a handful of her skirt before she was able to jerk herself free and hurry towards the door.

Her hands were trembling as she fumbled for the key at her waist and shoved it into the lock. The stubborn thing was old and unused, so it stuck, but she still managed to turn it, sliding the bolt into place with shaking fingers. He was rising by that point, but she did not dare wait for him and say the things she wanted to shout at him. She hurried down the short corridor and up the steps, his roar of outrage following her as she fled.

Cedric was waiting for her outside the door at the top of the steps. He had insisted on it since she had refused to allow him to go downstairs to see to the prisoner. She could have called out at any time and he would have come running to help her. She had not done so, because she had been so certain that she could handle the Norseman. Only, she had not planned on that kiss. Her face flamed as she imagined Cedric finding them like that.

What had she been thinking? How had she allowed that man to put his mouth on her? She waited for disgust to roil to life within her, but it didn't. Even now her lips tingled pleasantly.

'What happened?' Cedric's hawk gaze seemed to see everything.

Dear Lord, were her lips swollen? She touched them with her fingertips as she shook her head and locked the door behind her. 'He's doing well. Still not talking about who he is or why he's here.'

'But we already know that, do we not?' Cedric raised an eyebrow and crossed his arms over his chest.

'We do.' It seemed trifling for him to point that out, or perhaps she was overly sensitive because she did not know how to proceed. This inability to decide was something new for her and she did not enjoy how vulnerable it made her feel. Doing her best to appear busy sorting the keys at her waist so that she could avoid Cedric's knowing gaze, she said, 'I shall retire to my chambers after checking on Wilfrid.'

Cedric gave a huff of disdain when she stepped away. Whatever had made her think that he could be put off so easily, she did not know. He had never once been put off easily in all the years she had known him, so she paused and added, 'I know we cannot keep the Norseman prisoner for ever. I will decide by morning what is to be done.' Though how she would accomplish that she did not know. She could not bring herself to order his death, but there was no other obvious answer.

The creases between Cedric's brows relaxed and he nodded. 'That is wise. The sooner we have this business done with, the better.'

Annis gave him a nod of assent and hurried away. She looked in on Wilfrid only to find him in bed already, snoring soundly. Still shaken from her encounter with the Norseman downstairs, she hurried to her own chamber and suffered through the brisk administrations of her chambermaid. The girl had only been with Annis a year, taking the place of her mother who had served Annis all these years. Annis enjoyed Goda's company, but sometimes missed the wise words of the girl's mother. Perhaps she could have confided in her. She discarded the thought almost at once. She was in this alone. She could not endanger anyone else with the truth.

After she was changed into her nightdress and her hair was thoroughly combed and plaited, she bid the girl goodnight and took a candle to her bedside. Climbing up on to the down-stuffed mattress, she lay back and pulled the coverlet over her as she pondered what to do. Cedric was right. Death for the Norseman was the only reasonable solution. But it was so brutal that she could not do it, nor could she order it done. The events in Maerr were already black marks on her soul. She could not add the Norseman as well. However, she could not set him free either. He could very well murder them all with no hesitation. There was absolutely nothing to stop him from bringing back all the warriors in Maerr who might want vengeance.

Then there was the kiss. Even the memory had the ability to make her stomach swirl pleasantly. How could she have responded so completely to him? When she closed her eyes, she could *feel* the weight of him above her, the heat of his mouth on hers.

What could she do?

The question followed her into a fitful sleep where she dreamed of that stolen kiss.

\* \* \*

Rurik had very nearly bellowed his thanks to the gods when his foot had encountered the metal of her seax. The slim weapon had been lying on the floor of his cell, still warm from where it had been secured against her body. Their wrestling must have loosened it so that it had fallen free when she had been lying on the ground. Rurik had promised to offer up a proper sacrifice to whichever god was responsible for his good fortune when he was free. Then he had spent hours using it to work the lock on the cuff around his wrist. For something so obviously aged as the restraint was, it had taken a long time to break the mechanism holding it closed. Once that had been taken care of, he'd had to do the same for the lock on his cage and the lock at the top of the stairs.

Most of the night had gone by then, but that did not matter. His only objective was to find Wilfrid. The home was quiet and so dark that he had to stand very still for far longer than was comfortable for his eyes to adjust to the lack of light. A series of doors opened off a large atrium, each one appearing to guard dark chambers. The only light came through a crack between a large set of double doors. The wood was cold, nearly freezing, so he knew that they led outside.

Taking a deep breath and holding the seax in front of him, he pushed one open very slowly to find himself entering a garden. A single torch lit this area, revealing chambers along two sides. All seemed quiet, but one set of doors showed flickering light beneath. It was behind this door that he found an old man muttering to himself over a game.

Rurik knew immediately that it was Wilfrid. His

age and the status indicated by the comfortable fabrics and appointments in the room told Rurik as much. Whether Rurik lived or died, at least he had found the man at least partially responsible for his father's death, for Gilla's death, for Ingrid's death. So many dead.

'Wilfrid?'

The man looked up, his snow-white hair an unruly mane. Rurik knew a moment of shock at his obvious age. While he had expected a man of Sigurd's age, this one appeared at least a score of years older. The ruthlessness needed to kill innocents was generally found in younger men, or so Rurik had thought.

Though Wilfrid's eyes sparkled with intelligence, there was a childlike innocence about him that had Rurik proceeding with caution. He refused to kill innocents in his pursuit for revenge. It was possible he was wrong about the man's identity. As he approached, he found himself hoping that he was. There would be no joy in killing this strange man.

'Are you Wilfrid?' he asked again to make absolute certain, his fist tightening on the small dagger.

The man gave a jerky nod that had his head moving awkwardly. Rurik looked for an injury that would cause him to move like that, but could not see one.

'Welcome,' Wilfrid called out as if meeting a beloved friend, a hand raised in greeting. Whether he did not see the small dagger Rurik carried, or if he simply did not care, Rurik did not know. 'Come.'

The man's words were slurred. Having learned a bit of the Saxon tongue from his mother's servant at a young age, Rurik was adequate, but not advanced in the language. He could barely make the words out. It was Wilfrid's raised hand that bid him come forward. That and the man's obvious lack of a weapon.

'Sit,' Wilfrid said, gesturing to the chair opposite him.

Rurik let himself fall heavily into the chair, momentarily concealing the weapon in the folds of the fur cloak draped over his shoulders. In all his imaginings, he had never thought to meet Wilfrid this way. His fingers trembled with suppressed anger.

'Do you know who I am?' Rurik asked, knowing the man would not.

Wilfrid seemed not to hear as he leaned over the game, selecting a wooden figurine and moving it to an adjacent square on the wooden board set on the table. This man was not a warrior. He seemed hardly more than a child for all his white hair and wrinkles. He was simple-minded.

Rurik had allowed anger and the promise of revenge to fuel every decision he had made for almost two years, only to come to this end. If Wilfrid even remembered the murders in Màerr, he would likely not even be able to talk about them, much less answer Rurik's questions. His grip tightened again on the dagger. Did it matter that he was simple-minded? He had been involved in the murders. He deserved to die.

As the man leaned over the table, blissfully unaware that his death was imminent, Rurik stared down at the baby-fine hair on his pink scalp. He raised the dagger, but could not bring himself to allow it to descend to its natural conclusion in the man's neck. It did not seem fair. He had come for a fight, only to find this. He lowered the dagger and several long moments passed with Rurik pondering how to proceed when the door opened and fate delivered to him another prize.

## Chapter Five

In her dream, the face of the Norseman hovered above her, alternating between that of tender lover and vengeful enemy. He smirked down at her as he had after the kiss, only this time she was not offended. Her fingers traced the outline of that smile as he pulled one fingertip into his mouth. She gasped and pulled it away. He laughed and knelt to kiss her again. When she followed his progress, she realised they were in her bed, not in the straw, and he was lying between her naked thighs.

The shock of it jolted her away, making her sit straight up in bed as if she would find him there. Her heart raced and even though she knew that she was still in her nightclothes and that it had been a dream, she reached for the seax that usually sat at her waist. Not the dagger she had worn to take the Norseman captive, but the shorter, blunter one she wore daily.

It was not at her waist. Of course it was not. She was in bed and it was deep in the night. Her candle had long since sputtered out. The seax was in the chest where it was meant to be. She tried to let that thought soothe her back to sleep, but something nudged at the back of her mind. Something important. It hovered there, just out of reach, and all the more insistent because of it.

Was the seax in the chest where it belonged? She mentally retraced her movements of the evening. She had no memory of putting it away, nor of taking it off. Had Goda removed it and put it away? Annis could not remember. She had been so preoccupied with her thoughts about the kiss that she barely remembered interacting with Goda at all.

Rising from the bed, she hurried over to the chest that kept them. There were three inside and she traded them out depending on her mood for the day. Pushing the lid open, she peered into the shadowy interior. It was too dark to see very well, so she used her hands to find them. A sigh escaped her when she found the bundle all lying together. One, two… Where was the third?

Her heart pounded and dread settled heavy in the pit of her stomach. The Norseman had held her down, but he had not taken the seax. She was certain that she would have noticed him taking it. But then her thoughts had been preoccupied with his kiss. A quick search of her chamber revealed that it was missing.

Had he stolen it? She closed her eyes and allowed herself to remember everything that had happened in his cell. It might have happened at any point during the struggle that preceded the kiss. When she had left, she had been too unsettled to think clearly, much less search him for the seax.

The blackguard!

Drawing on a cloak, she grabbed her long dagger

off the wall. If the Norseman had her seax, then he could free himself. If it came to it and she could not recapture him, then she would kill him herself. She had no alternative. It was a choice that would haunt her for the rest of her life, but it must be done. The danger to everyone around her was too great to allow him the chance to get free. She could not allow him to harm Wilfrid or anyone else at Mulcasterhas.

The fact that he was the only man she had felt anything for since Grim could not sway her. She opened the door to her chamber that faced out to the courtyard, ignoring the cold blast of air. There was no guard here because they were all posted along the outside walls of the house. The night was still dark, but a single torch gave off a watery light. Wilfrid's chamber was directly across from her. The double doors were closed, but a flicker of light could be seen in the tiny crack between them. He frequently did not sleep well and Cedric or his manservant generally attended him overnight. But some instinct drew her closer to his chamber.

She walked silently along the tiled path, her gaze on the crack between the doors. Male voices came from inside. She instantly recognised Wilfrid's. After a series of brain attacks had left him weak on one side of his body, he could still talk, but his words came out as if he were speaking around a mouthful of wool. But the other voice was too low to be Cedric and not quite as deep as Irwin, the strong manservant who attended to Wilfrid.

Bracing herself for what she might find, she pushed the door open and crossed the threshold with her long dagger before her. Wilfrid looked up from the seat he occupied at his table and gave her his customary crooked smile with a cry of enthusiasm to see her. The table game *hnefatafl* was set up before him.

The Norseman sat across from him.

Annis arrived as if he had somehow summoned her. Her eyes were wide and fear filled. He knew a strange urge to call to her and soothe that fear, but it did not make sense given their predicament. She should be afraid. He would have to kill her if it came to it, wouldn't he?

Still somewhat stunned by the strange direction his plan for revenge had taken, he said, 'Close the door, Lady Annis. We have many things to discuss.' He tried to keep his stymied anger out of his voice, but it trembled with the absence.

Her astute gaze went to Wilfrid and then the seax. Rurik tightened his fingers around it, ready to use it should she decide not to comply. It was dull, but he knew his own strength. One quick movement would have the knife embedded in Wilfrid's vulnerable neck. Rurik could see the action play out in his mind and his body even tensed, muscles tight as they prepared to follow his command if needed.

It was his stomach that voiced a rejection. It churned, unwilling to accept what Rurik might be willing to do to mete out justice. He had never considered harming a woman or an invalid. The years since the massacre had wrought many changes in him, most of them bad. He had kidnapped, held a weapon on an innocent and many other things he would rather have missed out on in his life. Was he really prepared to add more atrocities to the list?

He hoped not to find out and clenched his jaw to hide his hesitation. The breath he had been holding slowly released when she reached behind her and closed the door. His hand kept its grip on the dagger, but his muscles relaxed, leaving his limbs numb with relief.

'Come and sit down.' He gestured towards the bed. 'Wilfrid and I have been having an interesting discussion.'

She did as he asked, closing the door and taking halting steps across the room. He allowed himself a moment to admire the upward tilt of her chin, the flaming hair that escaped her plait to sweep around her shoulders and the determined glint in her eyes. She was breathtaking. There was something about her— her strength, her innate integrity—that combined with her very pleasing looks to make her special.

Like someone he could care about very much given different circumstances. Or, perhaps, someone he might be coming to care about anyway, despite the circumstances. No, that could not be right. It must be that he was mistaking respect for genuine affection. That made more sense. He could respect her while still maintaining that she was an enemy.

Of their own accord his eyes dropped to her lips as the memory of their kiss caused an echo of his earlier desire to flare to life in his belly. She drew herself up when she saw him, the very sharp-looking dagger held before her, limbs braced for action.

When she was close enough, he reached out to take the sharp dagger from her, but she pulled it back. He could not blame her. Not when he knew the actions he would resort to if needed. Respect for her increased yet again in the tiniest measure. Inclining his head, he allowed her to keep it for now. He did not want to fight her for it and alert Wilfrid that something was wrong. The house was at rest and he would keep it that way while he could until he got some answers.

'What has he told you?' Her eyes were wide and focused, never leaving Rurik's, as she sat lightly on the bed. It was clear that she was ready to jump up and defend both herself and Wilfrid if needed.

'How long has he been like this?' Rurik asked.

Wilfrid, who had gone back to studying the table game, looked up. 'Annis,' he said, although it came out as one syllable with the sounds all running together. As if his speech was not to his satisfaction, Wilfrid slapped a hand on the table and gave one hard shake of his head.

Rurik glanced from Annis to the old man, taking in the lines of strain around his mouth and the deep grooves that time and pain had carved into his forehead. His hair was almost purely white and, though it was thin, it stuck out at all angles. As if noticing Rurik's censure and determined to present her father-in-law in the best light, Annis reached over and smoothed it down on his pink scalp. The man gave her a lopsided smile filled with obvious affection.

The simple action—her touching him with such affection and the warmth with which it was received—stirred something in Rurik's chest. He ought to look away from the tender act, but he could not risk that when she sat right there with her dagger ready. He had made the mistake of underestimating her once. The pain in his nose could attest to that. It would not happen again. The sharp bite of fury raced up to replace the tenderness. This man had ruined lives in Maerr. He was not entitled to Rurik's leniency.

Rurik met Annis's gaze. 'How long?' His voice was sharper.

She swallowed and glanced away, hesitant to answer. Finally, she said, 'A series of brain attacks have whittled away his abilities over the past several years.'

'But how long has he been witless?'

She looked as if he had slapped her. Rage mottled her face and her eyes turned as hard as marbles. 'He is *not* witless! He is a superb player of *hnefatafl*, routinely besting us still.' She gestured towards the game they were playing. Realising that her voice was raised, she stopped talking and looked over to Wilfrid who was examining them both in suspicion. In a great display of restraint, she nodded to him as if to tell him things were fine and reached over to the board.

'Here,' she said, taking up one of the game pieces before Rurik. 'Your task as opponent is to trap his King—this piece—' she pointed '—into one of the upper corners.' Her well-shaped fingers placed a figurine on another square and Wilfrid grumbled. It had apparently been a good move.

The older man did not immediately move his King or any of the other pieces. Instead, he looked at the people before him, his keen gaze going from Annis to Rurik and back again. Finally, he mumbled something that sounded like, 'Tell him.'

Rurik stared at him. He had to wonder if 'witless' was an apt description for Wilfrid. In those two words, he revealed that his mind was still active even if his person was starting to rebel against him. 'Yes, tell me, Lady Annis.'

She breathed out through her nose in frustration. The dagger lay across her lap, where her fingers worried with it. 'Several years ago he had a brain attack. Since then he has had many others. They come on suddenly, striking from nowhere and with no warning. Each of them seem to drain a bit more of his strength and leave him unable to attend to himself.'

She gave Wilfrid a quick glance as if to question whether she had said too much. He gave her a fractured nod and turned his gaze back to the table game. Her shoulders relaxed infinitesimally and she returned her attention to Rurik.

'What have you said to him? I must warn you that—' She broke off and glanced to Wilfrid again. Leaning towards Rurik, she lowered her voice and said, 'I must warn you that you cannot be allowed to upset him. Any variance from his normal routine can frustrate him and send him into another attack.'

She did not have to say that another attack just might kill him. He seemed frail and half-gone from the world as it was. If Wilfrid heard them, he did not acknowledge it. Rurik had already ascertained that the man was a bit hard of hearing, but he wanted to know for certain. 'Can he not hear you if you whisper?'

She shrugged. 'The hearing on the weak side of his body seems to have gone.' The older man's weak side was the side nearest Annis.

Rurik found it odd that he was being asked to not upset the man who had had a hand in his father's death. The very man he had come here to kill. His fingers clenched around the seax. One quick move and the man before him could be dead, his blood spilled all over his precious table game. The idea of it did not hold the same appeal it had a week ago.

What joy was there in killing a man who was simple-minded and half in his grave? Had not the gods already accomplished the justice that Rurik had been prepared to mete out? Impotent anger and bitterness roiled within him. He had come so close only to have his justice denied to him. There had to be someone else. Wilfrid could not have acted alone.

Annis's astute gaze saw his fingers and accurately read his intentions. Her own hand gripped the hilt of her dagger where it lay beside her on her lap. 'If you do that… I will kill you.' The words were low and softly spoken, but no less intense because of that.

'Perhaps I would forfeit my life to see him dead.'

Rurik's gaze turned from the old man before him, the man that he should hate, to take her in. She seemed unusually reserved and then he recognised that serenity for what it was. It was the warrior quiet. The calm before the storm of battle. He could easily plunge the small dagger into Wilfrid's neck, but then Rurik would have to face her. If she did not kill him, the sound of their battle would rouse other warriors. Rurik would not live out the hour. There was no question about him being taken downstairs to the cage, not when there was no reason left to keep him alive. Not when vengeance would burn in their own hearts as brightly as it had blazed in his.

Was he prepared to kill her as well? He would no doubt be forced to fight his way through her if he had a hope of making his way out of the house. The question made his fingers loosen on the seax.

'I have not questioned him yet, if that is your concern,' he said to her. 'I told him that we are lovers.' He could not help the satisfaction he felt at her reaction.

'What?' The colour fled her face along with her rage. She stared at him as if he had spoken in his own Norse tongue when he was very certain that he had used the Saxon words correctly.

He fought the smile that threatened to make itself known. He very much liked this sparring with her. 'Wilfrid wanted to know why I was here, who I was. All the normal things that a person questions when finding a stranger in their bedchamber. I told him that my name is Rurik and that I am here as your lover.'

She continued to stare as if his explanation had made no sense, so he asked, 'Would you prefer that I tell him I am here as your pris—'

'Do not say it.'

She spoke quickly so that he would not confess the truth and risk Wilfrid hearing. Interesting. He had no idea why she would want to hide the fact that he was a captive from her father-in-law, but he was beyond intrigued. Their voices had risen to a normal conversational tone, so Wilfrid had heard this part. He gave her a nod and reached across his body with his good arm and took her hand.

Strange. Rurik had expected anger and a desire for retribution, but Wilfrid seemed perfectly content that she had taken a lover. Who were these odd people? No one here reacted as he thought they should. Continuing the odd display, Wilfrid brought her hand to his face. He mumbled something, but Rurik could not make it out.

Her eyes glazed with tears that she hastily blinked back. Wilfrid released her and went back to the game as if he were alone. He moved the King, but then also one of the pieces Rurik was supposed to control.

'He behaves like a child.' Rurik lowered his voice again so as not to draw Wilfrid's attention. 'One moment he is alert and the next he is so absorbed in his game that he does not see us.'

She nodded as pain slashed across her features. 'I do not know if it is the result of the attacks, but there have been times when he does not even know me, but in the next instant he will call me by name.'

'That happens often?'

She shook her head. 'Only a few times and only late at night, like now.'

Her gaze went to Wilfrid, the table, the dagger… anywhere but Rurik. It was as if she did not want to meet his gaze and allow him to see the pain she so clearly felt. Wilfrid was beloved by her. Rurik tried to imagine his own father in a similar state as the old man found himself. Sigurd had been such a powerful man that it was impossible. Would Sigurd ever have sat so easily playing an amusement? Would he have finally welcomed Rurik's presence at his side?

Clearing his throat, he asked, 'Why does he not care if we are lovers?'

That question cut through the pain on her face, bringing her eyes sharply back to him. 'How could you tell him that? It is not the truth.'

'We *did* kiss.'

Her chin came up. 'You stole a kiss.'

'You would deny that you kissed me back?' There had been a glorious moment when she had welcomed his kiss, her lips moving beneath his, her tongue in his mouth.

'This is not appropriate conversation.' Seeming to gather herself so that she was once more the Queen, lowering herself to address a servant, she asked, 'Why are you here, Norseman? What do you want from us? Explain yourself.'

She was right. The game between them had gone on long enough. It was time to get to the truth. If the truth resulted in a fight, then Rurik would fight to the death if need be, but he would have answers. 'I want to know why Wilfrid would want my father dead.'

There was a flicker of knowledge in her eyes. It had gone as quickly as it had appeared, but Rurik was certain he had seen it. Even as she asked the next question, he knew that she already knew the answer. 'Who is your father?'

'King Sigurd of Maerr. Wilfrid helped kill him two years ago and I would know why.'

## Chapter Six

Annis had known all along that Rurik must have come because of the massacre that had happened in Maerr. She had hoped she was wrong, but deep down, where the scar on her soul was almost too much to bear, she had known. The wound had throbbed to aching life the moment she had heard that someone was in the village asking questions about Wilfrid. Rurik had come to avenge his father's death. More than his father. There were other dead, too. Possibly family members. She thought of the pregnant woman's face in the moment the woman had realised death had come to claim her.

Anger and sorrow spun around inside Annis so fast that she was not certain which one she should feel more. It had been the same ever since that day in Maerr—before then, if she was being completely honest. Losing Grim and the baby had been difficult, sowing the seeds for both the fury and the sadness. Maerr had only sharpened them both, putting an edge on an otherwise dull blade. An ache filled her throat so that it was a moment before she could speak.

She could not change her involvement with the past, but she could give Rurik his due. He deserved some sort of answer.

'I will discuss it with you, but not here.' She nodded towards Wilfrid.

Unfortunately, Wilfrid had already got wind of their discussion. He sat up straighter, his eyes as sharp and alert as they had ever been. 'What of Sigurd? Has he come back?' he asked in the garbled speech she had come to understand. His hand touched her arm and his gaze searched them both almost frantically, as if expecting the news that his enemy was approaching. Rurik probably had not understood every word, but he knew the word Sigurd. His eyes had sharpened.

'Father.' Rising, she set the dagger down on the coverlet and moved to his side, casting an anxious glance towards Rurik as she put her arms around Wilfrid's shoulders to calm him. 'I have told you before, Sigurd is dead.'

Wilfrid touched her hand and lowered his face. Remembering Sigurd would surely remind him of Grim. She had never seen him cry for Grim, but she knew that he still grieved the death of his son. His only son to reach adulthood.

'You're certain?' he asked. When she assured him that Sigurd was truly dead, he shook his head. 'I cannot remember. I have trouble remembering.'

'Perhaps you should lie down. The sun has yet to rise.' His mind seemed to be muddled the worst during these nights when he did not sleep well. She hoped his wakefulness now did not bode ill for the next day. Watching him struggle to remember the simplest things was a painful reminder of how she was losing him.

He agreed and she helped him stand. His muscles seemed particularly weak on these nights as well, so it was no surprise when his knee gave way. They would have tumbled to the floor had Rurik not grabbed her waist to brace her. Surprise and a strange sort of delight made her glance at the Norseman. He met her gaze, but his expression revealed nothing. His face was as strong and impassive as she had ever seen it. She gave him a nod of thanks and braced her weight under Wilfrid, helping him shift into the bed.

Before pulling the blanket up, he turned to look at Rurik. 'Good evening. I look forward to speaking with you later in the day.' The words were spoken as plainly as he was capable, a testament to how important the words were to him. Yet they still managed to run together.

Annis glanced at her long dagger, which had been pushed off on to the floor, and then at the seax in Rurik's hand. Only then did she notice his knuckles were raw, as if he had dragged them against the stone in his cage, a stark reminder that he was her enemy. There was nothing certain about Rurik not trying to kill them at any moment, yet she did not feel threatened any more. He could have killed them both by now if he chose. Nevertheless, the caution and discipline both Wilfrid and Cedric had instilled in her made her kneel down with caution to collect her weapon.

Rurik noticed. He seemed to notice everything, but his lips pulled tight as he stepped back towards the table. 'Until later,' he said to Wilfrid.

This had turned out to be one of the most peculiar

nights of her life. Walking in to find her enemy talking to her beloved father-in-law had been bad enough, but then to have to tend to him while Rurik waited to discuss the murder of his father was something she had never imagined would happen. And she had imagined plenty the many forms in which Sigurd's sons might deliver their retribution to her.

'Come.' She mouthed the word more than said it and was relieved when Rurik nodded and made to follow her. The blast of cold air when she opened the door was welcomed. It revived her senses, which she would desperately need as she faced off with the Norseman. Her next task would not be easy.

She stood there, momentarily uncertain where she should take him. When she had been certain just an hour ago that she would be forced to kill him, now she was prepared to explain Wilfrid's hatred of Sigurd. To hope that there could be a peace between their families. She wanted to lead him back to his cell, but that was obviously out of the question. Not only would he refuse to go there, if Cedric saw him walking free, he would almost certainly attack him on sight. The only answer was that they would have to talk somewhere more private where they would not be disturbed. There was only one place where that was possible.

'Will you agree to a short truce? We need to talk,' she said.

He stood beside her, tall and broad, but restrained. Perhaps it was the lingering effect of his earlier noble intentions when he would have saved her from her own men, or the way he had helped with Wilfrid. Or perhaps it was simply that she felt that she deserved at least some of his anger for his family's fate and she trusted in her abilities to put up a good fight. Whatever it was, she decided to trust him in this.

His suspicious glance took in the rectangular garden, looking for dangers hidden in the shadows. When none revealed themselves, he met her gaze. 'You have my word. For now.'

It was all that she could ask. Taking a deep breath of the cold, she said, 'Follow me', and led him to her chamber. Another chill came over her as she opened the door to let him inside. He followed her cautiously, the seax gripped in his fist as if he expected a guard to be within waiting for him. No one was there, of course, so he stepped into her chamber.

Closing the door behind her and moving by the dim orange glow of the fire in the brazier, she lit the small tray of beeswax candles on her chest and waved him over. Her chamber was smaller than Wilfrid's and she rarely took her meals here, so she did not have a table and chairs. Instead, she had stools and the chest, which was where she intended for them to sit.

Rurik took in his surroundings as he went, as if he were appraising the space for hidden threats. As a child, she had been relegated to one of the antechambers off the room belonging to Wilfrid's wife. The woman had died in her childbed the year Annis turned twelve. When Annis had wed Grim many years later, she might have chosen his mother's chamber for her own, but she chose this one simply because she liked the mosaic tile floor. Left over from the Romans, it was badly crumbled in spots and refurbished in others, but enough of the tiles were left to show olive trees surrounding what would have been a woman. Annis suspected the woman was a goddess, but she could not say which one. She'd had her choice of tapestries, so she had chosen forest scenes which meant the walls were decorated in faded shades of green and gold. It was quite nice in summer when the shutters could be opened to allow in the sunlight. In winter it reminded her that there was more to the world than their grey existence.

Gathering her cloak about her, she took a seat and faced him. He sat on the stool opposite the chest, though he did not relinquish the seax. Not that it mattered. He could take any of the weapons in the room if he wanted. She was taking a huge risk in trusting him, but it was necessary. Short of killing him, which she was glad she had not done, she had to convince him that they could find peace. To do that she needed to convince him that her revenge on Sigurd had been justified.

She nearly laughed aloud in self-mockery. She could not convince the son that the father had earned his death. To even think so was madness. Perhaps she could at least help him understand the why of it.

'I was not completely aware of it at the time, but it seems that your father, Sigurd, visited our area several summers past.'

'How many summers?' His strong tone brooked no omission of the truth.

'Four.' Had Grim been gone that long? Sometimes it seemed as if it was only months ago; sometimes it seemed as if it had been for ever.

The Norseman gave her a nod. To call it encouragement would have laughed in the face of his stern expression. It was more of an urging to continue. She could not help but notice how the flickering candlelight painted his features in a soft light, making his eyes mere slits of shadow that held his thoughts secret, while illuminating the pleasing turn of his jawline and high cheekbones. His hair seemed darker where he had pulled it back and secured it with a cord of some sort. The raw masculinity he exuded had her very aware that he was a man and he was in her bedchamber.

Turning her gaze from him while still keeping him in her periphery, she said, 'Until Sigurd's visit there were no Norse here. The Danes were well to the east and, while Wilfrid believed that they might attempt expansion, he had been able to negotiate a peace of sorts. He paid their taxes and no one threatened him. They were too busy with their other wars.' She took a deep breath, trying to articulate all that she had learned in the years since. 'Sigurd was an outsider. He did not bow to the Danes, so he would no doubt refuse to bow to Wilfrid. Wilfrid had heard that Sigurd was preparing to set up a camp just north of here. He sent word to the Danes, but he wanted it stopped. He could not wait for a reply before he and Grim—'

She paused, quite certain that the name Grim would be unfamiliar to him. Then another, far worse, thought came to her. Had Rurik been one of the warriors with Sigurd back then? Had he fought with him? Been one of the men to take Grim captive and torture him? This nightmare seemed to get worse. What if she had kissed the man who had delivered the death blow to her husband?

'Grim?' he prodded.

Her throat had seemed to close, as if the horror of that thought had been too terrible to let anything in or out. Finally, she was able to force out the words. 'Wilfrid's only son. My husband.'

Rurik's gaze had been on the candle, but it darted up to meet hers. Surprise lit his eyes and relief flooded her that he did not seem to know of Grim, but she had to know for certain.

'Were you there…to the north when Wilfrid and Grim met with Sigurd?'

'I was at home in Maerr.' He shook his head, but did not elaborate.

With no choice but to believe him, she continued. 'They took men north to confront Sigurd. I do not know the details of those talks, but I do know they ended badly.'

'Badly? How did they end?'

Death.

'There was a battle. Sigurd provoked it.' That was Wilfrid's claim. Unfortunately, unlike Cedric, Wilfrid had always had a temper that burned hot. She could very well see him insulting Sigurd and provoking a fight. Cedric had stayed behind to guard Mulcaster-has, because they had believed there could be Norse watching who would attack when Wilfrid left. That had turned out not to be true. For the thousandth time she wondered how things might have been different had his level head gone along.

'Wilfrid was injured. It was a head wound and soon after that he had his first attack, though it was not that one that left him as he is now. It was the first of many to come, each of them doing their part to whittle away his senses.

'Grim was fatally wounded,' she continued. 'A head injury… A gash in his side… His legs were…broken.'

Crushed would have been a more accurate way to describe them. Had he lived, he would have never walked again. She forced herself to swallow the lump in her throat and keep going. 'They brought him home, but he died in the days after.'

Rurik stared at her as if he could see every emotion she felt. Shifting under his gaze, she stared over his shoulder to the shuttered window.

'What are you not telling me?' he finally asked.

She meant to tell him more, but some things were too difficult to talk about. As the years passed, she had tried very hard to block out the horrible things that had happened to Grim at Sigurd's command. Locking the thoughts away in a chest buried deep in her mind had been an excellent way of dealing with them. Now, threatened with their release, she froze as a sort of terror overcame her. The last time she had unleashed them, innocent women had died. What if she unlocked them and could not put them away again? What if she could not hide her pain before this Norseman and he knew her for the weakling that she was?

Understanding that those concerns in themselves were indications of her weakness, she forced in a breath, making her lungs burn with the effort. Even difficult tasks had to be managed, she reminded herself, and clenched her hands so tightly that her nails dug into her thighs. The discomfort gave her an external pain to focus on, which helped to alleviate the swell of pain in her throat so that she could keep talking.

'I was told that after their initial talk with Sigurd yielded inadequate results, Grim crept past their guard and into their camp. I do not know for what purpose,' she said, noting the question on Rurik's face. 'It hardly matters. He was found out. By the time Wilfrid and the men freed him, he had been tortured for hours. His legs had been crushed. And his insides...' The lump in her throat made it impossible to talk. She took in a deep breath through her nose and forced herself to plough through. 'They were in the process of removing his—'

'I understand. They were trying to get information from him. Why would that be necessary if they had merely talked?' Rurik asked. He stared at her as if trying his best to cull the information out of her with his eyes.

It was enough to turn her pain to a much-easier-to-manage anger. 'Because they were barbarians out to cause him as much pain as possible.'

After hearing that story, it had been so easy to imagine Sigurd as a monster, a devil unleashed from the bowels of hell who cared for no one. To have his son sitting before her—a man who was clearly not a monster—was almost more than she could comprehend.

Rurik did not look away. 'There is more to what happened.'

'That *is* what happened. Grim came home and he soon died from the injuries that your father ordered. He was tortured and his death was excruciating.' She brought her hand up to her mouth to quell the nausea that had churned in her belly as she spoke. In the days that had followed his injuries, she had prayed for Grim's death as the only way to ease his pain. It had eventually happened, but not before he had experienced a pain so great she could hardly fathom it.

'Imagine praying for the death of someone beloved to you to spare them from pain. Only when you have done that can you imagine my horror.'

As if God had not thought their family punished enough, he had taken the baby growing in her belly. The only bright spot in that whole time was that Grim would live on in their child, but that had been taken from them, too. She had lost them both and it was Sigurd's fault.

Annis had hated him ever since. That hatred had given him an almost mythical aura. So much so that when she had finally laid eyes on him in Maerr, she had been surprised to find him a mere man. He had been tall and broad like Rurik, except his hair had been lighter and touched with grey. Though lean, he had gone a bit soft as older men were wont to do. He had not been the wrathful devil of her nightmares. In fact, he had been a proud father that day.

Thankfully, Rurik stayed silent, while his eyes seemed to see all. Finally, when she thought he would move on, question the why or how of Wilfrid's involvement in the Maerr massacre, he said, 'There is more.'

He leaned forward as if to get a better look at her in the meagre light. The result was that she could finally see his eyes. The pure blue stood out in the golden light of the candle. His gaze stripped her bare to her very soul, taking in the whole of her stricken face and demanding she hold nothing back. Anger flared within her again. How dare he make demands of her? Yet, just as quickly she found herself telling him.

'I was with child when they brought Grim home.' If he could understand her pain, then perhaps he would understand that both of their families had suffered. Perhaps that suffering could lead to peace. 'I tended to him day and night, hoping… Still he hung on, clinging to life. Perhaps I sat by his bedside too long… I do not know. I only know that I lost the baby…a boy.'

It was that loss that woke her from her sleep at night. It was that loss she remembered every spring when her boy would have been another year older.

'I am sorry for your loss.' Rurik let out a long-held breath as his hand came up to slide over the top of his head and settle on the back of his neck. He sounded as if he meant it, so she gave him a tiny nod of acknowledgement. The fact that he had recognised her loss was more than she had expected from him.

'I suppose that brings us to why Wilfrid hated my father so much. But how did he know to come for the wedding? How was it all co-ordinated so well?' His fingers made a steeple under his chin as he stared into the flickering candlelight, as if the answer could be found there.

He asked her these things as if she knew that Sigurd had been killed during a wedding. Perhaps he assumed that Wilfrid had shared the information with her. She let him have his assumption.

'Some of the men who went with Wilfrid to confront Sigurd the first time were not his warriors. They were mercenaries for hire. After the failure, they fled. Perhaps they were afraid to get caught up in the fight should Sigurd pursue Wilfrid and Grim home. I do not know their intentions or their thoughts. I only know that I thought I would never see them again. That they would never dare to set foot in Glannoventa again. But I was wrong.

'Two summers back, they came to Wilfrid, claiming to know of a way to get to Sigurd. It seemed that his son was getting married and everyone was invited. The guard in Maerr would be lax. There would be no better time to gain access to its King.'

She had not been present for that meeting because Wilfrid had wanted to take it privately. Even Cedric had not been allowed to stay in the chamber. Although his illness had taken its toll, Wilfrid had still been fully in charge of himself and his men. Not like now. Instead of leaving, she had hidden herself and listened anyway. The seeds of revenge had already been planted, but that meeting had encouraged them to flourish.

Wilfrid was too ill to go, but she was not. She would go and see Sigurd dead with her own eyes, then she would come back with the joyful news. Naively, she had imagined that Sigurd's death and the triumph that followed would bring Wilfrid back to himself. That somehow it would cure his grief and the wounds on his mind and make him whole again.

But that had not happened. It was only after Annis returned home, silent with the horror of what had happened tormenting her, that word of Sigurd's death had found its way back to them. A message sent by one of the assassins had delivered the news. It had been confirmed many times over by whispers of travellers who had heard it in other parts of Northumbria. A king's death, no matter how minor the king, was always good for a story on a cold night.

Her euphoria had never come. The sense of justice for Grim had never been felt. Grim was still gone.

Their babe was gone. Countless men—and women—could die and that would always be true.

How foolish of her not to realise that before leaving home. Not only had she brought back the internal pain of what she had seen, vengeance had physically come to pay them a visit in the form of Sigurd's son.

'Lady Annis?'

She jolted at the intrusion of his voice. She had been so consumed by her thoughts that she had not heard whatever he had said to her. He leaned forward now, hands on his knees as if braced for something.

'Who are these men?' he asked.

The way his eyes lit up with interest, she knew that he meant to go after them. Annis shook her head. 'I will not tell you. I will have no more blood on my hands.'

His head tilted, catching the nuance of her words. She said 'no more blood' as if she had indeed had plenty of blood on her hands in the past. Silently cursing her own idiocy, she held her back straighter, defaulting to the reserve of poise that had helped her through the last years.

His gaze sharpened, sizing her up as if he would be able to see remnants of that blood. Sometimes she was amazed that everyone could not see the rust-coloured stains. 'What do you mean? How do *you* have blood on your hands?'

The door burst open, saving her from answering. They both jumped in surprise, but the Norseman leapt to his feet, turning to face Cedric, who had come armed. His sword gleamed before him as grey light filtered in at his back. It was later than she had thought.

'The cell was open. I am glad I have not come too

late.' Though Cedric spoke to her, his eyes never left the Norseman who held the dull seax out before him. It was a paltry weapon compared to the sword.

'This is Rurik of the Kingdom of Maerr,' she explained. 'It seems he has come for an explanation of his father's death.'

That earned her a knowing look and a raised eyebrow from Cedric.

'I have not come for an explanation,' Rurik said, biting the words out through his teeth. 'I have come for vengeance and justice.'

He moved so quickly that, had she had even a little less training, he might have caught her. Instead, she moved backwards out of the reach of the swinging arm that would have grabbed her, toppling over the stool and stumbling to her feet. Apparently, their truce was over. Taking hold of the dagger with both hands, she gained her feet. Their eyes met and held. She did not *think* he wanted to harm her, but a cornered man was a dangerous man. Before he could decide if he would trade his honour for a chance at that justice, three more men rushed into the chamber.

# Chapter Seven

Rurik fought them like a beast being forced back to his cage. For that was exactly what he was and he had decided to embrace the comparison. He could have easily taken two of them on, perhaps even all four of them with a proper weapon. The seax was all but useless and he finally tossed it at one of them in favour of his fists. He landed several good blows, taking the first two down, but the older one hung back, wiser than the others with his years of experience.

Lady Annis hung back as well, her eyes wide and alert, but she had already come to the inevitable conclusion. He could fight, but in the end he would be dragged back to his cell like an errant mongrel. The assured resignation on her face fanned another blaze of fury to life within him and he fought with renewed vigour.

More men came in until the chamber seemed to overflow with them. Rurik felt as though he was drowning. One man was downed, but his place was taken by another, like treading water in the increasing fury of a storm. The heel of a boot kicked Rurik's leg out from under him, sending him down on one knee. That was enough to give them the upper hand. Faces closed in above him. Raising his arm to keep the fists away from his already sore nose, it was quickly jerked away and twisted behind his back. Another man grabbed the other. Rurik fought, but he was tired and outnumbered.

'That is quite enough.' Lady Annis's voice filled the room with authority. It worked to halt the blows, but his arms felt near to breaking. 'Take him below.'

'So much for our truce.' It was not wise, but he could not help the sneer that twisted his features.

'The truce? You tried to grab me!'

'Get him below.' Cedric interrupted their argument with the order. 'He broke the lock on the chain and the door. The one on the cell seems to be working.'

'Not for long,' Rurik promised as they dragged him out. He did not make it easy for them, but there was no escaping. They pulled him down the stairs and all but tossed him into the cell. At least there was no chain to bind his wrist this time. He ran at the cell door, but was not able to stop them from locking it.

'I will not be kept down here as a prisoner!' he yelled, knowing that his voice would reach the main floor before they closed that door. 'Lady Annis! Come and face me! We have more to discuss!'

The door closed with a bang on its old hinges, but he was not going to give up easily. He kept up the yelling all day, hoping that he was being heard.

The light that seeped through the crack in the stone had started to wane when Rurik heard the door over the stairs open. The familiar tread of her boots on the steps told him that Lady Annis had finally deigned to pay him a visit. She was dressed in the finery befitting her station when she presented herself to him before the bars. Her gown was a finely woven wool in a suitable but sumptuous golden colour. She wore no cloak tonight. Her fiery hair was tamed in a series of braids that wrapped around her head with a shiny fall of sunset-coloured hair over her shoulder.

Had he not despised her so much he might have found her attractive. That was not true. He still found her attractive despite the fact that she had broken their truce and imprisoned him again and he was all the angrier for it. Also, he did not *really* despise her. He hated that she had imprisoned him, hated that she was part of the family who had plotted to murder his father, but he could not find it in him to hate her. He wanted to, and in his darkest moments a tiny part of him did, but it never took. The grudging respect took over. In an attempt to disguise that, as well as because his throat was raw from all the yelling he had done that day, his voice came out more harshly than he had intended.

'Who were the men Wilfrid hired to kill my father?' he asked, picking up where they had left off.

She winced at the callousness of his tone and a thread of satisfaction wove its way around his spine, straightening it. As the day had worn on, Rurik found himself latching on to the idea of the assassins as a drowning man might grasp at a piece of driftwood. He had been denied the release of satisfaction he would find in killing a healthy Wilfrid, but had been gifted with the knowledge that there were others involved in the vicious plot. Just as the search for justice had led him from King Feann of Killcobar to Glannoventa, it appeared to be leading him to other men. Other warriors who had sought to end his father's life. Would the search never reach its own end? Would everyone involved ever be punished?

She shook her head and he grasped the bars in his fists, unwilling to be denied his justifiable revenge. This time she took a step back from him. He was reminded of where they had left off in the conversation before her men had intervened. 'What did you mean earlier? How do you have blood on your hands?'

This time she shook her head harder. 'There has been too much death in regards to Wilfrid and Sigurd and their dispute. I will not be the cause of more. There was enough with Sigurd. Let it end there and forget the men who came to Wilfrid.'

Before he could think better of it, he sneered at her. 'Forget. That is an easy word for you when your family wielded the last blow.'

She straightened her shoulders and became very still. 'They are not easy words, Norseman. I have lost as you have. I know what it is to have death change your entire life.'

Remorse hit him immediately. Of course she had lost. This was not a battle of losses; if it were she might have won, having lost a husband, a babe and very nearly her father-in-law. Rurik had lost his father, but no one belonging to him. Gilla and Ingrid had been kind women, but he had not known well. Their losses had been keenly felt by their families. Rurik's pain had come from how Ingrid's death had nearly destroyed his eldest brother Brandt. How his brother

Alarr had almost lost his legs. How his family had been nearly destroyed.

In terms of personal loss and pain, Annis had him bested. Her family had been destroyed as well, coupled with numerous personal losses.

'There were more killed than Sigurd. Innocents.'

Her brows drew together, not in anger but compassion. 'I know. It was a terrible thing that happened to your family. If I could go back and change this whole mess, then I would. I have no stomach for revenge. Not any more.' She drew in a breath and he could not help but study how her bottom lip trembled with it. 'I am here because I have a proposition for you.'

'You are not here because my yelling drew you down?'

Her eyes narrowed while a white line appeared around her lips and another zing of satisfaction surged through him. She had heard him and been annoyed by him. He would be content with any small blow he could land to her regal composure.

'Wilfrid is asking for you,' she said, continuing without acknowledging his question.

'I am surprised he remembers me.'

'If I'm honest, so am I. He has a keen mind much of the time. There are days when he seems to forget almost everything, but other days when he remembers. This is one of those days. Unfortunately, he remembers what you told him…about us.'

The blush on her cheeks reminded him of his comment about them being lovers, something he had almost forgotten. It had been a stroke of brilliance to unsettle her in that way and watch her squirm so prettily. Rurik's gaze dropped to her lips, remembering how soft and warm they had been beneath his. Even knowing who she was, he would enjoy having her beneath him once. To his immense surprise, she was looking at his mouth, possibly remembering their kiss. She did not look disgusted. When her gaze flicked back to his, there was a moment of awareness that passed between them before she forcibly looked away.

'Is he angry?' he asked.

'He...he wants you to dine with us. He wants to meet you again to discuss matters, he says.' She said this with a raise of her chin as if she had been caught doing something wrong and was willing to face her punishment.

'He's not angry that we're lovers?' He found that impossible to believe.

'Concerned, perhaps, but he isn't like any man you have met before. He knows how much Grim's loss meant. He seems content that I have found a bit of happiness.'

If that were true, then Wilfrid was indeed like no man he had met before. Propping his arm on the bars, he enjoyed watching her obvious embarrassment play out on her face. 'And your proposition is...?'

'I would like you to dine with us. Pretend to be my...who you said you were. We must be very careful about upsetting him. If he is stirred to anger, it could bring on another attack. Strong emotion has brought them on before. Therefore, you must agree not to mention your family. We will say you are an emissary from Jarl Eirik—'

'You would have me pretend to be a Dane?'

She frowned at the interruption. 'A Dane sent by Jarl Eirik to check on things here. We have successfully avoided the Jarl's meddling for several years. Wilfrid will believe that we were finally forced to accept a visitor.'

'You would have me pretend to be someone else to pacify the man who was involved in plotting to kill my father?'

She blinked and took a step back. 'You are right. It's unconscionable. I do not know what I was thinking.' She turned and would have hurried out, but he realised at that moment that this very well might be his only chance to negotiate with her.

'Wait.'

She had the decency to look sheepish when she turned to him, her gaze trying to dip down, but she visibly forced herself to meet his eyes.

'You said a proposition. What do you plan to give me in return?'

Meeting his gaze, she said, 'You can move upstairs into a chamber there. It will be more comfortable than your straw.'

'You expect me to pretend to be someone else for only a bed?'

'After tonight, we can discuss a way for you to earn your freedom. I would not be opposed to setting you free if you could somehow persuade us that you intend to leave and not harm us.'

He thought of what leaving would mean and even glanced towards the steps that would lead him out of here. He could go, but what then? There was nowhere for him to go. Home to Maerr was out of the question. The kingdom that should rightfully belong to Brandt had been given to another. He could go back to Éireann.

But, no. Even as the idea crossed his mind, he pushed it away. His mother had been Irish, but it was not his home. Rurik was Norse, but he did not belong there any more than he belonged in Maerr. Bastards rarely had true homes, he was learning.

All he had was his need for justice. He needed to prove his family innocent in plotting against his father—he and his brothers had been declared outlaws in the aftermath as baseless rumours had circulated that they might have wanted Sigurd dead for their own gain. Rurik needed to know that those who had plotted against his family had been brought to justice. He could not leave without knowing the names of the assassins.

'I need to know the names of the men who were with Wilfrid.'

She paused. 'I have already told you that I cannot give you that.'

Gripping the bars, he stood as close to her as he was able. 'I have to find justice for my family, for those innocent people who had no say in what Sigurd did, but paid for his perceived crimes anyway. Please...' It was the first time he had pleaded with her. She drew in a shaking breath and seemed to drop the regal demeanour she adopted so easily. Perhaps it had never been real at all.

Nodding, she said, 'If you agree, then we can discuss it further.'

It was all that he would get from her, but it would have to be enough. At least he would be a step closer and away from this cage. The truth was he was looking forward to a hearty meal. Thanks to his exertions last night, he had not been given food yet today. He would agree, but first he wanted to make certain that his knife was returned to him.

'I will have your promise that my weapons will be returned to me.'

'When you leave, perhaps.'

'The bone-handled knife has meaning to me.' He despised giving her that information, because it was always possible that it could be used against him, but he found himself trusting her a little more every time they met. He needed to know that it would be kept safe. 'I will have your promise that it will be safe until such time that it is returned to me.'

She gave a brisk nod and the tightness in his shoulders eased. 'It is in the armoury. No harm will come to it.'

'Do you not think he will question why the Jarl's emissary is beaten?' He indicated his nose. Most of the other bruises were hidden by clothing.

'We will say you were attacked on the road.'

He nodded, accepting the opportunity she was giving him. 'Then I will need a bath first.'

## Chapter Eight

An hour later, Annis sat at the table with Cedric across from her and Wilfrid to her left at the head. Her stomach churned as she waited for Rurik to make an appearance. After leading him up the stairs from below, she had seen that he was given access to the bathing chamber. Two men had been assigned to guard him, but she was not at all certain that two would be enough. Others were stationed in the house, but after seeing him in the fight in her chamber that morning, she had gained a newfound respect for Norse warriors. He had fought with an unbridled passion that had sparked as much admiration within her as it had fear.

Had she let a wild animal loose in her home? Or had she done the only thing that was morally acceptable in the face of her own transgressions: given him a chance for freedom? She did not know. Her only comfort was the fact that he had not killed Wilfrid last night when he had the man defenceless. Only time would tell, however, if his mercy would continue.

Cedric raised a silent brow at her from across the table. They had argued before she had gone below, he again for Rurik's death, her for his eventual freedom. That brow seemed to declare he had been right all along. If Rurik did not show, she would expect to hear the roar and clang of battle very soon.

The harsh tread of boots at the entrance drew her attention. Rurik stood there in borrowed clothing and his own boots, freshly cleaned. She did not know where the tunic had come from, but it was well made and deep green in colour. His trousers seemed to have been made for him, hugging his thighs just enough to display their power. His dark hair was clean and still damp, pulled back from his face, but left to fall to his shoulders. His short beard had been groomed, so that the strong build of his jaw could be seen. It was a fine jaw for a fine face. He appeared every bit a king's son as he strode into the room with his shoulders back and his eyes, intense pools of blue, focused on his adversaries. Only the mark on the bridge of his nose from her forehead and a slight bruise on his temple indicated that he had recently been a captive.

'Good evening,' he said to the room at large as Cedric came to his feet. Wilfrid made a motion to rise, with his manservant Irwin at his back to assist him if needed. Cedric took an almost defensive stance, his shoulders stiff and a hand at his hip where she had no doubt he kept a dagger. Wilfrid was smiling his crooked smile.

'Welcome,' Wilfrid said and settled with a soft grunt back into his chair, waving Irwin away.

Rurik inclined his head before looking at her. His eyes were narrowed to barely more than slits and they singed her skin when his gaze fell upon her. Her stomach flipped over itself. He had come to do battle. 'Good evening, Lady Annis.'

She nodded at him because she could not speak, then watched in dismay as he approached the place that had been set for him at the end of the table. Instead of taking his seat, he grabbed the silver, chalice and platter and walked with them before very deliberately setting them down at the place beside her. A look of unmistakable victory flashed in his eyes as he took his seat.

The man was dangerous and unruly. This had been a terrible idea. A quick glance at Cedric, who was in the process of taking his own seat, confirmed his agreement. His jaw was tense as he stared at Rurik, as if to look away would encourage the Norseman to strike. It was too late now to stop the plan that had been set in motion. The die had been cast. Not for the first time, she wondered if they had gone too far in their attempts to keep Wilfrid placated, but he had been very insistent about meeting Rurik. It was difficult to deny him when he showed so little interest in things these days.

After she settled herself, she waved Leofe over to begin serving. The girl presented a platter of roasted meats and vegetables, while another poured wine for the table. There had been a time when Annis was growing up that the table had often been filled to overflowing. Wilfrid and his wife had liked to have people around. In addition to the main table, others had been brought in and arranged throughout the hall. Sometimes the warriors and their wives would fill them. At other times, visiting lords and their families. The hall had held many banquets and long meals deep into winter nights. After Wilfrid's wife had died, the frequency had died with her, but the evenings had ceased completely with Wilfrid's illness. In order to make certain that he was able to keep his place as Lord of Glannoventa, it had been necessary to keep him isolated. Now their meals were passed in polite silence as she and Cedric watched him decline with every season.

Seeing the way Wilfrid's eyes lit up at Rurik's company, she could not help but wonder if they had done him a grave disservice by keeping people away from him. Another wrong to add to her list of wrongs. The wine tasted particularly bitter as she swallowed it.

'Rurik,' Wilfrid said, his speech marginally better than it had been when he had spoken to Rurik the previous night. It was still garbled a bit from using only one side of his mouth, but it was clearer, betraying his excitement. 'It is good you have come. Was your journey well?'

Rurik looked at the old man and then at her. After softly repeating the man's question, she tried to plead with Rurik with her eyes to stay with the story they had invented. 'Well enough.' He kept his gaze on her as he spoke. If his journey had been well, his arrival had not, his eyes seemed to say.

Finally glancing back at Wilfrid, Rurik picked up the mutton shank Leofe had served him and took a bite. His strong white teeth bit into the flesh and he made dramatic work of pulling it from the bone. Grease shone on his lips as he chewed. 'Thank you for your welcome and generosity,' he said around the bite in his mouth, his eyes sparkling with mischief as they met hers.

He planned to play the heathen Viking. Lord save

her. Her heart pounded against her ribs and she took another drink of her wine.

'We do not often have Danes at our table,' said Wilfrid.

'You do not have one tonight, for I am no Dane.' He gestured with the leg bone and spoke loudly in deference to Wilfrid's hearing, but his tone was casual, as if he had asked for a second portion. Annis nearly choked. From the corner of her eye, she could see Cedric lower his hand, probably to the blade at his side. She should have known better than to believe Rurik would go along with their plan. And why should he address the man he believed to have killed his father with any civility?

Wilfrid gazed at Rurik in open curiosity. 'Not a Dane? But you have the look.'

Whether Rurik understood that or inferred the meaning, he replied easily, 'I am from the North. I was raised Norse with my father's family, but my mother is—was from Éireann.'

'Éireann?' Cedric spoke the word in a clipped voice, his eyes alert as they settled on Rurik as if looking for signs in his features that he spoke the truth.

Rurik's hand settled on her shoulder and her eyes widened at the physical contact. Squeezing gently, he tilted his head a bit to look down at her. 'My father kidnapped her and made her his concubine…or slave, depending on who you ask.'

He was taunting her, trying to unsettle her. She was ashamed to admit that it was working. An image flashed through her mind of him standing over her, much like he had looked down at her after their kiss, his eyes livid with desire. The very same look that was in his eyes right now as he stared at her before Wilfrid and Cedric and whomever else bothered to see it. Only, in her imagination, she was his…she belonged to him in a way that was so completely consuming that it lit a fire inside her. A shrug of her shoulder dislodged his hand, but only to have it move down her spine in a slow caress that ended at the small of her back. Tingles of a pleasant sensation followed the path, unsettling her more than his words could have.

She did not *want* to belong to him or anyone else but herself. Then why on earth would she find anything pleasing in anything that he did to her? Or in that image that had been planted in her head?

'How did you…?' Wilfrid's voice trailed off as he stared at them. His eyes were more alert than they had been in a long time and she had the oddest feeling that he knew more than she wanted him to.

She opened her mouth to answer his unasked question, uncomfortable beneath his scrutiny, as Rurik's hand seemed to burn right through her clothing. Her own husband had never touched her this way. Rurik certainly did not have that right. She had already planned to explain to Wilfrid that Rurik had misspoke, or perhaps been too eager in his word choice when he had said they were lovers. Rurik touching her now and looking at her as he did would not help convince her father-in-law of the truth.

'Rurik misspoke last night,' she said.

Wilfrid's gaze turned questioning.

'We are not lovers…not the way you think he meant it.'

Rurik moved his palm from her back, but only to grab her hand with his, making hers feel small in the confines of his larger palm. 'Certainly, the things that have passed between us deserve that description.' He smirked, clearly challenging her to deny him.

His thumb traced a path from her wrist to her palm, stroking a small circle in the centre. The warmth of his touch felt so unexpectedly good on her cold skin that she jerked her hand away. His grin widened and, mercifully, he did not reach for her again as he went back to his meal. Of its own accord, her hand found its way to her lap where she cradled it. Her thumb absently tracing the path that his had taken, trying and failing to recreate the heat.

'I am…f-fond of you.' The word tripped over itself as she said it. 'But we must respect propriety.'

He smirked behind the chalice as he brought it to his lips and took a long drink. She could not help the way her eyes dipped down to his neck to watch the way it moved as he swallowed. She could imagine pressing her face there so easily that it scared her into looking away. Unfortunately, her gaze caught Cedric's disapproving one.

'At least one of you can remember your decency,' said Cedric.

Her face flamed, so she stared down at her food. Somehow this evening was getting away from her. Damn the Norseman.

'Dane or not,' came Wilfrid's voice, 'Jarl Eirik's men are welcome here. It is the least I can do after…' Wilfrid's words sputtered out. Annis was not certain if he was simply grasping for the correct word or if he had forgotten.

'After what?' Annis urged.

As usual, Cedric seemed attuned to Wilfrid in a

way that anticipated his words. 'After the way in which he and Jarl Eirik parted at their last meeting,' Cedric explained.

Annis jerked her head to stare at her father-in-law. 'What do you mean? His last visit was…' She thought back. 'Why, it must have been after…after Grim's death? He and Lady Merewyn had come to pay their respects.'

She remembered the visit well. Having had a significant hand in raising Annis for the first years of her life, her Aunt Merewyn held a special place in her heart. Annis had been comforted by the visit, confessing the loss of her child to the woman. Aunt Merewyn had three small children at home at the time and had professed to losing a babe early in pregnancy between her second and third child. At a time when Annis had felt that no one could understand her grief, the shared experience had been a comfort to her. The visit had been a timely and well-received one.

Or so she had thought.

Wilfrid gave a jerky nod in agreement. 'He had the… He spoke of a marriage for you. Grim was not even… He was hardly in his grave.' His eyes hardened as if the mere memory still had the power to stir the fire of anger to life within him.

She reached out to him, wanting to be able to reassure him that he did not have to think of it if it would upset him, but she could not say it. She was too shocked. 'I had no idea.' There had been rumours that the Jarl meant for her to wed, but she didn't know the subject had come up so soon after Grim's death.

'I did not want you to… Too soon.' His gaze trailed off across the room, as if he were lost in his thoughts of the time. Tenderness swelled in her chest at how he had shielded her from what would have been a painful thing to handle at that time.

Cedric gave her a warning glance, both of them aware of how dire the consequences could be of upsetting Wilfrid, and he reached over and placed a hand on Wilfrid's shoulder, his touch lingering. 'Eat, Wilfrid, while the food is still warm.'

Wilfrid's food had already been cut into tiny pieces before being served to him. It spared him the indignity of having it cut and prepared in front of him. He could no longer use a knife, nor could he chew anything too large or too tough. His meat was specially chosen for him, so he received only the tenderest morsels. She hated that Rurik would be a witness to Wilfrid's weakness, but he hardly seemed to be paying attention as he ate his own meal with enthusiasm.

Wilfrid took a bite, chewing slowly and thoughtfully. She wanted to give him time to eat, but she did not want to let this moment of lucid reminiscing pass. It was not often that they were able to speak of the past so openly. Waiting for him to finish chewing another bite, she finally asked, 'What else did Jarl Eirik say of a marriage?'

'Tell her,' Wilfrid said to Cedric, already showing signs of strain around his eyes. His voice was fading as well. It was evening and his interrupted sleep the night before had taken its toll.

'He wanted you to marry one of his Danes, to assure our allegiance,' said Cedric. 'Things in the south were still unsettled. He did not want to risk you marrying a Saxon enemy and the fight for control that would result from that. He was inclined to arrange

a marriage for you. Someone from Alvey in Berni-
cia, but I cannot remember the names he put forth.
It hardly matters. Wilfrid told him that he would not
agree to such a marriage. At least not until you were
out of your mourning. Harsh words were spoken and
Jarl Eirik left soon after.'

'And he has been pressing for my marriage ever
since?' She knew it was true, but she wanted the rumours confirmed. The look that Cedric gave Wilfrid
substantiated them.

'We can speak of it later,' said Cedric.

The urgent sound of his voice made Wilfrid pause
with his fork raised. 'Speak now.' His tone left no
doubt that he still felt himself Lord here.

Sighing, Cedric set down his fork in favour of his
chalice. 'Every year he sends an emissary. I kept it
from you, but he says that you are not to wed unless
he approves the match. It seems he still intends you
to marry a Dane. It is likely that he has men in the
village making certain that you do not wed without
his permission.'

'You have kept this from me?' Wilfrid asked.

Cedric opened his mouth to reply, but then closed
it and took a drink of his wine. Annis knew then that
Wilfrid had known, had likely been a party to these
meetings. It was simply that he had forgotten.

Wilfrid trained his gaze on Rurik. 'Are you here
to marry her?' Only the last words were clearly in-
telligible.

She gasped aloud before she could help herself.

'No.' Rurik's voice was calm, immune to their family strife. 'I was told of no marriage and have brought
no messages about that.'

Wilfrid seemed to relax, but he asked, 'Then why has Jarl Eirik sent you here?'

Silence descended over the table. When Wilfrid stared at her, she repeated the question in case Rurik had not understood, though it nearly killed her to do so. 'He wants to know why you're here.'

Several moments passed until Rurik finally broke it. 'King Sigurd of Maerr was murdered. Word has reached us that someone here might have knowledge of the crime.'

Annis wanted to hide her face from the world. Their plan to not upset Wilfrid had not worked out as she had hoped.

# Chapter Nine

Rurik stared at Wilfrid as his words settled over the room. He was looking for any sign that the man was surprised, any hint that Wilfrid remembered the part he had played in what had happened in Maerr. The man went still, his cloudy brown eyes meeting Rurik's as his brow furrowed. 'You will find no one here with that knowledge.'

The words were somewhat garbled and Wilfrid's face was drawn tight with strain and fatigue. Whether he was lying or if he truly believed that, Rurik could not tell. Frustration made him drop the last of the leg bones so that it fell with a clatter on to the pile.

'I am weary,' said Wilfrid, turning subtly to Cedric.

This spurred Annis into action. Though she had barely eaten anything, she pushed back from the table and rose. 'Let us bid you goodnight. I will see Rurik settled for the evening.'

She made to leave, grabbing his arm none too gently to prod him from his seat. He wanted to refuse—though his belly was full, his wine had not been finished—but then changed his mind and grabbed his chalice as he rose from his seat to follow her. Not knowing how dire Wilfrid's physical health was, he decided that it was best not to chance the man having another attack, thus potentially robbing Rurik of the chance to ask any questions at all. He would work on getting the information from Annis until he was given the chance to talk to Wilfrid again.

'I should send you back to your cell.' Annis spit the words out through her clenched teeth the moment they left the hall. They were standing in a wide corridor with faded and chipped frescoes of some long-forgotten Romans on the walls.

'You would add liar to your growing list of crimes?' He could not help but enjoy taunting her, though genuine anger simmered beneath his words.

Her eyes flashed at him and then settled on his chalice as if she wanted to knock it from his hand. Deciding not to chance losing it, he took another long swallow of the rich wine. 'You did not uphold your end of our agreement,' she said.

He shrugged, knowing what she meant, but unable to deny himself the pleasure of her anger. 'How so?'

She nearly screamed her outrage, but glanced back at the closed double doors of the hall and tempered her words. 'We agreed that you would pretend to placate him.'

'Ah, but then you are the one who told him we are not lovers.'

'Only in the physical sense. We could still pretend to have a fondness. Why could you have not said that you were sent here to see if I was ready for marriage and left it at that? Cedric nearly fed you the words you were meant to say.'

Anger rose within him. 'Because I am here to find my father's murderer. Do not forget that. I kept up our deal while still doing my part to find the men responsible.'

'You upset him.' Her voice was raised and she pointed towards the hall as she said that.

Rurik was dimly aware of the warriors who had stood on either side of the door closing in on them, faintly confused and ready to intervene if they were needed to subdue him. However, the bulk of his attention was focused on the woman before him and the way her cheeks went rosy in her anger and her eyes flashed with heat. For a moment he wondered what it might be like to have all of that intensity beneath him, her eyes alight with a different kind of heat.

He blinked to break the spell she had cast and took a step back. 'You do not even begin to understand how upset he has made me—'

Surprising him, she closed the distance between them to bring her face close to him. She was tall, but still had to look up to meet his gaze at so close a distance. 'Do I not, Norseman? You might have lost your father, but I lost my husband…along with any hope I have of a child.'

Pain had replaced the heat of her anger, leaving her eyes shining up at him. A tender swell in his chest made him forget his own fury for a moment. 'I did not mean it in that way, Annis.'

She blinked—whether it was at his conciliatory tone or the fact that he had used her name, he did not know. Shaking her head as if to clear her thoughts, she stepped away from him, visibly relaxing her stance as she took in a breath. Her hands unclasped and she turned away from him. 'Follow me,' she said, not even bothering to look back to make certain that he had obeyed.

Then again, she did not have to make certain. The two warriors who had apparently been appointed his guard stepped closer, their eyes making it clear they would carry him if he did not comply. Cursing under his breath, he took the last swallow of wine before tossing the empty chalice away where it bounced off the stones and rolled towards the wall. One of the men gave his shoulder a rough push and Rurik began to follow her.

His gaze took in the house as he walked. Torches lit the way, lighting up the tapestries he passed and reflecting off the stone floor, turning it a deep orange. It felt old, but in a way that conveyed years of knowledge and living rather than decay. It should have felt forbidding and menacing—it was his prison, after all—but it did not. Strangely, it felt like a home, cosy and a refuge from the world. Cold winter wind howled outside, but, aside from an occasional flicker of the light, it did not touch them here.

The creak of a door drew his gaze to Annis as she disappeared through a doorway. This chamber was off the atrium and not the garden like her own chamber and Wilfrid's had been.

'Here' came the voice of a guard at his back as they approached the open door.

Wary of what might be inside, Rurik paused at the threshold, taking in what appeared to be a bedchamber almost the same size as Wilfrid's, but not nearly as well appointed. A large bed sat in the centre of the room with a few chests and tables scattered about.

Otherwise the chamber was bare, making it appear as if it were not currently occupied. One of the guards pushed him and he stumbled into the room. He turned, drawing his fist back to drive it into the man's smirking face, but he moved backwards too quickly.

Annis gave the man a harsh glare before turning her attention to Rurik. 'Your new home. For now.' She stood near the head of the bed, her features closed as if she had overcome her anger.

'It is much better than my cage, I will admit,' he said. He could not help but eye the bed with longing as he approached. Last night had been long and it seemed ages since he had slept in a good bed: the straw pallet in the cage, the boat and, before that, his time in Killcobar with Alarr looking for King Feann. They had slept on the ground and in dirty hovels much of the time.

His body longed for rest, but he could not forget the important task before him. He had to get closer to Annis somehow, to get her to confide in him, at least until he could make more progress with her father-in-law. 'Will you share it with me?'

Her glaring disapproval answered him even before she said, 'Never.'

He could not help the grin that spread across his face. Something about her simply begged him to unravel her. 'I meant the bed, not your body.'

She swallowed hard as he walked closer. 'Why would I do that?'

He shrugged. 'Wilfrid already believes us to be lovers.'

Shaking her head, she said, 'Not physically. I explained to him, you heard me.'

'I know what you explained.' Coming to a stop before her, he gave her a long look up and down. He wondered at how she seemed to trust him. He could hurt her now, quickly before the guards could get to him if he wanted. Did she even realise how she trusted him? Whether she did or not, he found himself liking that.

'But you do not realise how beautiful you are. No man would be a lover to you in fondness only as you explained to him. Wilfrid might be physically deteriorated and he might have memory problems, but he is not a daft man. Were you mine, I would have you in my bed every night and again every morning.' His voice had lowered as his words lit a fire in his belly. He had to clench his hands into fists to keep them from reaching for her.

She gasped and he did not miss the flare of heat in her eyes before she took a step back. 'Nevertheless, we are not lovers and we will not be lovers. Wilfrid can think what he wants.'

'Then I will ask that you stay.'

'Why?' She tilted her head to the side.

'Because you are the only one I trust here.'

'Why would you trust me?'

He grinned again. 'Because I am not dead yet. I have no idea of the intentions of others, but you do not seem inclined to kill me.'

She gave a harsh laugh at that. 'I can assure you the guards have been ordered by me not to harm you unless you give them reason.'

He glanced back at the two men near the door. They were not who he was worried about. 'And Cedric? He also has been given this order and he abides by your decision?'

A look of uncertainty crossed her face before she smoothed out her features. 'You need not be concerned with Cedric.'

Her assurance did not have the ring of truth. Cedric saw him as a threat. Cedric had stormed into her bedchamber in the early morning hours because he had found Rurik's cell empty. He hadn't forgotten the man had gone looking for him in the dead of night. Whether or not Annis realised it, Cedric would rather see Rurik dead than see him become a complication. Rurik had no doubt of that. 'You are certain he will not come in the middle of the night and slide a dagger between my ribs?'

She glanced at the door and then back at him. 'You will have a guard just outside the door. This chamber has no windows so there is no other way to gain entry.'

Lowering his voice so that only she could hear, he asked, 'And you are certain that the guards are loyal to you and not Cedric?'

She opened her mouth to speak, but then sent a quick look to the two men standing inside the open door. She was not certain. She might want to believe it, but there was something there that made her hesitate. As a woman, there were bound to be warriors who were loyal only to Cedric. Gratified to find that his hunch had been right, he drove the point home. 'I would prefer to have you as my own personal guard.'

Her troubled gaze lighted on him briefly before going to the bed. She looked very much like a reluctant bride who was about to be forced to endure a wedding night.

'You have my vow that I will not touch you. Unless you want me to.' He could not help but add that last part.

'I would be a fool to accept your vow on anything.'

She was right. Not that he would touch her against her will, but that he was willing to say almost anything to get the answers he wanted. Before he could challenge her, she said, 'If I stay here with you, you will be chained.'

'No.' He said the word so harshly that she straightened, clearly stunned by his vehemence.

'You must. You cannot expect me to sleep here, to lower my guard, based solely on your word that you will not touch me.'

'I will not be bound again.' The very idea of it set his blood to boiling.

'If you will not agree to be bound, then I will not stay.' Her chin went up a notch, a move he was coming to know meant that she was holding her ground.

'Then I will be so loud that no one will get any sleep tonight. I am certain I will be louder here than below stairs.'

Anger flared to life again in her eyes. 'Then I can bind your mouth.'

He stared at her, trying to determine if she was bluffing. He knew that his captivity did not sit well with her. She was not glorying in her ability to hold him prisoner. Would she actually see him gagged for the night? 'You would not.'

Whether it was his direct challenge or her own guilt at keeping him captive, he could not say, but something made her walk behind him to the guards.

'Make certain everyone believes I am in my chamber for the night. No one is to know I'm in here. I'll tell Goda that I am not feeling well and do not have need of her tonight.' Relief lightened his shoulders. She was staying. But then she mumbled something to the guard and it was so low that he could not hear enough to make out the commands. One of them ran off as she turned to him.

'Chains, or we do not have a deal.'

# Chapter Ten

The look of satisfaction that adorned Annis's face as the guard pulled the leather restraint tight on Rurik's wrist was unmistakable. Rurik knew that he had got under her skin and this was her way of getting her revenge. Thank the gods she did not have a vicious streak in her, or the punishment could be worse.

'On the bed,' the guard said. When Rurik glared at him mulishly, the man shrugged. 'Unless you would rather stand for the night.'

Apparently, it was not enough that his hands would be bound, she wanted him chained to the bed as well. He scraped his free hand across his jaw as he stared at her. She seemed to stifle a laugh as she turned to give him a modicum of privacy. In the time it had taken the guard to retrieve the restraint—a suspiciously short amount of time—Rurik had been divested of his boots and tunic, so that he stood in only his trousers and undershirt.

With an inward sigh of frustration, he climbed on to the bed and held his hands up to the headboard. The guard pulled the restraint around a sturdy piece of wood and fastened the cuff to Rurik's free wrist, effectively chaining him to the bed for the night.

'I find it odd that you have all these chains and restraints at your disposal. Do you make a habit of befriending men in taverns and bringing them home to chain them up?' He could not seem to help his unhealthy obsession with goading reactions out of her. She made it far too easy to want to ruffle her. The fact that she usually responded as he wanted her to only sweetened the enticement.

She whirled around as he had known that she would and gave him a critical glare, her chin notched up just slightly. 'None of this is necessary. There are no windows. No escape except through the door which will be heavily guarded. There is no need to chain you if you are in here alone.'

'And wake up dead? I would rather not.'

She laughed and it was not bitter or derisive. For the first time, he thought that perhaps she enjoyed his goading. Perhaps having everyone around her bowing down to her every whim had not been very satisfying.

'It is done,' the guard said.

She nodded her thanks. 'Go and take your position outside the door, Alder.'

Rurik called after the man, 'No one in or out for the rest of the night. If you hear screaming, it will be from pleasure.'

The door closed with a bang and Annis shook her head. 'You hold yourself in too high esteem.' There was no bite to her words and her eyes shone with mirth.

'You could find out.' Rurik raised a brow at her. 'No one has to know if you are very quiet.'

She rolled her eyes and walked to the far side of the bed, perching on the very edge. She divested herself of one slipper and then the other, keeping her feet and ankles well below the side of the bed so that he could not see them.

He decided to give his chains a quick test. Grabbing a section of the restraint with each hand, he pulled tight. She glanced up in surprise at the movement. The wood groaned a bit in protest, but stayed in place. He did not think it could withstand a prolonged assault and would eventually give way. The problem was the noise would draw her attention or even the guard at the door before he could break it. To make a quicker escape, he would have to roll up and give the wood bar a swift kick that would likely splinter the wood. It was a measure he would take only if Cedric or someone else came in to end him, but it was reassuring to have a plan.

So that she would not catch on that he was coming up with a plan for escape, he said, 'There is no chance that I can touch you. The wood is strong. You might as well get more comfortable.' He gave a shrug as well as he could with his arms pulled up past his ears.

'Thank you, but I will be fine.' Moving back on to the foot of the bed, she pulled her feet up so fast he barely saw the flash of her light skin before they were hidden beneath the deep amber of her skirts.

'Whose chamber is this?' he asked.

'It belonged to Wilfrid's wife. She died many years ago when I was still a child.' Her gaze touched briefly on the space between them before she looked away. It was a telling gesture, as if she thought the bed was smaller than she remembered, or perhaps it was simply that she felt uncomfortable being so close to him. He shifted a bit, making certain that his legs took up more space than was strictly needed.

She did not move away and instead asked, 'Would you mind explaining something to me, Norseman?'

His plan was to get her to talk with him openly. If he could get her to understand him, even sympathise with him, he just might get the information he sought. 'I will if you call me Rurik, not Norseman.'

She glanced at him and he read hesitance in her eyes. Almost a sort of fear. Interesting. Instead of responding to that, she asked her question. 'How is it that you are here on your father's behalf, as his son, if your mother was a slave?'

Noticing that he had to crane his neck to look at her, she moved on to her knees and leaned over him to adjust the cushion behind his head. She smelled fresh and faintly sweet with a hint of the outdoors about her, like a field of wildflowers in early summer. He closed his eyes to breathe her in more, searching for the musk of her layered underneath the scent, but opened them again as soon as he realised what he was doing. He could not allow his attraction to her to undermine his strategy.

'Because I am still my father's son.'

Her lips pursed in obvious displeasure at his answer as she sat back on her knees beside him. 'But you would be a slave as well?'

He stared at her, wondering why he was so compelled to answer her question. Yes, he wanted her to know him, but this could easily become too intimate, yet he was compelled to answer her. Was it simply that she was a woman to whom he was attracted?

'My father acknowledged my brother and me from the beginning. We were never slaves.'

She nodded and understanding dawned across her face. 'Ah, so then your mother was a true concubine and not a slave.'

'My parents had a complicated relationship.' Truer words had never been spoken.

'Will you tell me of it?'

He never spoke of his mother to anyone except for his twin and even then the conversations were brief and rare. She had died when they were young and ever since he had felt that talking about her might somehow take her further away from him. As if speaking of his memories would release them into the air so that they might evaporate and be gone for ever. As a result, he held them close, unwilling to part with the few he had.

'Why?'

She shrugged and he was struck by how vulnerable she seemed now. Without her guard, with Rurik bound, with her slippers on the floor, she seemed less Queen and more woman. He quite liked the transformation.

'You do not know this about me, because, as you are a prisoner, we have not had much opportunity to talk.' Her eyes sparkled as her tone became teasing and he found himself dangerously close to being enchanted by her. 'But I enjoy learning about other people. Wilfrid once had a warrior with dark skin who claimed to be from Córdoba. He would talk of great, domed buildings and fantastic battles. I like to imagine them.'

Rurik could not quite keep himself from staring at her. It crossed his mind that she might have figured out his ploy to get under her skin and was using it against him. If she had, she was being very effective. As wary as he was of her new-found enthusiasm, he decided it would be best to keep her talking. With that in mind, he resolved to tell her a bit of his parents, while keeping his own personal memories to himself.

'I am told that when she was young, men came from all over Éireann to seek my mother's hand. She was a princess—Saorla the beautiful.' As a child he had thought her beautiful in the way every child thinks a loving mother beautiful. Only now that he was an adult could he think back on her and appreciate her true beauty. With dark, flowing hair, green eyes and a small frame, she had stood out among the women back home in Maerr. Even knowing that she belonged to Sigurd, many men had admired her. 'She refused all offers of marriage until my father visited. It seems that even he was intrigued by her, despite having a wife at home already.'

Clearing his throat, he swallowed down the bitterness that accompanied those words. Most of this he had learned only when he and Alarr had gone to confront King Feann. He had not known Feann was his mother's brother and that he had confronted Sigurd to avenge the injustice done to her. His father had not told her he was already married, all but stealing her away from her home in his bid to possess her.

His mother had deserved better than the life she had had with his father. 'My father charmed her and when he left Éireann he took her with him.'

When he paused, she asked, 'Saorla went willingly, then? It was not a kidnapping?'

A bitter smile turned his lips. 'I suspect it was a

seduction. She left with him willingly, but only because he lied to her and promised her marriage. She
would not have accepted anything less. My brother
and I were born less than a year after they met. My
father's wife, as you can imagine, did not take to my
father having such a beautiful concubine. My mother
was relegated to little more than a slave. She asked to
go home many times, but he refused to part with us,
holding my brother and me hostage.'

He had not meant to tell Annis that much. It was
too close to his memories. He could see his mother
shaking with anger after Sigurd had refused her request to allow her to go home yet again. Could remember climbing into bed with her to comfort her at
night when she cried. An unwelcomed swell of guilt
thickened his throat. She might have returned home
to Éireann and had a good life had he and Danr not
bound her to Maerr. Or perhaps Feann was right. Her
pride held her there away from those who loved her.

Fascinated by the story, Annis asked, 'Why would
Sigurd keep her? Would not letting her go have been
simpler for him?'

Clearing his throat again, he said, 'I think he cared
for her in his way.'

'And what way was that?'

The way of a tyrant unwilling to part with something every other man wanted. 'He was not an easy
man. He was brash, arrogant, unwilling to give up
things he wanted.'

She sniffed. 'He sounds like a child with a trinket.'

Rurik laughed, surprised to find humour in the telling of the story. 'He may have been. Perhaps it was

possessing her that drove him to keep her rather than a tenderness for her.'

But that was not precisely true. Just as he remembered the anger and pain, a few of his earliest memories were the rare times Sigurd had visited their small home on long winter nights. He would open his arms to the boys and tell them stories for hours. Saorla would look on with a smile and, afterwards, long after Rurik and Danr were supposed to be asleep, he would hear them talking softly and laughing. That was long before their relationship had become more bitter than sweet.

'Why are you here fighting so fiercely in your father's memory? If you are...' She seemed reluctant to say the word. It was a harsh word, but it was one he had heard often enough.

'If I am a bastard?'

Her cheeks went rosy, a pleasing look on her, and she nodded.

'My brother and I were acknowledged by our father. We have the same advantages as our brothers born to Sigurd's wife.'

She frowned. 'You Norse are a strange lot.'

'Why? Because we believe that children have value, no matter whether their parents were wed or not?'

She sucked in a harsh breath. He had not meant her child, but somehow the words had struck that way. 'We value our children,' she said.

'I did not mean you. I meant that your people tend to disregard the babes born out of wedlock. Do you not send them to monasteries or send them out to be fostered by strangers? Are they not barred from their

rightful inheritance?' There was truth to his words—
she could not deny that.

'But surely, not all slaves are as fortunate as your
mother. Is it not still up to the man to acknowledge
them?' she asked.

And he could not deny the truth in that. 'That is
true.'

'Women, doomed to have no choice in many cul-
tures.'

For some reason, he longed to push the strand of
hair back that had fallen down over her cheek and was
glad for once that the restraints bound him. 'You seem
to have managed your choices quite well.'

She smiled, but it held a bit of sadness. 'I am lucky
to have found Wilfrid. He cares nothing for what people think and allowed me freedoms denied to most.'

'Wilfrid, is it? What of your own father?' Rurik
was genuinely curious about her now.

She frowned and he knew there was something
there. He was stunned at his own sense of betrayal
when she shifted positions, grabbing a cushion and
settling herself as if for sleep with her head at the
foot of the bed.

'That is not fair. I tell you of my life, while you
hold back.'

'You are a prisoner,' she said easily, ploughing a
fist into the side of what appeared to be a very hard
cushion. 'Life is not fair for prisoners.'

He laughed a mirthless laugh at how she had bested
him. The woman was a fierce adversary, and, despite
himself, he found he admired her even more. 'Tell
me, please.' He could probably count on one hand the

times he had begged in his life and here he was, begging again with her.

She had rolled on to her back and became very still at his plea. Finally, without looking at him, she asked, 'Why do you wish to know of my family?'

'Because you fascinate me,' he answered honestly. 'I have never met any woman like you.'

One long heartbeat later, she rolled to her side to meet his gaze. He was struck anew by how heady it felt to hold her undivided attention. 'I have met no man quite like you either, Norseman.'

His breath caught in his throat as he sensed more to her words. There was the flicker of interest in her eyes and, if he was not mistaken, her gaze had dipped down to his chest, perhaps lower, as she spoke. He was forced to grind his molars together to stop the surge of heat that wanted to warm his blood.

'Then you will tell me?' he asked to cover his response and draw her gaze back to his.

## Chapter Eleven

Annis knew what the Norseman was hoping to accomplish. If he could get her to see him as a person, a man who was part of a family with his own needs and goals, then she would naturally feel less inclined to see him meet his end. It was a clever move, though not particularly inventive. The problem was that she already saw him in such a manner. Her guilt had forced her to ever since he had first shown himself on the shores of Glannoventa. Perhaps it was that she was not particularly good at holding people prisoner, or perhaps it was that her prisoner was him—a man she was coming to know as endlessly fascinating. Either way, she was faltering in her bid to keep herself from feeling anything where he was concerned.

'What is it that you want to know, precisely?' A need she did not understand made her talk to him. All the while she knew that this path led to danger, but she could not stop herself.

'You seem to have been with Wilfrid and his family a long time. Why did your parents send you away?'

It was an easy enough question to answer without

allowing him to get too close to her. Rolling on to her back, she stared at the ceiling which was quite dark in the dim light. 'I grew up in the east with my family. My father's sister, Merewyn, lived with us. Because he was quite a bit older than she, my family took her in when their mother died. We were very close when I was quite young.' In many ways, Merewyn had been a mother to her when her own mother had been busy with the other children and running the household. 'One morning, a group of Danes visited our shores. It was a raiding party. They burned and looted, taking anything of value they could find. One of them took a liking to Merewyn, so he took her, too.'

'Ah!' He said it with such satisfaction and confidence that Annis was compelled to raise up on her elbows to look at him. 'Now I understand why you despise me so much.'

'I do not—' She broke off abruptly. It would not do to allow him to understand her true feelings, that she was coming to admire him and hoped for a way out of this mess they were in without his bloodshed.

'You do not...?' He asked the question, but his eyes told her that he knew what she had meant to say. Everything had changed between them in the space of the past hour. She did not know how or why and could not name the many ways that it had, but it had.

'I do not despise all Danes or Norse.'

He grinned. 'I vow that I have not come here to pillage and take you home with me.'

The queer little flutter in her belly had no right to be there in response to the idea of being pillaged and taken home by him. It was a terrible thought, for to belong to him would make her little more than his property, but it made itself known regardless. 'Of course you have not.' She sniffed and laid back down to stare at the ceiling, her palm going to her belly to calm it.

'What happened after that?'

'My parents sent us all away, hoping to avoid disaster should the Danes return. I was sent to Wilfrid because he and my father had already been arranging a marriage with Wilfrid's oldest son. We were betrothed with the promise that I would not wed Grim until I was older.'

'What happened with the Danes?' His expression had gone pensive, as if he were evaluating their actions. 'They must have returned.'

'The Danes returned in the spring, as expected. Jarl Eirik took over our home and my father was sent as a representative to the King. He had no choice in the matter.'

'And what of Merewyn?'

Secretly pleased that he would concern himself with her, Annis smiled. 'She happily married her Dane, Jarl Eirik, and they still live there, raising their children.'

'It is becoming clearer now why Jarl Eirik would be so adamant about you marrying. You are his relation and his responsibility.'

She shrugged, not particularly interested in discussing that topic again. 'Grim has been gone for several years now and I have managed to avoid Jarl Eirik's decree that I marry. I imagine that I can hold him off for a while longer.'

'Do you not want to marry again? Have children?' The teasing in his voice had gone. This was spoken softly and without mocking.

A cold hollow opened up in her chest as it always

did when she thought of Grim and her lost babe. There had been a time when she had thought of nothing more for her life than being a good wife to him and a good mother to their children. But that had changed. With Grim's death and Wilfrid's poor health, more of the responsibility of running not only the household, but the larger issues in Glannoventa, had fallen to her.

Two summers past, she had organised the early summer planting. Cedric had been preoccupied with a threat to their southern border and Wilfrid had only recently been seized by another attack. It had been a small thing to gather the men and convey to them a directive she had been forced to claim had come from Wilfrid himself, then to make certain the task was followed through to the end. Small as it was, it had filled her with a sense of pride and purpose. Ever since, she had been the one to receive villagers with Wilfrid in the hall every month. When his last attack had left him disfigured, it was she who continued to meet with them, conveying his wishes and resolving disputes, often without going to Wilfrid because she was capable all on her own.

Grim had been a kind and patient husband, but he would not have allowed her such freedom and autonomy had he lived. The truth was that Annis found she quite liked making her own decisions and shouldering the responsibility of her people. If she married, she was almost certain to lose that.

Rurik's voice broke through the silence that had fallen as she pondered his question. 'You were right. I do not know what it is like to lose a wife and a child.' He had obviously mistaken her silence for anger, but she was too shocked to correct him. 'I do not know why I keep reminding you of their loss.'

It was an apology of sorts. The only type she was likely to get from him, but it was no less surprising for its abruptness. She swallowed, only to find that her tongue felt thick in her mouth and her throat had closed. Instead of responding to him directly, she finally said, 'Why have you not married yet? You must be of age.' He was probably around the same age Jarl Eirik had been when he had wed Merewyn, making her think that his culture was similar to hers when it came to marriage.

'I saw no great need to rush into marriage after watching what happened with my parents, and Sigurd and his wife.'

'Perhaps you could learn from their mistakes. Do not seduce another woman after you have wed and you can avoid their difficulties.'

He laughed. 'Wise advice.'

She smiled. 'I am certain Sigurd's true wife was angry with him.'

Rurik laughed, a dry yet rich sound that made her want to make him do it again. 'She was, and angry with my brother and me for existing.'

Her smile fled as she thought of him alone and facing her wrath. 'What happened to you after your mother died?'

A moment of silence passed during which she dared not look at him, then he said, 'Hilda despised our presence, but there was nothing she could do. Our father welcomed us into his home and we did our best to stay out of her way.'

She tried to imagine how it must have been to be

a child whose very existence was seen as an affront to the woman in charge of his care. She could hardly do it. Her parents had been often busy and rarely tender, but Annis had always felt that she belonged with them. That she belonged in her family. She also tried to imagine what it would be like to have her husband bring home his bastard children and put them under her care. She could not. Sigurd must have been a fool.

'Did you…?' She thought perhaps she should not ask, but then there seemed to be no rules tonight. 'Did you feel as if you did not belong?'

He grew silent, so much so that she could not hear his breath for a time. When she glanced at him, it was to see him staring up at the ceiling the same as her. 'Yes,' he finally said.

She wondered then if that was the true reason he had come all this way seeking to avenge the death of a father he had not been particularly close with. Perhaps he was hoping that it would make him belong at last. Why did that thought make her so sad when she hardly knew him at all?

A prickling heat spread over her skin and with it came clarity. She knew why the image that had come to her at dinner had sent a flutter of longing through her belly. It was not so much that belonging to him excited her, it was the idea of him belonging to her that did it. She admired him. Like her, he had harboured a deep need for vengeance to restore his family honour. He had nurtured that need for years and travelled far to see it accomplished.

Also like her, that need had been fuelled by so much more than the wish to restore honour. When the layers of that need were peeled back, the heart of it was so much more. The heart of her need had been an inability to accept the losses. Perhaps his was a hope to find his place.

No matter what it was, she could not help but admire the strength it had taken him to consider the fact that there was something more driving him forward. It was silly to give the imagining any credence. He would not belong to her and she would never belong to him. But it made her feel better to know why the thought had provoked her.

Rolling away from him on to her side, she closed her eyes and tried to find sleep.

'You never answered my question.' His voice had her opening her eyes. She need not ask which question he meant. She knew.

'I do not intend to wed if I can help it. My freedom is too important to me.' Hoping that would suffice, both for him and herself, she closed her eyes again.

Rurik awoke to the feel of a woman's soft curves pressed against him. It had been a long time since he had awakened to such a simple pleasure, so he took a moment to enjoy her. The sweet scent of her filled his nose, wildflowers and the salt of her mingled together. He gritted his teeth, both enjoying and bracing himself for the sensation that moved through him when she shifted and pushed back, her lush bottom shoving gently against his hip. The blood thickened in his veins and his thoughts turned carnal. They seemed especially powerful because Annis was the woman in bed with him.

The attraction he felt for Annis was one that he could not deny any longer, not that he had been very good at denying it from the first. She was beautiful and strong and talking to her last night had only whetted his appetite for more of her. She was perceptive in a way that would have been unnerving if he thought he had anything to fear from her. True, he was currently chained to a bed and her prisoner, but she had obviously found it distasteful to keep him chained in that cage and saving him from Cedric's rightful caution was the reason they were here. In this bed. Together.

He had to open his eyes because the imagery that thought provoked was too tempting. He could not lie with her and there was no sense indulging the dream. She still lay on her side, facing away from him, but at some point in the night she had covered them both with a thick blanket that they now shared. It was the only thing saving his rather obvious erection from making itself known to anyone who might walk into the room.

Shifting his hips to ease the pressure in the confines of his trousers, he disturbed her and she rolled on to her back, spilling flame-coloured hair across the bed. Whether she had released it from the intricate plaits or whether it had come loose during the night, he did not know. He only knew that it was the most fascinating colour and he itched to have it wrapped around his hands so he could feel the silk of it.

Forcing his thoughts from her and how strangely good it felt to wake up next to her, Rurik thought of what had passed between them the night before. No matter how he tried to go over the entire conversation, he kept going back to the end, when she had asked him if he had felt he had not belonged. Her startling perception had given him pause. That feeling of not belonging was one that even he had not allowed himself to dwell upon. It seemed odd that the one place he had lived his entire life, surrounded by people who had known him since birth, would not feel like home. So instead of facing that, he had found ways to simply not face it. Women were one distraction of many. He had thrown himself into training, learning to best his brothers and the older warriors from a young age. He had focused on guiding other warriors, becoming someone that his father had trusted to send out to speak on Sigurd's behalf.

Now he realised that he had done those things not because he held a deep devotion to his people, but because he had always been looking for that moment when he might finally belong. If he became the best warrior, the trusted advisor, the one to find his father's murderer, then it might all somehow come together.

The thought settled in his stomach like a coal, glowing and hot. His plan might not work. What if he found the men responsible and still did not belong? Not the way Brandt belonged, the oldest of the brothers. He should have come into his own and replaced Sigurd as King, but had been denied by Harald because of the taint the unavenged murders had brought to their family. The familiar anger came back to Rurik, easing the uncertainty and idea that he did not belong.

Anger was manageable. Anger was something he could hold on to and use against the world. It beat the vulnerability of doubt, so he held on to it tighter. He held on to that anger and allowed it to fuel his determination. He would find the killers and afterwards perhaps they could all find a way to help restore Brandt to his rightful place. Nothing mattered but that.

Annis shifted, one leg stretching out on the bed as she slowly started to come awake. Her foot peeked out from beneath the blanket and then a trim ankle, followed by a shapely calf, firm with muscle. Desire flooded him, warring with the anger for control. They threatened to mingle and become something he did not understand. But then she made a soft sound in the back of her throat. A sound that meant she was waking up. A sound that fascinated him. He wanted to hear it again, wanted to hear all her sounds.

Her eyelashes fluttered and she opened her eyes. To his amazement, a smile gently lit her face as she set her gaze on him. That smile softened him, taking his anger and engulfing it in the soothing embrace of hope and warmth until it was little more than an afterthought. A slow burn beneath the surface of his skin that could be attended to later.

He might have started to respond. His mouth might have turned upwards in a smile, but he could not be certain. Before he could even think, she remembered who he was and where they were and sat up with a sheepish expression on her face, pulling her leg back beneath the blanket.

'Do not worry.' He smirked at her. 'I kept my hands to myself.' He rattled the chain against the wood of the headboard for extra effect, wincing at the pain that shot through his deadened arms. It worked and she did a very bad job of hiding a grin while huffing out a breath as she swung her legs over the side of the bed.

'Good morning, Rurik.'

His greedy eyes took in the vivid length of her hair and the soft curve of her hip as she leaned down to put her shoes on. As strange as it seemed, he was sorry to see their night end. Gaining her feet, she started to walk towards the door, but his voice halted her.

'You will not leave me here like this all day, will you?'

She glanced at him, her eyes dropped in a hint of shyness before she gathered her reserves and met his gaze full on. She was as fascinated by him as he was by her. That subtle move proved it. His breath caught in his throat when she took a few steps towards him. It was a depraved thought, but he wanted her to peel back the blanket and crawl into the bed with him. Perhaps a few hours would be enough to slake this wild desire he felt for her. He was almost willing to give it a try, even if she was supposed to be his enemy.

'I will send Alder to release your restraints. You can have the freedom of this chamber, but you will not be allowed outside it.'

'And when will you grant me another audience with Wilfrid?'

She took in a wary breath and chewed the inside of her bottom lip as if she was thinking of the best way to deny him.

'I will have the names of the assassins before I leave here,' he warned.

'I do not know. Last night was straining for him. I imagine rest will be best for him today,' she said, but there was a hesitance in her tone that put him on guard.

'Tonight, then.' It was more demand than request.

'I will let you know after I have seen him today. It will not do to overexert him.' She turned swiftly as if she did not wish to discuss it any longer. He watched her leave and for the first time he wondered if there was something she was not telling him.

## Chapter Twelve

'You spent the night with him?' Cedric had barely waited for her to settle herself at the table before he asked the question.

Despite his harsh tone, the smile on Annis's face refused to fade away. What should have been a very strange night, and had been in many respects, had not resulted in her losing any sleep. If anything, she had slept very soundly, better than she had since they had learned the Norseman was in the village asking questions.

'Good morning, Cedric. How is Wilfrid this morning?'

'He is overly tired. He was awake much of the night. Last evening was a task for him.'

She nodded. Those details were what she had expected. Wilfrid rarely joined them for their meals any more and, when he did, he usually took to his bed the next day. Last night would have proven even more trying for him, especially since Rurik had decided to break the news about Maerr. Any bit of upset seemed to send Wilfrid into a decline that took him several days to overcome.

She waited for the serving girl to fill her cup, before she said, 'Thank you, Leofe. You may leave us alone now.' She had no desire to have this discussion before the servants. They must all be talking as it was.

The girl gave her a nod and set her pitcher down among the others before taking her leave. Cedric heaved an impatient sigh as he waited, though Annis assumed the sigh was meant for her and not the girl. When the door closed with a soft echo, Annis finally allowed herself to meet his gaze. His brows were drawn together in a scowl she recognised all too well.

'I spent the night in his chamber, if you must know,' she said and found that she could not meet his gaze after all. While the night had passed innocently enough, she could not understand her response to Rurik this morning. There was a peacefulness about her that had not been there before sleeping beside him. Until she could figure out exactly what it meant, she did not want Cedric to root out the information with his all-knowing gaze. Instead of meeting his eyes, she focused all her attention on her food. Honey cakes always made her feel better anyway.

'He was concerned that someone might attempt to bring him harm in the middle of the night,' she added.

Cedric huffed across from her. 'He does not trust our hospitality.'

'Would you? He has been chained in a cage and then reluctantly given a chamber. He does not believe that you do not mean him harm.'

'The Norseman is wiser than I gave him credit for.'

'Why would you not believe him to be wise?' she

asked, mildly annoyed on Rurik's behalf though she could not understand why she would care one way or the other for Cedric's opinion of the man.

Holding his spoon poised above his porridge, Cedric said, 'Primarily because he arrived in Glannoventa to face us alone. He should have brought an army.'

'Perhaps he has no army. Had you seen the massacre you would know that dozens of warriors were killed. I do not know the details of the aftermath, but it seems that the kingdom is in chaos.' There was no reason for her to try to get Cedric to understand Rurik, but she could not seem to stop herself.

Cedric harrumphed and took another bite. 'Perhaps. I still say it was a foolish decision.'

'The alternative would be to give up the search for justice.'

He nodded. 'Sometimes wise men know that justice is not worth the risk.'

That message had been meant for her. Her eyes jumped to his and he met her gaze briefly before going back to his food. She understood then that this was why she was so determined to defend Rurik from Cedric. His search for justice was so much like her own, perhaps she was defending herself in the process. Her own search had come to an end, but it had brought her no peace. Would Rurik's search be the same?

Deciding not to comment, she took another bite as the doors were suddenly flung open. Alder hurried into the room with a stranger at his back. The man was unkempt and dirty, and he had clearly been riding for several days. Cedric rushed to his feet.

'Apologies for interrupting, but a messenger has arrived,' said Alder.

The man rushed forward, hardly waiting for Alder to finish speaking before he said, 'I would speak with Lord Wilfrid.' His gaze flitted back and forth from Annis to Cedric, seeming uncertain upon whom he should focus his attention.

Annis rose to her feet. 'Lord Wilfrid is indisposed this morning. I am Lady Annis, his daughter by marriage. You may speak to me in his stead.'

The man gave one last look to Cedric, waiting for his nod before turning his full attention to her. Although the man's need for confirmation was not unexpected, it still made her grit her teeth in consternation. It was more proof that she would never be completely accepted as a leader here.

'You have my apologies and condolences, my lady. It is my sad duty to inform you that King Ricsige of Northumbria has died.'

Cedric cursed and crossed himself all in the same breath. Annis was too stunned to respond right away. King Ricsige was the last true Saxon King of the North. Jarl Eirik had gained an uneasy truce with him and they had found peace for the last few years. However, with his death, the future was even more uncertain and unstable. Either the Danes would take over all of Northumbria, or the Saxons would install their own leader. Any uncertainty for Northumbria meant uncertainty for Glannoventa. Uncertainty for her.

Regaining her senses, she asked, 'What has happened?'

'He became ill. It was a natural death, I am told, my lady.' What he did not say was that poison often seemed natural because there was no trace of it. No one would know for certain which would lead to bitterness and betrayal.

'Thank you for bringing this message to us.' He inclined his head in answer. 'Would you stay with us?'

'I am sorry, my lady, but I must continue on. I have many more to tell.'

Nodding, she said to Alder, 'See that he is given food and a fresh horse. He may rest before continuing onwards.'

She waited until the door closed before sinking down into her seat. Cedric took his as well, though neither of them seemed inclined to finish eating.

'You know what this means, Annis.' He whispered it, as if to say it too loudly would bring the devil himself down upon them.

She could not answer him immediately. It was as if the blood in her veins had grown too cold to flow and sat pounding in her head. Only when she could rouse herself did she say, 'It might not mean that, if King Ricsige has named a—'

Cedric shoved back from the table, impatient with her. 'You know that it means you must marry now. Annis, this wavering has gone on for too long. Wilfrid is dying and he has no successor. If you do not marry, then Glannoventa and Mulcasterhas can be taken from us. Someone else will be brought in and God only knows how inept he might be. These people need you.'

She shook her head. Even knowing that he was right, she could not allow herself to believe it. 'Wilfrid is still alive. No one, not even Jarl Eirik, will allow him to be removed from his position.'

Scratching his jaw in frustration, Cedric said, 'That

might be true, but that was when the King still lived. What do you think will happen when Jarl Eirik comes to our door? What do you think will happen when he sees Wilfrid with his own eyes? We have been fortunate to have kept Wilfrid's state quiet for the past year, but when Jarl Eirik sees for himself that he is little more than an invalid—'

'He is not an invalid!'

'Isn't he? God knows that I love him more than my own family, but we cannot continue in this vein. Wilfrid cannot make sound decisions as he once could. You and I have been working on his behalf. If it were just us, then I would say that we could continue.' He paused and the slight wobble in his voice had gone when he spoke again. 'But it is not only about us. We have all Glannoventa to consider. The people—farmers, fisherman, even children, Annis. Think of them, if no one else. You have the responsibility to make certain that their futures are secure.'

Flushed with anger, she rose. 'Of course I am thinking of the children, and their parents, and the barren, and the very old, and even the criminals. All of them matter to me. Glannoventa has thrived in recent years. Our fields are fertile and our lakes are bountiful. No one is hungry.'

'That is precisely why we must act now.'

'Why? I am perfectly capable. Glannoventa is thriving because of me.'

Cedric shook his head. 'But it will not matter. You will not be allowed to rule alone. Jarl Eirik has made this clear. Whoever this new King is, he will almost certainly not agree to you ruling alone. Glannoventa is ripe and, while we have been left alone in the past, we will not be left alone now. One side will claim Glan-noventa, which means that one side will claim you. Now is your chance. You will either have a husband forced upon you, or you can choose your husband now and pre-empt them.

'Which will it be?'

'That will not happen, Cedric.' She shook her head emphatically, as if that would help make her words true. 'We can make an arrangement with the Danes. If Jarl Eirik comes—'

'*When*, child, not *if*. Jarl Eirik has likely already heard of King Ricsige's death. Make no mistake. He may even now be on his way.'

A shiver of unease ran through her, but she held her shoulders straight anyway. 'When he comes, I will explain to him. He cannot deny success when it is right before his eyes.'

Cedric struck the table with the flat of his hand, but he did not refute her.

'I must go and see to the messenger's care. Excuse me.' Angry and hurt that Cedric would give her advice that would betray everything she had worked for during Wilfrid's illness, she left the room.

It was strange how the morning had started with such a feeling of well-being and peace, only to disintegrate in less than an hour. The King's death was ominous, but it was not as dire as Cedric made it seem. Annis was certain that Jarl Eirik would be content to allow her to rule. The alternative was unthinkable.

To Rurik's frustration, he had been largely ignored for the day. The accommodations were vastly improved from the cage, but with no access to Annis, he was making no progress towards his goal. At least he was left with the run of his chamber and someone brought him meals, but he was greeted with stony silence when he demanded to see Annis.

He was perplexed to admit that he was a bit hurt by her absence. Their night together had seemed to have forged a connection, at least in his mind, but apparently not hers. He told himself that it was not the connection he missed, but the progress he had made in gaining her trust and co-operation, except even he did not believe the lie.

She interested him in a way no one ever had. He had never met anyone with her particular mix of boldness and vulnerability and he was not one to hide himself away from things that he did not understand. Only, in this case, the person in question seemed to be hiding from him.

Rurik rose to his feet when he heard the click of the door being unlocked. Even though it was early in the evening, his stomach grumbled in expectation of the evening meal, but he ignored it. He had already decided that he would refuse all food until Annis came to see him. It was either that or attack his guards and force his way out. While that option held its own allure, it would not tell him the names of the assassins he sought. Annis was strong, but her obvious guilt at keeping a prisoner was a weakness he planned to exploit. It was in his best interest to play the mild prisoner, for now.

Instead of food, the woman herself stepped inside. She was wearing a violet frock made of the finest wool he had ever seen. Despite himself, he took in the pleasing way the fabric clung to the curves of her hips.

'Wilfrid has requested your presence.'

He met her gaze at that, but her eyes were hooded. Strange. There was something she was not saying. Experience had taught him that a direct question would not get him to the bottom of that mystery, so he simply nodded instead of asking why she had avoided him.

'Good. Is he ill?'

A flash of pain crossed her features before it was quickly extinguished. 'Not ill, but tired.'

'Has something happened?' The question was out before he could stop it. 'I only ask because I thought I would be given more access to him.' He did not want to remind her of their deal, but he could not deny the flicker of annoyance that threatened to become a full-blown fire within him. Even a day wasted was too much.

She opened her mouth to speak, gave a shake of her head and crossed her hands in front of her. He had noticed that she tended to do that when she felt uncertain. A wild need to go to her nearly made him move forward, but he held it in check.

'King Ricsige has died.'

Rurik knew of the struggles Northumbria had faced to keep itself from falling entirely to the Danes and Norse, but he did not know precisely why this news seemed particularly disagreeable to her. To him it was inevitable that the Danes would install their own ruler who was not Saxon.

'Did you know him well?' he asked.

'I had not met him.'

'Did you—'

'If you will come with me, I can take you to Wilfrid before we have our meal in the hall.'

This was obviously a subject she did not want to speak with him about, so Rurik kept silent and gave her a nod of assent. 'Lead the way, Lady Annis.'

His tone was meant to provoke her and he was thrilled to get a slight roll of her eyes in response. She turned on her heel and headed out of the room, and his eyes had free rein to roam down the length of her strong and graceful back to the sway of her hips. In his abundant free time in the chamber, he had imagined that backside more than he wanted to admit.

She glanced over her shoulder, catching him, and her cheeks pinkened, but she did not reprimand his wandering eyes. The knowledge settled deep within his chest and warmed him. Perhaps she had stayed away *because* she had felt their connection. It was the first time he had allowed his thoughts to go in that direction and the result was too pleasing for him to allow them to linger there. He could not forget that this connection between them was only temporary and only to serve a purpose.

With that in mind, he forced himself to stop looking at her. Instead, he took in the wide corridor. More men were stationed here than last time. Aside from the two outside his door, there appeared to be two at either end of the corridor to block an escape attempt. There were also two at Wilfrid's door. Rurik had no doubt there were others he could not see. He felt naked and exposed without his weapons, making him realise how much trust was implicit in this captor/captive relationship they had.

She paused outside the old man's door and looked up at him. Her eyes were wide with uncertainty and a suspicious shimmer. 'Please do not tell him who you are. I beg you.'

He put his hand on the door to disguise that he had almost touched her to comfort her. 'I will adhere to our agreement, but I do need answers.'

She nodded, but then tilted her head to the side as she studied him more intently. 'What do you think you will do with these answers once you have them?'

'I will find the assassins and kill them,' he answered, matter-of-factly.

'And then what will you do?'

He paused, not quite certain what she meant.

His confusion must have shown on his face, because she elaborated. 'If they are dead, your father will not be brought back to life, nor will the others.'

'Ah, but my goal is not to bring them back. It is in part to punish those responsible.'

Her brow creased. 'And what is the other part?'

'To help clear the way for my brother Brandt to take back what should be his.'

'And what if you find these people you are killing have families?'

'I assume that most people have families of some sort. It did not stop these men from bringing terror and death to my home and family.'

She stared at him and he wasn't certain how, but he got the distinct feeling that he had disappointed her. He did not like that feeling. It settled heavy on his shoulders and in the pit of his stomach.

'The doors,' she said to the guards and the doors to Wilfrid's chamber were opened. 'After you.'

## Chapter Thirteen

Rurik walked into Wilfrid's chamber to find the man sitting at the same table as the first night with the wooden game board before him. He was not as lively as that night. He sat a bit slumped in his chair with a brow furrowed as he stared down at the pieces. Something had changed and Rurik would bet his life that it was more than the death of a king. Or perhaps it was what the King's death meant.

'Father, I have brought the Norseman as you requested,' said Annis.

So he was the Norseman again instead of Rurik. Interesting.

Wilfrid looked up and his eyes brightened slightly at the sight of them both. Raising a hand, he beckoned them over. The knuckles on that hand were swollen and red, while the fingers on his unusable hand were bent in on themselves. His skin was ashen, the only colour in his face around his eyes.

'Good evening,' he said in his usual laborious speech.

'Good evening.' Rurik walked over and took the

chair across from him. Annis followed, but she hung back, almost as if she were watching them rather than planning to participate in the conversation.

They sat in silence for a moment, until Rurik reached forward and moved one of the figures. Wilfrid's chuckle started deep in his chest and never managed to make its way out before subsiding. He swiped the figure from the board. It rankled to play so poorly, but Rurik reminded himself that he was doing this only for the man's amusement which he hoped would eventually get him to discuss Maerr. Rurik moved again and this time Wilfrid did not react so happily. Slightly mollified, Rurik sat back in the chair only to look up to see the old man watching him.

'I am sorry you lost your father.' The words were a bit garbled, so Rurik did not quite believe what he heard. He glanced at Annis whose eyes were wide. She slowly walked forward, her hand shaking as she reached out to touch Wilfrid's shoulder.

'Did he say...?' Rurik paused at her nod and turned his attention back to the older man. 'You know who I am?' His heart pounded behind his ribs.

'I am as near to death as a man can be while still breathing, but I—'

'Father—' Annis began, but he raised his hand to stop her. She gestured to the guards who quickly left the room.

'I must say this, Annis.' He paused and took several breaths, as if the words had made him use up all his air. 'I have not lost all of my reasoning.' He paused again for another breath. 'As soon as you said you were Norse and then mentioned Maerr...' a pause for breath '... I knew that you were Sigurd's son.' Wilfrid stared at his eyes, not looking into them, but at them. It was almost as if he was seeing someone else there. 'Your eyes are his eyes.'

Danr looked like Sigurd, while Rurik's features tended to favour their mother. However, their eyes were the same and those were Sigurd's eyes. Rurik had not thought to anticipate that part of him would be recognised.

'When you hate as much as I hated your father, you remember things.' His gaze looked off across the room as if he were remembering things about Sigurd. 'I have not seen him since Grim…in many years, but I remember.'

Rurik had already begun to suspect that Wilfrid had been too ill to travel to Maerr, but he needed to ask anyway. 'Did you not go to Maerr and see him one last time?'

Wilfrid gave a jerky shake of his head. 'I would have gone had I been able.'

The world spun around him. Rurik closed his eyes to quiet the spin. All this way and not only was Wilfrid an infirm old man whose death would provide no sense of justice, but he had not even been in Maerr. He told himself it was enough that he could be led to the assassins, but the victory felt hollow. The door of the chamber opened and Rurik did not have to look to know that Cedric had walked in. The air changed with the man's furious vigour. A quick glance confirmed the suspicion, though Cedric kept away, only standing inside the door.

'I believe you,' said Rurik.

Wilfrid took in another shallow breath. 'You came for revenge.'

'For justice.'

Wilfrid smiled, but it looked more like a sneer as only one side of his mouth twisted upwards. 'What is justice?'

'A chance to right the wrong.'

'What of our wrong? Annis told you of Grim?'

Annis was looking at Rurik again, only this time her eyes seemed to glow with her pain. 'She told me,' he answered, unable to look away from her. 'I am sorry for Grim.' He said it for Annis, not for Wilfrid or Cedric. He was sorry for the pain he saw in her eyes every time she thought of her late husband. For the days she had spent caring for Grim in his pain. For the babe she had lost.

Her eyes glistened, but she did not look away from him. The sight of her so vulnerable made his throat ache. He wanted to hold her in his arms and give her pleasure to take the pain away.

'You are sorry, yet you bring vengeance to our door.' This was from Cedric and effectively broke the spell Annis had cast over him with her eyes.

Rurik stood to face the man. 'I have brought only myself seeking the truth.'

'You came to kill Wilfrid.'

He could not lie. 'Obviously, that will accomplish very little.' No one would say it, but he would be surprised if the man lived out the winter.

'Then how will your justice be served?' asked Cedric.

'There were assassins. I can find them.' Not only did he want to punish them, but he needed to find out what they knew. Others had participated in the attack and he was almost certain that someone was responsible for bringing them all together. Rurik needed to find out who it was. For himself, his family and especially for Brandt.

Cedric's heavy gaze levelled on him before moving to Wilfrid and then settling on Annis. 'I am told that you are the son of a princess as well as that of a king,' he said to Rurik.

So Annis had told him. Rurik did not know whether to feel glad she had spoken of him or to feel betrayed. He decided to feel nothing and see where Cedric would lead. 'I am.'

'That means you can bring the warriors of Maerr as well as those of an Irish king down upon our heads were we to let you go.'

'My father's warriors were killed in the massacre. Those that are left serve a new king now.' There were rumours that the sons of Sigurd had conspired to kill their own father, along with rumours that they had plotted with their father against Harald Finehair himself. The fact that they were conflicting rumours did not seem to matter—the remaining warriors had still fled and now the brothers were scattered. King Harald would not be inclined to believe him. 'Besides, my own uncle conspired to kill Sigurd. Any proof I could bring would be suspect.'

Unless he could bring Annis. In the space of a heartbeat, his gaze flicked to her, taking in the smooth skin of her cheek and her soft, lovely mouth as she stared at Cedric. The base appeal of taking her was one he could not deny. He despised how his father had taken Saoria, but only now did he understand the allure. Annis called to something fierce and wild inside him. The idea of having her to himself was nearly irresistible. It was only the memory of his mother's pain that made him push the idea aside. For now.

'Then that only leaves your Irish uncle.' The way Cedric said that made the fine hairs on the back of his neck stand on end in warning.

'King Feann will see Glannoventa punished if I am killed.' The heat of Annis's body warmed his back as she came close, but he could not look away from Cedric to see if she was there in support or opposition to him. He supposed if he felt a knife slip between his ribs soon, he would have his answer.

'Cedric,' she said in warning.

'We should have killed him the first night you brought him here. I will remedy that now.' Cedric moved forward, pulling a dagger.

Rurik tensed, prepared to defend himself with his bare hands if necessary. Hot oil from one of the lamps scattered about the room could hurt Cedric enough to slow him down. He made to move towards one, but Annis stepped in front of him. Her back was to his chest as she faced Cedric.

'He will not be hurt. I won't stand for it.'

A swell of tenderness came over him, completely at odds with the fury of the fight burning in his veins. She stepped back so that her body touched his, a human shield. His arms ached to hold her, but he would not allow her to stay between him and the dagger, not when he didn't know if Cedric could be trusted with her.

Cedric paused, but did not lower his dagger. 'We cannot let him go. It will only be a matter of days before someone else is here for retribution. Their death will be followed by another seeking vengeance, and another in a never-ending cycle that will persist until a great war swallows us all whole.'

Rurik stepped to the side, but Annis followed him, keeping herself between him and Cedric. She grabbed his thigh and a frisson of longing rippled beneath his skin. He took her wrist, intending to pull her away from him, but his hand lingered instead. 'I will go in peace as long as I have the names of the assassins,' he said.

Cedric raised a prominent brow. 'And we cannot trust you. There is no trust between enemies.'

'Then we are at a standstill.'

Silence descended on the chamber, only broken by the sound of Wilfrid's harsh breathing. A gleam shone in Cedric's eyes and the corner of his mouth tipped up in a slow smile. 'There is one option left unexplored.'

'Cedric, do not!' said Annis, the panic in her voice suggesting that she still believed he meant death.

Whatever the man was about to say, Rurik had the strange feeling that the conversation had been leading to just this moment all along, that Cedric had manipulated them towards it. He held his breath.

'You could marry Annis.'

Marry Annis? He could hardly put the two words together in his mind. 'What?'

'If you are Lord, you will hardly be inclined to bring destruction down on your own people. One would hope you would not want to harm your own wife, but if you did, there is the threat of death from Jarl Eirik to stay you. When you think of it, short of your death, it is the only way to protect Glannoventa from you.'

Whether that were true or not, Rurik could not say.

He could only stare in disbelief. When he could finally draw a lucid breath, he moved to look down at Annis. Her face was pale with two spots of colour riding high on her cheeks. She seemed to be as shocked as he was, which indicated that she had not spoken to Cedric about this. It was not planned. Or at least, not with her knowledge. He quickly looked down at Wilfrid, still seated at the table. The old man did not appear shocked at all. The glimmer in his eye indicated that he and Cedric had discussed this.

'I do not understand,' Rurik said. 'How did we go from my death to this?'

Cedric returned his dagger to its sheath and stood as if he had not threatened Rurik only a moment before. 'Our meal is on the table. Let us discuss it as we eat. Wilfrid needs his rest.' Before anyone could reply to that, Cedric left.

'Did you have a hand in this?' Rurik knew it was unlikely, but he had to know.

Annis shook her head. 'Not at all. This is not something you should consider. I will discuss it with Cedric.' Turning her attention to the large manservant hovering behind Wilfrid's chair, she said, 'Irwin, see that Father is comfortable.' Then she leaned down and placed a kiss on the old man's cheek. 'You have been plotting, I see. We will talk about this when you have rested.'

He made a sound that might have been a laugh or a grumble and then she walked out after Cedric. Rurik watched the guard close the door behind her and felt as if his legs were wooden and his feet stuck to the floor. He could not go after them even though every part of his body urged him forward. They would not move.

'Rurik,' Wilfrid said in that way of his that fused the *R* and *K* sounds together.

'You agree with Cedric? You believe that marriage is the best way forward?'

The older man gave a jerky nod.

'Why? What do you get out of this? You would marry Annis to the son of the man you claim to despise?' Because Rurik was so shocked, his words came out more harshly than he intended, but Wilfrid did not seem to take offence. Instead, he gestured that Rurik should retake his seat. After some negotiation with his still-reluctant legs, Rurik accepted and sat down heavily.

'I get to die knowing she is well.'

'I came to kill you. How do you know that she will be well?' None of this made any sense to him.

'You've not killed me and you've not harmed her.' His words were halting now as if he were having more trouble forming them. 'You had chances. You didn't do it.'

'Perhaps I am simply biding my time.'

For the first time Wilfrid looked impatient. His face flushed and it seemed as if the words wanted to spew out of him, if only his body would co-operate. His hand slammed down on the table, rattling the wooden figures and knocking a few to the floor. No one moved.

'Cedric will tell you. Her options are few.' The breath moved in and out of him in a slow and harsh rhythm. Irwin came forward and touched his shoulder, urging him to bed, but Wilfrid shook him off. 'Take Glannoventa, take Annis and be done with vengeance.'

\* \* \*

'What have you done, Cedric?' Annis could not keep her voice from trembling as she faced him in the hall. She was too angry and bewildered to even try.

'It's not I. This was Wilfrid's plan.' She had caught him as he was about to take his place at the table, so he faced her with the well-laid table between them. 'He conceived of it. He proposed the idea to me. We discussed it at length and, after a time, I understood him to be right.' His voice was so calm in the face of her displeasure that it was a bit off-putting. It had the ominous tone of something that had been decided and now she was to receive the speech that had since been prepared to deal with her discontent.

'You both discussed it, did you? And when did you think you would discuss it with me? Was I to wake up one morning to a wedding?' A pang of regret crossed his face, and she felt a stab of victory.

'I am sorry for the way that happened. It wasn't my intention. Of course, I meant to speak with you first.' He went to sit down, remembered himself and gestured to her own seat. 'Please. Let us share a meal and discuss it.'

The last thing she could do right now was eat, but she sat because she wanted his full attention. 'There is nothing to discuss. I cannot marry the Norseman. There will be no good to come of it.'

'You can and you should.' He picked up a loaf of black bread and pulled off the heal. The words *and you will* floated silently in the air between them. 'Let us run down your list of choices, shall we? If you marry fast, your options are Lord Strang and Hrypa of Whalley. The first is older than Wilfrid and the

second would embroil us in a war to bring Mercia
back to its former glory. I would advise against him,
as sinking Glannoventa into war is not something you
want. You are welcome to the first, but he has three
sons and they would tear you apart in the fight that
would ensue after his death. If you do not choose to
marry fast, then you will either wait for another king
to be chosen, or you will wait for Jarl Eirik to arrive,
whichever happens first. The new King will likely
send a man to you who will aid an alliance to usurp
the Danes. This will anger Jarl Eirik and we will be
sunk into another war with the Danes. Or, far more
likely, Jarl Eirik is on his way here now and will arrive with a Dane for you. You will be married on the
eve of his arrival—my guess would be week's end—
and have a Dane's spawn planted in your belly before
the year is out.'

Her hands had come together during his speech and
were clasped over her breasts with her heart pounding beneath them. She longed to refute every word of
what he said, but she could only watch as he dipped
the bread into his stew and took a bite of it. The problem was that it all made too much sense. Her options
had been laid out before her and she did not like any
of them. She hated them, in fact.

'Then I am to marry the Norseman by week's end
and have his—' she could not say the crude words
'—have his child, instead?'

Cedric's eyes gentled as they landed on her stricken
expression. 'The way I see it, you have to marry—and
soon. You have five options before you. Choose one.'

Were they even really options when none of them
were what she wanted? It was all so unfair that she

wanted to plant her fist into the face of the first man who arrived hoping to claim her as his wife. After years of avoiding this discussion, it all seemed to be coming to a head at once. The only ways to avoid war were to wed the Dane Jarl Eirik put forward or the Norseman. Or were they? 'How do you know that Jarl Eirik will not declare war once he learns I have wed the Norseman?'

'Good question,' Cedric answered between bites. 'I do not know, but Wilfrid and I believe it can be avoided. Jarl Eirik is known to have a tenderness for his wife. If we are lucky, he will arrive with her. If we are not, then she may still have a gentling affect from afar. When he arrives you will believably profess your great affection and admiration for your Norse husband. Rurik will do his part to convince the Jarl that he will work with him. It will take a bit of doing, but I believe, in the end, Jarl Eirik will relent. Rurik has no allegiances that I'm aware of. I believe he can be convinced to align himself to the Jarl. Jarl Eirik might even consider it a boon that Rurik has ties to King Feann.'

Whether that was true or not, she could not say. She rather believed that Cedric thought the Jarl to be rational when she held no such illusions. However, there was a bigger issue with her marrying Rurik than Jarl Eirik. 'I cannot marry him.' When he paused in his meal to look at her, she took a steadying breath and continued in a lower voice so as not to be overheard. 'I was in Maerr. I was *there*, Cedric. Once he knows, he will not want to marry me when killing me will be so much more satisfying.'

'You will not tell him that.'

It shouldn't surprise her that he would feel that way, but it did. 'I cannot marry him and *not* tell him.'

'You can and you will.' He dropped his spoon and levelled a finger in her direction. 'This will be the last we speak of this. You will not tell him. It is not information he needs to know.'

'But he does. I cannot marry him under…under false pretences. It would be vile of me to do so.'

'It would be vile of you not to do so.' Cedric countered. 'You must think about your people. Not yourself. Not even Rurik in this. This is about doing what is right for Glannoventa. These people have become your responsibility. You have spent the last years of your life shouldering that responsibility. You cannot, you *must* not, shirk it now.'

Bristling under the weight of his displeasure, she drew herself up. 'I have said nothing of shirking my responsibility.'

'Fine. Then you can marry whichever Dane Jarl Eirik puts forth to you.'

'I… That… I…' Annis was aware that her mouth was opening and closing like a fish tossed up on the shore gasping for air. She simply was not able to stop doing it. This was all too much and far too soon.

'The Norseman, then?' He raised a brow.

'How can you expect me to decide so soon? For that matter, how do you know that he will not wed me only to slit my throat as I sleep? You are putting me in a very difficult position.'

'It is not me putting you in this position, Annis. It is simply the situation we find ourselves in.' Cedric sighed. 'Rurik could already have harmed you if that was his plan.'

'But once he finds out about Maerr—'

'You will not tell him!' His voice rose so that it echoed off the high ceiling. 'Never speak of that time again. You put all of us at risk, but especially yourself.' Pushing back from the table, he came around to kneel before her. His hands took hers in a rare sign of physical affection. 'Please, Annis. I know that you feel compelled to honesty, but it will not help you here. By all means, tell him if you must, but later. Much later. He is still a stranger to us in many ways. If you tell him now, he could very well marry you anyway with no one to stop him from carrying out his revenge on you. My protection can only extend so far.'

He did not say it, but they both knew what he meant. At night in her chamber, no one could intervene. Though she had no doubt that Cedric would knock down doors to get to her, there were things the Norseman could do that would not be heard. A coldness crept over her and she had to fight to keep her limbs from trembling, though Cedric must have felt it in her fingers because he tightened his grip. 'Have you told Wilfrid about Maerr? About me?'

He shook his head. 'I saw no need to share that. We both know the risk of upsetting him. Even that scene just now left me frightened for him. Wilfrid prefers Rurik because he wants to end the need for vengeance after he is gone. It does not hurt that marrying the Norseman will likely annoy Jarl Eirik. He does enjoy thwarting the man.' He grinned in fondness.

The door to the hall opened and Rurik stood there framed by two guards. She wanted to believe that he could be the saviour that Cedric, incredibly, believed that he could be. A large part of her trusted him, whether she wanted to or not. And the night they had spent talking had made her feel closer to him than was comfortable. But what did they know of him? What decision would he make if he knew her part in the massacre?

Perhaps he would take the choice from her. Perhaps he wanted no part of Glannoventa and would leave at first light.

But he stepped into the hall and took that final hope away from her. 'I will wed you, Lady Annis.'

## Chapter Fourteen

Life could change in a day and sometimes in an instant. That had been proven to Rurik more than once. His mother's sudden death from an illness, the wedding attack, finding out that King Feann was actually his uncle and now this. He was to be married into the same family he had come to destroy. As improbable as it seemed, with a night to sleep on his decision, he still believed he was making the right one.

In truth, he could remember very little of the previous evening. He remembered clearly right up until the moment Cedric had suggested marriage. After that, the bits of memory became vague and matched together in a way that did not seem to follow a logical trail of time. There was Annis's horrified expression. That particular memory kept coming back and it smarted. There was Wilfrid and the almost sage way he had pressed Rurik to consider marriage. There was Annis's face again when Rurik accepted. She had excused herself, but he honestly could not remember if she had accepted as well. Cedric had spent the meal—all with guards still present—droning on and on about Glannoventa's great history, but Rurik did not recall a word of it.

Earlier that morning, Alder, the guard who seemed to be assigned to him most and the one who had hit him that first night outside the tavern, brought him food and requested he ready himself for an outing. He half expected that Annis had arranged for his imminent demise. A little while later he had been given his fur and led out a set of doors and was now standing in a courtyard. A low wall surrounded it with a gate that was open to the outside. Alder disappeared into a stone building that seemed to house horses if the smell of manure and straw coming from it was any indication. The warrior returned, leading a mare, just as the doors to Mulcasterhas opened.

Annis and Cedric stepped outside, Annis with a look that suggested she was being led to the gallows, though Cedric seemed more resigned and less likely to stab someone at a moment's notice.

'Good morning,' Annis said. He noticed she left off any form of address. 'We thought that you might like a tour of Mulcasterhas and Glannoventa, before…'

'Before our wedding?' He supplied the words, while gauging her response.

She flinched, an unusual reaction for her, and glanced at a boy who brought out two more horses. Instead of answering, she walked past him to her horse, a sturdy-looking animal that whinnied in greeting at her approach. She stroked his muzzle and he dipped his head to get a scratch behind the ears.

Rurik found himself admiring her tall, lean frame as she moved. He had always found her attractive, but now that he had agreed to wed her—and it seemed that she had accepted him—his interest intensified. His body knew that she was his even if his heart and mind were slow to catch up. He liked the way she took the time to stroke the animal, before making use of the stool placed down for her to assist in mounting. He liked how she still crooned to him softly from his back as she settled herself. He liked how she sat in her saddle, both graceful and strong.

'Will you come with us?' she asked, when she caught him watching her.

Surprised to see that Cedric was already mounted, he hurried to the horse Alder had presented to him. She waited long enough for him to settle himself in the saddle, before leading the way through the gate. Cedric dropped behind with the three other guards who trailed along, allowing them a modicum of privacy as she showed him around. Mulcasterhas and the surroundings were on the remnants of a Roman fort and much of the original was still visible. Stone stalls had been converted to living quarters and wattle-and-daub huts had been built more recently to replace the ones that had disintegrated with time. The barracks had been rebuilt and enlarged to more comfortably house Wilfrid's warriors…soon to be *his* warriors if all went as planned. A new weight came over him as this realisation settled in. This would be his. An arrangement he was not likely to find in Maerr, even before the massacre.

The responsibility and the opportunity it presented was appealing. To rise from a barely tolerated acknowledged bastard to lord of all this was a heady proposition.

She showed him all of it with pride in her voice.

The barracks had been a project she had instigated and they were well done.

'How many warriors?' he asked.

Pride threaded her voice as she gave him an accounting of the warriors stationed here and those that could be called in if they were needed. He followed her arm as she indicated the endless hills that rolled far beyond their corner of the world. All of that would be his. 'Come.' Giving him a hesitant smile, she led the way up the stone steps to the top of the wall that surrounded Mulcasterhas.

And what a world it was. He had not had the time or inclination to appreciate the beauty of the landscape when he had arrived. But now, it was impossible to miss. Despite the fact that winter was upon them and white dusted the tops of the highest hills, the abundant evergreens kept the world from turning completely brown. Sunlight shimmered on at least two lakes hiding in the valleys where a silver thread of water snaking through the hills joined them together. He imagined how lush and verdant the summer would be and felt a pang of longing for Maerr and what had been lost.

But look at what he had found. It was not until that moment on top of the wall that cordoned Mulcasterhas from the rest of the world that Rurik truly understood the task he was taking on. His heart jolted with the first burst of excitement.

Warriors sparred in the valley below the wall and some of them had stopped to take notice. He had no doubt that talk of their possible marriage had already reached the men. The clang of the swords and shields of those in the distance continued on. The fight to gain their loyalty would no doubt be an uphill battle, but he welcomed the challenge. He had come to Glannoventa for vengeance and justice. While he had not found vengeance, perhaps this truly could be his opportunity for justice. A chance for all this to be his.

Theirs. He looked over at Annis, who stared back at him with a wariness he was beginning to understand stemmed from fear.

'You do not give this up by marrying me,' he said, keeping his voice measured so the conversation would not travel to Cedric and the others. He resented that he had not had a moment alone with her since agreeing to this match the night before. Now he thought perhaps it was her own doing. She might have been avoiding him because she was reticent about the match and rightly so.

A wry smile curved her lips as she looked out at the hills beyond. 'As I am a woman, you will rule here. Not I.'

Closing the small distance between them, he stood so close their shoulders touched and he took her chin in his palm. 'As my wife, you will sit beside me. I am certain we can come to an agreement for a suitable division of duties.' He did not quite understand why he was saying this. It was his right to do as he wished and she would have no choice but to answer to him, yet he wanted to see the spark return to her eyes. It had been there from the first and was one of the many things he admired about her. He did not want to be the reason it faded. From all accounts, she had done well on her own. He saw no reason to disavow her skills now. Not when he wanted things to be good between them.

Her eyes widened as they met his. 'You do not mean that.'

He could not help but smile at the challenge. Strangely, he enjoyed that about her. 'Do you question your lord?'

He teased her on purpose and was gratified when the spark returned to her eyes and she tilted her head. 'Daily.'

He could not help the chuckle that came from deep in his chest. His fingers tightened a little on her soft cheek as he drew closer to her. It did not matter that Cedric and the others were near, or even that several warriors watched them from below. He wanted to kiss her, to claim her in a way that suddenly felt vital to him. The way her gaze touched on his lips made him think she wanted it, too.

'I want to kiss you,' he whispered. Remembering their last kiss, he added, 'But I do not want to risk a broken nose.'

'Then you do not want to kiss me badly enough,' she said with a devilish gleam in her eyes and pulled herself free. She glanced back over her shoulder at him as she made her way down the steps.

Far behind her and over the opposite wall, the cold sun glinted off the small portion of sea that was visible. He had crossed that sea less than a week ago, but it might have been a lifetime. Little had he known that he might find a home waiting here for him. Or that he might find her.

Tendrils of auburn had escaped their confines to trail behind her in the wind. They beckoned to him and he was helpless to resist their call. With the exhilaration of a promise to come burning in his belly, he followed her.

The rest of the day was spent exploring the village. Her eyes lit up with love and enthusiasm as she showed him each shop or greeted a villager. It was clear that she loved this place. If the truth be known, he was a little envious of how she belonged here. It made him want to marry her even more. Not only so that he could belong to her, too, but so that he could protect this for her.

By the time they were heading back to Mulcasterhas, Rurik had almost forgotten that the marriage had all but been arranged. Had life been different, and she a woman back home in Maerr, he would have pursued her. But life was not different for them, nor would it allow them to forget who they were. A warrior left the gate as they approached and met them halfway up the road. Cedric rode ahead to intercept him, but after a rushed conversation turned back towards them with a grim expression on his face.

'Jarl Eirik is on his way,' he called out. 'He should arrive by tomorrow evening at the latest. Earlier if he doesn't stop tonight.'

Annis took a breath on a swift intake. Rurik wanted to reach for her, but he doubted she would find comfort from him. Instead, he tightened his grip on the reins, making his mare prance a bit in place. 'We must marry tonight.'

Cedric nodded. 'Agreed. Tonight, and by tomorrow he will not be able to question the validity of the marriage.'

A quick glance at Annis found her none too pleased, but she straightened her shoulders and her chin went up a notch. A sure sign that she was resigned. Rurik stifled a curse that it had to happen this quickly. They had had no time alone. Other than his hasty reassurance, she had no guarantee that he would hold to his word. He did not want a marriage like his father's, but under the circumstances he was not at all certain how to avoid it.

The wedding took place that evening. A simple affair with Cedric, Wilfrid, Rurik and herself, along with a few words. There was no banquet or long list of guests as had been present with her first wedding, but then Annis did not really require those things. It was only that it all happened so fast that it did not even seem to be real. How could a few spoken words change things so completely?

As impossible as it seemed, they were man and wife. The meal passed in relative silence, with no one eating very much. While she was worried about the night to come, the men were more worried about Jarl Eirik. The conversation centred on what might happen tomorrow and strategies on how to approach the man. Annis thought she participated, but she could not be certain. She was too focused on the Norseman at her side.

Her husband. He had promised to divide the duties between them, but nothing else had been spoken about that. Would he follow through with that? No one would force him. Had he merely said that to gain her co-operation? He need not have. She had no better options. She would have wed him regardless.

Would he be rough with her tonight? He had not changed physically in the hours that had passed that day, but he somehow seemed larger, stronger, bigger boned than she had noticed before. He had been kind to her that day when he could have been harsh. Then again, he had come here to destroy her family. What if he had decided that if there was no satisfaction to be had in punishing Wilfrid he would punish her instead? What did she really know of him?

Without realising it, she found her thoughts propelling her to her feet. All of the men except Wilfrid stood abruptly and he looked at her in confusion.

'I am tired. I wish to retire.' It was the only explanation she could think of, when she was actually going off to question her very sanity.

'I'll come with you,' said Rurik. His eyes were slightly hooded as he took her in and there was a softness about his mouth. There was no doubt to anyone what he was thinking, but she could not face that yet.

'Stay and finish.' She spoke too quickly, so she made her voice calm as she continued. 'I will be a while.'

He nodded, but she noticed his jaw hardened. He was not happy about staying. Perhaps it would have been better to stay at the table. She did not know and, as panic began to overtake her, she did not care. She had to escape, to be alone for a few precious moments before facing the coming night.

## *Chapter Fifteen*

Annis was still pacing her chamber when a knock sounded at her door. An hour must have passed since she had left the hall. It was hard to tell as, after Goda had finished helping her change and brushed out her hair, she had spent the ensuing time pacing the length of her chamber. She kept eyeing the Norseman's bone-handled dagger lying on a chest, but her normal ways of protecting herself would not work this time. The marriage had to be consummated before Jarl Eirik arrived.

Before she could make herself cross to open the door, Rurik pushed it open as he let himself inside. His eyes took her in—her hair was unbound and fell to her waist, and she wore a simple, linen underdress— before stopping on her face. The look he gave her was one that threatened to swallow her whole. She took a step back from him as he closed and locked the door behind him without looking away from her. He wore a long, dark tunic that was open down the middle and secured with a belt and his bare feet were peeking out from the bottom of the long hem. It was not until he stepped closer that she realised he only wore trousers. The fabric parted to reveal his bare chest beneath. Thankfully, he did not take it off, but she got a glimpse of firm, sculpted muscle. She shivered both in fear and a sort of anticipation she did not know how to manage. There was no question that she had been attracted to him from the first, but to have him here in her space, like that, was too much.

Reacting in the only way she knew—to take control—she crossed to the bone-handled knife and picked it up. Laying it across her palms, she turned back to him. Her brain could not quite believe that he had been a guarded enemy, a prisoner even, the night before, and now she was handing him a weapon. Cedric had insisted on keeping men posted in the corridors for safety, but they would be too late to help her if she truly needed them.

'The knife,' she said. 'The other weapons are in the armoury. We can retrieve them tomorrow if you like.'

Her heart pounded as she awaited his reply, anticipation at his pleasure in seeing it threaded with fear. She could hardly miss the way his eyes lit up when he saw it. His fingers touched the hilt with the same reverence in his gaze as he took it from her and turned it over in his hands. 'Thank you.'

The appreciation startled her. She had imagined him to be a bit more self-righteous in his acceptance of it. The tension in her shoulders relaxed ever so slightly. 'You're welcome. I know it is important to you, so I wanted you to have it with you.'

The hint of a smile touched his mouth. 'My mother gave it to me not long before she died. I think she knew she would never see her home again. Feann had given it to her.'

'Is it the only thing you have of hers?'

He nodded and walked to place it back on the chest. 'She gave it to me, because I was the older. I don't think Danr ever forgave me for being born moments before him.' When he turned around she could see the teasing light in his eyes and relaxed a tiny bit more.

'You and your brother are twins?' Shock coloured her voice. She had heard of the phenomenon, but had never actually seen twins. 'Do you look alike?'

Walking slowly towards her, he explained. 'Only a little. He is known as Danr the Fair because he is blond and favours our father. I am called Rurik the Dark.'

'Rurik the Dark. Hmm… Perhaps that is how our people shall know you.' She forced a lightness she did not feel and was surprised when he laughed. How was it so easy to fall into this familiar play with him? She had been terrified until he walked into her chamber. Perhaps it was her own imaginings causing her to be so afraid rather than him.

Even so, she could not help but let out a small gasp when he came right up to her and put his hands on her arms. She was not accustomed to him touching her at will.

'Are you afraid?' he asked, dipping his head down slightly to meet her gaze.

Admitting to her fear seemed almost as bad as having that fear to begin with. 'I am not.'

'I will not hurt you, Annis.'

The solemnity in his eyes made her believe him and a little more of the tension holding her rigid began to ease. However, she also knew not to expect the coming night to be particularly comfortable. Grim had taken his time with her and, while the intimacies between them had been far from terrible at the beginning, it had taken some time before they were more than tolerated on her part. She had no reason to believe it would be different with Rurik.

To delay the inevitable, she said, 'Earlier you mentioned an agreement. Things happened so fast that we were not able to properly discuss it, but I had hoped that things could be settled.' She braced herself for his disappointment and possible anger.

'Ah.' He dropped his hands from her arms. 'You are right.'

He did not seem particularly angry as he walked the short distance to her bed and sat down. The heavy brocade fell open, revealing the broad planes of his chest, lightly furred with hair, and the slight ridges of his stomach. If nothing else, he was an attractive man. A surprising urge to press her hand to his chest came over her. Would the hair there be coarse or soft? To stifle it, she made a fist and shoved her hands behind her back.

'If it is a separation of duties you want, then I will require supervision of the warriors and their training.'

Though Wilfrid and Cedric both had seen she was trained in the use of weapons, she claimed no knowledge of warfare. 'Of course. Cedric has always had that responsibility. I am certain he intends you to have a place there.'

'And you will have the run of our home?'

Her heart fell. This was sounding more and more like the type of arrangement she had expected. 'That is typically the case with the lady of the house.'

His eyes sharpened as he picked up on her dissatisfaction. 'What is it that you want?'

'I want to have an equal say. I want to be part of solving the problems that face Glannoventa. Every week Wilfrid sat for meetings with the farmers and villagers, but it is something he has not done for a while, so I have continued that.'

'Then I have no issue with you continuing.'

It seemed too easy. 'Truly?'

'I am a man of action. My father had days like that back home and I despised the sitting and endless negotiating of grievances and disputes. He would often send me and one of my brothers out to some of the far settlements in his place. It was a task that I detested. I would prefer not to deal with those, unless, of course, I am needed.'

She had not once allowed herself to imagine that he would not fight her on this. 'Then you will leave the smaller disputes to me?'

'All of them, unless you need to discuss them with me.'

'What of the larger decisions that affect Glannoventa? What if the crops fail one season, or once, years ago, there was a red tide and the fishing did not recover for two years, what happens—'

He rose and walked over to her. This time his hands fell on to her shoulders and he squeezed gently. 'From what I have seen today, Annis, you have done an admirable job in the years you have taken over for Wilfrid. I have no wish to take anything away from you. I would be a fool not to see the benefit you bring here and I assure you that I am no fool. We will face those decisions together.'

She smiled as the full weight of her fear of the future lifted. She had allowed her fear of marriage to colour her perception of this man. Despite the fact that he had been her prisoner for most of their acquaintance, he had proven his honour and goodness. He was a man of his word and she felt shame that she had ever convinced herself that he could be otherwise.

Of course, that did not address her immediate fear of the coming night.

His large palm cupped her cheek, while the other smoothed down her arm, leaving her skin to prickle in pleasure. 'I told you a bit about my father. There were many things I admired about him, but I do not wish to repeat the mistakes he made with my mother or his own wife. I want us to agree now that we will work to make this a true marriage.'

'A true marriage?' She was struck speechless so that she could only echo his words.

He nodded and his thumb stroked over her cheekbone. She could not quite explain how, but she felt an echo of his touch deep in her womb. 'It seems to me that a man and a woman can come together in marriage and still like and respect one another. I admit that the how of that is a mystery to me, but I can promise you honesty.'

'And that you will not take a concubine?'

He grinned at the reminder of their earlier conversation in his bed. 'I will not seduce another woman.'

She found herself smiling back until she remembered that she could not be honest with him in return. Turning away from him lest he see the guilt in her eyes, she remembered Cedric's words to her. He had begged her to stay silent, but didn't Rurik deserve the whole truth? He would not take out his wrath on the whole of Glannoventa now, would he?

'There is something you must know.'

Taking her by the shoulders again, he pulled her back against him. She did not even realise she had closed her eyes until the hard length of him nudged the small of her back and her eyelids shot open in surprise. His hands began a slow and delicious descent down her body, skimming past her breasts to settle on her hips where he held her against him.

'Do you not want the same thing?' he whispered, his breath touching her ear and making her skin prickle with gooseflesh all over.

'Of course I do.'

'Do you promise not to take another man aside from me?'

'Of course.'

His hands found her waist and he turned her in his arms. 'Then no more talk tonight. No more negotiating.' He leaned down until his mouth was only a breath above hers.

'There are things you must know.' Her voice was a whisper because she did not seem capable of more. She was trembling inside, so she set her hands to his shoulders to hold herself steady. They were so hard and powerful beneath her palms that she squeezed a little. 'Things that might change how you feel.'

'Then I will know them later. There are things I have to say to you that cannot be said with words. Let me show them to you tonight.'

She moistened her bottom lip in anticipation of his kiss and excitement began to coil tight in her belly. Still, as much as she wanted his kiss now, it would not be fair to him to go forward without telling him the truth. Even as she opened her mouth to tell him, Cedric's words came back to her.

*You must think about your people. Not yourself. Not even Rurik in this. This is about doing what is right for Glannoventa.*

Annis was very much afraid that she did not know what was right any more. Everything seemed to be turned on its head. 'What if the thing I have to tell you changes your perception of me?'

He smiled and it lifted her heart because smiles from him seemed so rare. She placed the memory of every one in a secret chest inside her head. 'You will be my wife, Annis. Whatever you have to tell me will not change that. We will face it together.'

'Then—'

'Later.' He was quick to add, 'We will face it later. Right now we must face the coming night.' His fingertip stroked a path from her cheekbone to her lips. She took in a sharp breath at the contact, unprepared for the shiver of pleasure that snaked down her spine at the simple touch.

Right. They must get through tonight to face tomorrow. Tomorrow would bring yet another battle with the arrival of Jarl Eirik.

'Why do you say "will be"? I'm already your wife.' She could not seem to stop talking. It was the only way to calm the trembling that threatened to overtake her.

'Where I am from, a man and woman are not truly married until they have joined together.' His finger dropped from her lips to toy with the string holding the neck of her underdress closed. He gave a tug on the looped end, pulling the linen across her breasts which made her nipples tighten. 'Will you become my wife in truth, Annis?'

There was a pulse deep inside her belly in response to him. His eyes had darkened so there was little of the pure blue left. It very much felt as if he wished to devour her. The odd thing was that she very much felt she would enjoy it.

When she nodded, his lips split in a grin that bared his teeth to her. They were straight and white with pointy eye teeth, making him seem quite wolfish. Why did her heart leap in anticipation?

# *Chapter Sixteen*

His lips were warm and soft when they touched hers. There was no urgency so the press of him was light and pleasant. Annis closed her eyes and allowed him his leisure. A strong hand cradled the nape of her neck, his long fingers sliding into her hair, while his other moved down her back, slowly drawing her closer to him until his heat was pressed against her front. Her lips parted with surprise at the breadth and strength of his hardness against her belly, so close to where it would eventually nestle inside her.

His fingers moved in soothing circles at the small of her back, not letting her retreat, but not pulling her forward. Instead of pressing his advantage, he placed tiny kisses along the rim of her lips, reminding her of a bee sipping nectar.

'It's been years.' She did not understand her need to explain her hesitance. It must be obvious to him. She simply did not like to behave in such a way. When the world required her to be resolute and forceful, this reticence was new.

He raised his head enough to look into her eyes.

'There is no rush tonight, Annis. You will be mine before morning no matter how fast or how slow we proceed.' The thumb on the hand at her nape stroked up and down across her frantic pulse. 'Would you like to touch me?'

Releasing her, he took her hands in his and brought one to his mouth where he placed a moist kiss on her wrist. Threads of pleasure wove their way up her arm before he dropped her hands to rest on his chest. She luxuriated in the warm, hard feel of him, letting her fingers slip beneath the soft fabric to push it further back. He did not react as he watched her face. His muscles were firm beneath her palms as they roamed. He was so hard and somehow supple at the same time. Her fingers curled in the light mat of fur, marvelling at how it could feel both coarse and soft at the same time. This man was a contradiction. She was starting to think that it might very well take her years, perhaps a lifetime, to learn all his nuances. Perhaps she was even looking forward to that.

Feeling braver and more herself, she found the nipples hiding in the fur and traced her fingers over them. The muscle beneath them flexed and his skin drew taut. She glanced up to see him studying her intently, his eyes deep pools of need. Satisfied with his response, she moved her hands up his chest to his shoulders, pushing the fabric away as she went. Neither of them seemed to notice when it fell to the floor. Her fingers traced the ropes of muscle that wrapped his shoulders and upper arms. Grim had been solid and strong, but not like this. There were angles and valleys where muscle met muscle. Each one of them seemed to flex as her fingers found them, which delighted her.

Skimming down his arms, she let her fingertips
dance across the hair on his forearms and thick wrists
to his hands. They were broad and strong like the rest
of him, but his fingers were long and graceful. Turning his hand over in hers, she traced the calluses at
the base of each finger. She brought his hand to her
face, remembering how he had gently cupped her chin
earlier that morning. He did it again now, letting his
thumb stroke her mouth. On impulse, she pressed a
kiss to the rough pad, drawing a deep sound from the
back of his throat.

She met his gaze and the naked desire there sent a
flood of heat low in her belly. Giving him a hesitant
smile, she let the tip of her tongue taste the salt of his
skin. His eyes flared, but he made no move to touch
her otherwise. Satisfied that he would cede her con
trol for now, she let his hand fall to her hip while hers
went back to his chest. Only this time, she let her curiosity take her downward, over the ridged planes of
his stomach. He was as lean here as Grim had been,
but somehow harder.

Her fingers found the waist of his trousers, but fal-
tered in their exploration. She wanted to touch the part
of him that made him a man, but it felt wrong somehow. He had been her enemy mere days ago. Her fingertips fluttered at the waist as she debated. They fell
away, but he was fast and caught her hands with his.

'Do you want to touch me there?' His voice was
rich with a husk she had never heard in it before. The
vibration of it raked pleasantly across her skin and
down her spine.

She nodded, her mouth suddenly gone too dry for
words. Slowly, and with the lightest touch on her wrist,

he brought one of her hands to that hard part of him hidden within the confines of his trousers. The shape of him was clearly outlined, a long, thick ridge that reached for his navel. She traced it experimentally with her fingertips, delighting in how it seemed to jerk. Then she shaped it to her palm, marvelling at how he was longer than her hand. She could not properly compare him to Grim in this area, because she had never once touched her husband like this.

How was it so easy to do with this man who was nearly a stranger? But to call him a stranger seemed terribly wrong. Some part deep within her knew him.

Her thoughts shuddered to a stop and corrected the sentiment. This man was now her husband. Not Grim. Not any more. She might have pulled away as the realisation washed over her, except a blast of cool air touched her breasts. Rurik had been busy loosening the drawstring that held her clothing together while she had been lost in her thoughts. His fingers gently and deliberately drew the linen down until it was beneath her breasts, framing them for his gaze.

His forefinger traced an invisible line from the hollow at her throat to the pink tip of one breast. Her breath caught as he circled the nipple, watched it draw tight and then pinched it lightly. She could not stop the gasp that escaped her as she watched him roll the tortured and eager nub between that finger and his thumb. When he tugged a bit, a bolt of heat travelled down to that hot place between her thighs. She watched eagerly as his other hand cupped the breast that had been neglected and gave it similar treatment. By the time he took them both in his hands, kneading a soft rhythm, her knees were ready to give way beneath her.

She sighed in genuine regret when one of his hands released her to roam down to her waist and curve around her back to draw her against him. His palm moved down to cup her bottom, making her stomach flutter in delicious anticipation. His short beard rasped her cheek as he sought her mouth, taking it in a deep kiss. She only had time to open for him before his tongue sought hers, invading her in a way that was reminiscent of how his body would join with hers very soon.

Want was quickly becoming need as she kissed him back, touching his tongue with hers as she sought to learn the taste of him. He growled softly deep in his throat at her response and the sound emboldened her. Her hands found their way to the nape of his neck where her fingers curled into his hair. When she tugged, he made another throaty sound and released her lips to drag his mouth down the column of her neck. He found a sensitive spot beneath her ear and touched it with his tongue, nearly making her jump out of her skin.

Grinding his manhood against her hip, he said in a broken voice, husky with need, 'I want to be inside you, Wife.' To emphasise the words, his teeth scraped her soft earlobe, the pain of it mixed with the pleasure coursing through her blood so it was impossible to distinguish the two.

She was surprised at how the words made her feel anticipation instead of anxiety. She also realised that he had said them as a sort of request, wanting her to give him permission. Drawing back slightly, she cupped his cheek, moved by the genuine tenderness in his eyes, though it was mixed with a healthy dose of lust. This could have been over in moments, but he was holding himself back for her.

'Soon.' She smiled at him and took his mouth in a brief kiss before moving back to put a breath of air between them. Her fingers went to the neckline of her clothing and tugged, letting it fall down her body to land in a heap at her feet.

His eyes went wide before narrowing in desire again as his gaze roved down her body at will. 'You are beautiful.'

Her face burned with the compliment. She was bold, but not bold enough to stand before him naked for any length of time. Not yet. Her fingers trembled as she pulled down the coverlet and slipped underneath, quickly moving over to make room for him in the bed. 'Now you,' she said from the safety of the blankets. Her bravery in this extended only so far.

'Do you wish to see me?' he asked with a devious glint in his eye.

She nodded, astounded at how badly she wanted to see him as her gaze drank in the sight of his muscled torso.

His hands came up in what seemed to be a deliberately slow movement to draw on the fastenings of his trousers. He pushed them down, first revealing the dark trail of hair that led downward from his navel, before giving her a glimpse of his manhood. The tip of him glistened. He pushed the trousers down his muscled thighs and she finally got a glimpse of his perfect length as it stood proud with his need for her. A few veins stood out against the smoothness of his skin there as it rose flawlessly from the dark patch of fur to lie against his belly.

Instead of crawling into bed beside her, he pulled the blankets back and knelt before her. His eyes were fevered and demanding as he took her in. A flush of embarrassment mixed with her own desire overcame her as she brought her knees to her chest. A grin twisted one corner of his lips as he ran his palms up and down the length of her calves.

'Your legs are very pretty, strong and lean, but they are not what I wish to see.'

When had her breath become this ragged? She stared at him, somehow unable to comprehend what he must mean. 'Do you…do you mean that you want to see…?' She could not bring herself to say the words.

Thankfully, she did not have to. 'Open your legs. I want to see your desire for me.'

His words only made her thighs press further into her chest. Grim had never asked this of her before. He came to her in the dark, or sometimes by the light of a candle that had not yet sputtered out, but he had never looked at her *there* to her knowledge. Perhaps a glimpse, but nothing more.

His eyes all but dared her to comply, while his hands encircled her ankles. She startled when the backs of his fingers stroked against the tender flesh of her inner thighs, dangerously close to that part of her.

'Why do you hesitate?' he asked. Although his eyes were still fierce with need, his voice was soft and unhurried.

'Because…it's indecent.' Was this the price of marriage to a pagan? Even while she asked the question, she could not deny that a part of her thrilled at the prospect of complying with his request, of having him see her there—perhaps he would even want to touch her there. Damp need accompanied that thought and she worried that he might know. What would he think if he saw her like that?

Obviously, she understood that it was part of the process. The times she was damp there had been the times Grim's invasion had not pained her. But to have it known was something altogether different.

Thankfully, Rurik did not seem to be at all bothered by her internal debate. He had taken an ankle in hand and drew it to his mouth. His lips touched the arch of her foot before trailing to the soft divot near her ankle. She watched, breathless, as he kissed his way up the inside of her calf and she seemed helpless to resist when he said, 'Lie back.'

Her eyes closed as soon as her back touched the soft mattress. How easy it would be to close her eyes and let him have his way with her. Reflex made her grab the edge of the blanket and pull it over her breasts, but that was as far as it went to cover her nakedness. She gasped when his hot mouth touched her inner thigh and his tongue traced over her skin. When he gave a gentle nudge, her other knee fell to the side. She would not think of the fact that she was exposed to his gaze. If she did not open her eyes, he could look and she would not have to acknowledge that he had seen her.

Nothing could have prepared her for the hot dampness of his mouth when it found her, or his eager tongue stroking between the lips that guarded her there. Eyes opening in shock, she sat up and grabbed his hair even as the hot flame of pleasure bloomed to life deep in her womb. 'Rurik! You cannot!'

He grinned up at her like a cat that had made a glutton of itself on ill-gotten cream. 'I would know your taste as any mate should.'

She stared at him, speechless in the face of that odd logic. He continued to smile as he placed another kiss to her curls, knowing full well that she watched him do it. 'But you are right,' he continued. 'That will have to be later. You are more than ready for me now.'

His strong body rose over her, forcing her to lie back. Resting on an elbow above her, he took her leg and fitted it around his hip, opening her to him in a way that had her angling her hips, eager for him despite how he had shocked her. As his gaze met hers and locked, his fingers worked between them and found her opening. He was right. She could easily feel how damp she was when a long finger slipped inside her. She clenched around him, arching her hips for more. He watched her face as he pressed another in, stretching her. There was a slight burn as her body adjusted, but it gave way quickly to greedy need as he moved them in and out in a slow rhythm that had her hips responding.

She had never felt this mindless with her need. In the space of a few moments, she had gone from being conscious of her own nakedness to preening under his touch, heedless of what he was doing to her as long as he kept touching her. A whimper escaped her throat and he groaned in response, dropping his mouth to her exposed neck. Her hands clutched at his hips, trying to draw him to her in her need to be filled. His manhood, hot and thick, brushed against her inner thigh, then the curls that guarded her womanhood.

'Please,' she whispered, wanting more than his fingers inside her.

That got an immediate response. He released her and rose fully above her with his palms flat to the bed, his hard shaft poised against her nether lips. 'Please what?' he whispered. His gaze was hot with his desire, his eyes unfocused.

'I need you inside me.' The words were barely discernible, but they made him groan.

Flexing his hips, he pushed into her, slipping in easily at first and then meeting some resistance. He pulled back, nearly all the way out, then resettled himself on an elbow to lie over her, grasping her beneath her hip with his other hand. The new angle lifted her slightly so that when he pressed forward again, he pushed in all the way. She gasped at the sensation of being filled as his hips came to rest against hers.

He was motionless for a moment, his breath harsh and laboured against her ear. 'Annis,' he whispered.

Something about her name on his lips at such a moment sent a tender pang through her chest. Her fingers buried themselves in the hair at the back of his head and she pulled his mouth to hers as she raised her hips. The low rough sound in the back of his throat as he kissed her without restraint was nearly her undoing. She felt full of him and more wanted than she had ever felt in her entire life.

His hips moved in a slow, searching rhythm that increased with the intensity of their kisses. Finally, it was too much to do both, so he broke off and buried his face in her hair as he increased his pace, his breath hot against her ear. A pressure began low in her belly and coiled tighter and tighter with each stroke. She could not get enough of him. It was not enough to be owned by him, to become his wife, she also needed to be possessed by him it seemed.

'Rurik,' she whispered, though she had no idea why.

He whispered back, speaking to her in his own language. The words ran together, leaving her no hope of remembering them to try to discern their meaning later. He rose over her and brought his hips against hers in a powerful thrust. She cried out at how the hard friction drove that coil of pleasure to tighten. She whimpered with her need, clawing at his shoulders in her bid for more. He obliged her and then his fingers found her where they were joined. A stroke of his thumb had her cresting a wave of exquisite pleasure as he moved within her, then hurtling over the brink with a cry. He gave a series of shorter, ungraceful thrusts and then stiffened, his own cry of pleasure filling the chamber before he fell over her.

She was amazed at the swell of affection that overcame her as he lay above her. He was her husband now and somehow that seemed all right. If he was this tender with her at night, she had hope that the daytime would be tolerable. She ran a loving palm down his back, which he must have taken as a sign that he was too heavy. He shifted and pulled out of her, leaving her aching and still somewhat needy for him.

Rolling on to his back with an arm thrown over his face, she found herself reluctant to let him go, which was silly. The deed was done. They were well and truly man and wife now. There was no need for anything more. She wasted no time in grabbing the blanket and pulling it over herself, both relieved and sad to have the initial act over and done with. Having not expected to enjoy it nearly as much as she had, she did not quite know how to face him now that the haze of pleasure was fading.

After taking a moment to regain his breath, he lowered the arm that had covered his face and looked at her, unconcerned with his nakedness. His manhood lay against him, still half-rigid.

'Did I hurt you?' he asked.

She shook her head. 'Not at all.' Try as she might, she could not prevent a blush from staining her cheeks.

It was only then that he smiled and turned on his side, raising up on an elbow to look down at her. 'You are my wife now, in all ways.'

'And you are my husband.' She still was not quite certain what that meant to her or for their future, but the tenderness in his gaze as he smiled down at her was more than she had ever hoped for.

'Do you wish to sleep?' he asked, stroking the ridge of her cheek.

The simple touch stoked the simmering flames of desire in her belly to vibrant life. It was nearly overwhelming how she could want to experience that again with him so soon. That, as much as her own uncertainty at how things would be between them now, made her nod. Dropping his arm, he pulled her into his side. She stiffened in surprise.

'Will you not go back to your chamber?' she asked. Grim had always left her soon afterwards.

'No, I sleep with you.'

The way he said it was almost as if he meant that he would sleep with her for ever, not just tonight. She did not want to ask, because whichever way he answered would leave her confused. Fatigue was already making her eyelids heavy and the pleasure he had given her made her limbs cumbersome and weighted. There had been too much change for one day. Instead of arguing, she allowed herself to relax into him and enjoy the weight of his arm across her body. He smelled the way he had that night in the tavern, of the outdoors and a deep, rich spice that was his alone. Turning her face towards him, she placed her nose very near the hollow of his neck where she could breathe him in.

Tomorrow would be soon enough to face Jarl Eirik. After the Jarl left she would consider how to tell Rurik about Maerr. Tonight, she would bask in the simple pleasure of sleeping near this man who by a strange twist of fate had become her husband.

Rurik could not sleep. Too much had happened in the past day to allow him a peaceful rest. And with Jarl Eirik expected to arrive tomorrow, there was even more in store for them. But that was not why he could not take his eyes from the woman slumbering at his side. In her sleep she had turned to him and now her head rested pillowed on his shoulder, while he gently twisted a length of her auburn hair around his finger. He took in her sleep-softened features, greedy to savour them before the single remaining candle burnt itself out.

She was beautiful, but he'd had beautiful women before. She was courageous, but he had known many courageous women. No matter how he studied her features, he could not understand exactly what it was about her that drew him in. Or why joining with her had felt as if he had given her a piece of himself that would belong to her for ever. It must have been the words he had spoken when he'd been inside her. He had bound them together, saying the only vows that mattered to him as he took her as his wife and gave himself to her as her husband.

The immediate closeness with her was both welcomed and unsettling. It seemed only right that he would feel this with his wife, but it was, nonetheless, unexpected. Drawing a length of her hair to his nose, he breathed in the soft and sweet scent of her. The heavy mass fell through his fingers to lie on her breast where the blanket had pulled down. Her pink nipple peeked out at him through the auburn strands.

He smiled and stroked it with a fingertip, watching it draw up as if eager for more of his touch. His shaft swelled immediately, ready for more of her, but she needed her rest. And if he was being honest with himself, a very real part of him was afraid of what might happen if he allowed himself to have her too often. What if every time they came together he gave her another piece of himself? What if soon she had all of him?

What if it was already too late to worry about such things?

He wanted a true marriage, but the truth was that he didn't know if he was ready for that closeness. Only now, after glimpsing how good things could be with her, was he coming to appreciate the vulnerability required for what he wanted. He'd not had much experience of leaving himself defenceless. Life had always been about strength and fortification for him.

Pulling the blanket up over them both, he hugged

her against him and closed his eyes, willing sleep to claim him. Tomorrow would be the first test of their marriage and he planned to meet it with a clear head.

## Chapter Seventeen

Rurik would be proud. Sandulf Sigurdsson surveyed the mean chamber where the assassin had attempted to hide like a rat run to ground. The stench of the overturned sweet wine vied with stale sweat and the reek of death, getting into his lungs. Sandulf breathed shallowly through his mouth, keeping the roiling in his stomach down.

The memory of his first battle and its aftermath swamped him—his distress had amused his father. After he'd scrubbed Rurik's boots clean, his half-brother had given him invaluable advice on how to control his wayward stomach.

Sandulf plucked the golden-arrow pendant which his mother had once worn from the corpse's fist. The dead man had tried to bargain with it, pleading for mercy. Sandulf had given it—a clean death, far more than the worm deserved.

His next target lay far to the north and west. Glannoventa in the Kingdom of Northumbria and the woman he had marked. Two dead, two to die before he embraced his brothers. He carefully closed the door with a click and strode towards the port.

## Chapter Eighteen

The insistent pounding on the door woke them long before either would have risen on their own. In the cocoon of their bed, Rurik had found the best sleep of his life with Annis cuddled next to him. He had woken several times, but only long enough to pull her against him and hurtle headlong into sleep once more. He meant to do that again, especially when she curled her fingers against his neck and let out a soft breath, but the pounding would not stop.

He opened his eyes to faint morning light coming in through the small cracks in the shutters. Covering her ear, he held her face cradled to his shoulder as he called, 'What is it?'

The reply was muffled, but the name Jarl Eirik set him on alert. Sliding out from under her, he grabbed the discarded tunic and slung it on, heedless of the fact that he was half-hard with wanting her again. By the gods, he must have passed the entire night in that state. Opening the door a crack, he found Alder scowling at him.

'You had better have a damned good reason for waking us.'

'Jarl Eirik has been sighted. He will arrive soon,' said Alder.

'How soon?' Despite the fact that seeing to Jarl Eirik was important, Rurik wanted to see to his wife more. He had anticipated at least a morning in bed with her. He was starting to resent the lack of time they had been allowed alone together.

'Within two hours.'

He had not yet met the warriors at any length, but he had no problem coming up with orders for them. 'Gather the warriors. We will not meet them with weapons drawn, but they need to be ready.'

Alder nodded and turned to leave, but Rurik's voice stayed him. 'Send food. The lady and I will take our meal in our chamber before leaving.'

'As you wish, *my lord*.' The peculiar tone Alder gave the words was unmistakable. Rurik knew that it would be an uphill battle to gain the respect of the men who had so recently taken him captive, but it was a fight he was prepared to win.

Closing the door, he turned to find his wife staring at him from the bed, the coverlet pulled up loosely to her chest. She was dishevelled and sleepy and infinitely attractive. She looked well tumbled and a certain part of his body noticed.

'What did he say?' she asked, her eyes wide with concern.

He relayed the brief conversation all the while stalking towards her and calculating how fast he could have her again before the world would intervene. If she was as responsive as she had been last night, it would be easily possible.

'I ordered our meal to be brought here, so we needn't rush to the hall…yet.' As he sat on the bed, he brushed the hair back from her shoulder and replaced it with a kiss.

'Good,' she said, disappointing him by not acknowledging his kiss. 'We must eat fast so that we can discuss strategy with Cedric and Wilfrid.'

When she would have risen to dress, he grabbed her hand and tugged her down to his lap. She let out a surprised gasp and braced herself on his shoulders.

'Must we rush?' he asked.

'Rurik.' She was smiling, but the concern had not left her eyes.

He placed a kiss on her neck, working his way up to her lips as he spoke. 'Last night was not enough time with you. I need you again.'

'But it is daytime.'

'My need for you does not know time, nor does it care.'

She giggled at that and took his face between her hands. He loved that things were easy between them again. 'But Jarl Eirik is coming. We must prepare ourselves to face him. I cannot do this with you while having a lump in my stomach.'

'Why do you have a lump in your stomach? Are you afraid of him?'

Shaking her head, she said, 'I cannot explain it. I am not afraid of him. I know that he would not hurt me, but I confess to being afraid of what he might do with you.' Her eyes dipped and he gently tipped her chin upwards so that she would meet his gaze. 'What might happen to us.'

Understanding dawned and he relented. He would not have her again this morning, but he would have her before the night was over. 'We are married now. No man can come between us, not even the Jarl himself. You are mine and I am yours.' A sense of breathlessness followed that statement. No one had ever belonged to him before. It pleased him greatly that she was the one who did.

One of her hands fell to rest above his heartbeat. He stilled at the implication of the innocent touch. 'Last night was not what I thought it would be.' Her voice was soft and when her gaze met his again, it held. 'I believe that we might be able to have what you want. A true marriage. I am only afraid that we won't get the chance.'

Tenderness made his chest feel tight. Closing his arms around her, he held her against him and spoke against her temple. 'You are my wife, Annis. Jarl Eirik will not change that.'

She took a hesitant breath before pulling back enough to meet his gaze. 'What did you say last night...during...?' Her glance drifted to the bed behind him.

He couldn't stop the smile that curved his lips as he closed the slight distance and kissed her. She was always so certain of herself, but in this they were both in new territory. Keeping his voice low, he explained, 'That I take you as my wife, making us one in body and spirit. I pledged my protection to you even at the cost of my life. I meant every word of it. You are mine and I am yours and nothing that happens today will change that.'

She stared back at him, her lips parted as if she wanted to say something, but couldn't find the words. A knock on the door signalled that their breakfast had arrived, effectively ending the moment.

'Tonight, then,' he said.

Regaining herself, Annis nodded and climbed off his lap.

Nearly two hours later, Annis stood next to her husband in the hall as they waited for Jarl Eirik to walk through the open doors. The thunder of a small army of hooves had rumbled through their peaceful home only moments ago as he and his men had filed through the gates, filling their small courtyard with unease and tension. While everyone knew that he had not arrived with death and destruction at his heels, a small army of Danes was never an easy thing to accept.

As strange as she might have found it days ago, she was glad to have Rurik at her side. His quiet strength was a source of reassurance that she needed more than she had known. While shouldering the bulk of responsibility for Glannoventa over the years had been a burden she had gladly borne, she was coming to believe that sharing it with him might not be as dreadful as she had feared. Their marriage was still very new, but so far he seemed willing to shoulder it with her rather than take it over completely.

The doors of their home opened, the heavy scrape of the wood echoing down the corridor. Rurik's strong hand found the small of her back in silent assurance. From the corner of her eye, she saw his jaw work as he clenched his teeth. Whether he was worried about the confrontation to come or simply steadying himself for it, she could not say. There was much about him that she did not know, but she found more and more that she was looking forward to finding it all out.

Her heart stopped when a man came through the doorway. Jarl Eirik walked like someone determined to get to his destination, his long powerful legs eating up the distance. A handful of men followed him into the hall, but she knew that there were at least a score more waiting in the courtyard, and possibly triple that waiting in the lands and forest surrounding Mulcasterhas. She held her shoulders rigid as he came closer. His tunic was weathered and lightly soiled from days in the saddle, and his blond hair was left to fall around his shoulders, looking more unkempt than she had ever seen him. Though she conceded that she had never seen him arrive with such haste.

With the eyes of a woman, and not the girl she had still been in many ways the last time she had seen the Jarl, she could admit that he was quite attractive. At only a few years over thirty winters, he was still virile and commanding, exuding confidence and authority. His eyes gave her a quick glance, but they settled on Rurik as if identifying a threat and sizing up an enemy. For his part, Rurik had donned the weapons he had arrived with, not that he would need them. Her stomach roiled, but she did not allow it to hinder her. She would not be cowed by the Jarl.

'Good day, Uncle.' She made certain that her voice was strong and even. 'I hope your trip was uneventful.'

He seemed reluctant to take his eyes from Rurik, but he finally looked at her. 'What is the meaning of this, Lady Annis? I have been told that you are wed to a Norseman. I presume this to be him?'

She had hoped that bit of information would be left for her to reveal. It had probably been too much to hope for. 'Uncle, I would like to present Rurik from the Kingdom of Maerr, my husband. We were wed last night.'

'Maerr?' His brows drew together. 'By the gods, you were meant to marry a Dane!'

Her heart pounded against her ribcage and she glanced at the handful of men fanned out behind him. They were all younger than the Jarl, warriors in their prime. She had no doubt that the man he intended her to wed was among them, but she did not care. 'I always maintained that I would only wed the man of my choosing. And I have chosen Rurik.'

'That was not your choice to make, unfortunately.' He shook his head. 'It is not valid. He was not approved by me or your King.'

'It is valid.' Rurik spoke for the first time, impressing her with the volume and vehemence of his tone. 'Vows were exchanged and it was consummated. There are witnesses if you care to confirm it for yourself.' His hand briefly left her back to indicate Cedric whom she had forgotten was standing a few paces behind them. Several warriors waited around the periphery of the chamber, but it had been decided that to keep things calm it would be best not to meet the Jarl with an army at their back.

'You allowed this to happen?' the Jarl asked Cedric, his eyes accusing.

'There was no King to consider when they were wed. However, even if there had been, the wedding will stand,' Cedric answered as he walked the few steps necessary to stand on her other side.

'That does not answer my question.'

Cedric took in a weary breath. 'You know that Wilfrid would rather die than see her wed to a Dane. He has pledged you his loyalty, but he refuses to give you his daughter. This cannot come as such a shock to you.'

Jarl Eirik's mouth twisted into a bitter smile. 'Then why is he not here to tell me that himself?'

'Wilfrid is ill,' offered Annis.

A vein in the Jarl's temple throbbed as he stared from her to Cedric, as if wondering how much of the truth they were telling him. 'Take me to him.'

Annis had known that it would come to this, but the knowing did not make the actual facing of it any easier. He would see how ill Wilfrid truly was and demand an explanation for why he had not been told. It could not be helped, however, so she gave a nod and led the way to Wilfrid's chamber with Rurik at her side and Cedric falling in line behind them.

There was no need to knock on the door, because Wilfrid had been prepared for the meeting. He sat at his table, staring at the door. Though his colour was still not very good and he sagged a bit, obviously tired, Irwin had dressed him in his finery. Pain squeezed her heart as she noticed the tunic looked far too big for him. How much longer would he be with them?

'Lord Wilfrid, it is good to see you,' Jarl Eirik said as they all filed into the chamber.

'Welcome, Jarl Eirik.'

Annis watched the Jarl's face as he registered Wilfrid's irregular speech. His brows lowered and he glanced at her before addressing Wilfrid. 'How are you feeling?' He walked closer, as if studying Wilfrid to note all the signs of his illness.

'Good, good,' Wilfrid said, though clearly he was not at his best. 'Annis and Rurik…' He gestured with his good arm, drawing Jarl Eirik's attention to the fact that his other arm was all but immobile.

Her heart broke that they had to go through this needless display. 'We shared our good news,' she said, drawing the Jarl's attention back to her as she went to stand beside Wilfrid. 'The Jarl was overjoyed.' She gave both men a wry smile.

Wilfrid gave a bark of laughter, his shoulders shaking with the effort. When he finished, he was still smiling, eyes crinkling in the way that had always made her think he had probably been quite gallant as a young man. An unexpected lump rose in her throat, forcing her to swallow it down before a shimmer of tears coated her eyes.

'No Danes here,' he said and the words were as clear as she had ever heard him speak.

Suddenly she felt a bit lighter, understanding that he had needed this moment whether it had left her uncomfortable or not. It was his last chance to prove to the Jarl that he would not bend to the wishes of the Danes. Although Wilfrid had come to a sort of truce with them, and an uneasy friendship with Jarl Eirik, he delighted in being his own man. Her hand came to rest on his shoulder, hoping that it conveyed the affection she felt for him.

'So you made clear on my last visit,' the Jarl said, his tone dry. 'I never thought you would allow a Norse into your home after Sigurd.'

Wilfrid sobered instantly and his gaze unfocused slightly, his head turning as if searching for someone among those in the room.

Afraid that he was going to fall into a panic again at the mention of Sigurd when he had been doing so well, Annis said, 'And as you can see, Lord Wilfrid needs his rest. Let us return to the hall. We have refreshments before you rest from your trip.'

Jarl Eirik's keen gaze never left Wilfrid as he sized up the situation. She had no doubt that she was not fooling the Jarl in regards to his condition. 'It was good to see you, Lord Wilfrid. We will leave you to your rest.' The Jarl left them there to return to the hall and she let out a breath that he had not insulted Wilfrid on his way out.

They all followed and as soon as the doors to his chamber had closed behind them, Jarl Eirik said, 'How long has he been out of his senses?' Anger was evident in his voice.

Before she could reply, Rurik intervened. 'He is not out of his senses.'

Jarl Eirik glanced at him in warning, but did not utter another word until they were in the hall. Annis gestured to the table and that they should sit, but the Jarl shook his head, still obviously upset.

Withholding a sigh, she said, 'Since the last time you visited, he's had roughly one to two brain attacks a year. The last one was the worst and resulted in what you see. He cannot easily move one side of his body.'

'And yet no one informed me of what had happened to him, so I could appoint someone to manage in his stead?'

Annis forced a calmness to her voice that she did

not feel. When would she stop being forced to defend herself for running Glannoventa confidently? 'As you can see, Glannoventa has been well managed. Wilfrid has been competent enough to offer opinions and guidance, but in the times when his illness proved him incapable, I was glad to take over.'

'You? You took over?' He glanced to Cedric as if for reassurance and, at the man's nod, he looked back at her.

'I took over,' she said. 'After your meal, I will show you the records we have kept. Glannoventa is profitable and has not struggled since Wilfrid's decline. You've received your taxes as promised.'

He still seemed unconvinced. Rurik took her hand in his. 'You will see that you were very lucky to have Lady Annis here. She has managed with a level head and an even hand.'

Her heart swelled in her chest at the fine words.

'And you.' The Jarl addressed Rurik. 'We have heard of your father's death in Maerr. Is that why you are here?'

'Initially, yes. I came because I thought Wilfrid had a hand in my father's murder.'

'But you do not believe that now?'

'I believe that Wilfrid hired assassins in a failed attempt to right a wrong.'

Guilt made her stomach roil again and she tightened her fingers around his hand. He spared her a fond glance, but it only made the guilt expand, nearly forcing all the air from her lungs. She had to tell him the truth. He should know that his wife was as much a part of that failed attempt as Wilfrid. He should know that the woman he had taken to bed was beyond redemption.

Cedric caught her gaze, his eyes rather severe as he gave her a barely imperceptible shake of his head. Not while Jarl Eirik was here, he seemed to say. Glannoventa needed Rurik. She knew that if he cried off, then the Jarl might very well find some way to end their marriage and appoint a Dane to take over.

Taking Rurik's hand with both of hers, she stared down at the fingers that had given her so much pleasure, that had continued to touch her with nothing but gentleness. He had claimed he wanted a true marriage, one built on trust and respect. She vowed to give him that as soon as the Jarl left.

## Chapter Nineteen

The day had been long and tedious. Jarl Eirik had insisted on laying his eyes on every record that Cedric and Annis had created since Grim's death. Once he had been partially satisfied that taxes were still being collected—he'd do a more thorough audit of the records later—and the farmers, fishermen and villagers had not staged some sort of revolt, the conversation had progressed to Rurik and their marriage.

Rurik had been picked apart by the man. From his childhood with a slave mother to his dubious claim to land in Killcobar with his Uncle Feann to his plans for Glannoventa and Annis, he had spent the better part of the afternoon and evening humouring the Jarl's questions. In the end, he felt that they had come to a sort of understanding. Rurik would not be cowed by the man, nor would he give up his claim to Annis or Glannoventa. Jarl Eirik had seemed to come to an acceptance of the new arrangement.

Tomorrow would be soon enough to tell. The plan was to head out into the villages as the Jarl surveyed their progress. Rurik was looking forward to the ride and laying his eyes on the land that was now his. However, he was exhausted and would think of tomorrow in the morning. He had sent Annis to bed earlier in the evening when she had begun to sag in the chair beside him at the table. She had surprised him by leaning down to place a chaste kiss on his cheek, while whispering, 'Wake me later.' Ever since, he had been rigid with wanting her, counting down the hours until the seemingly tireless Jarl sought his own bed.

Two candles still burned low in the chamber as he crossed to the bed. She lay on her stomach in the middle, her auburn hair spread out across the blankets. He was struck again by her beauty and the sense that she was his. His responsibility. His wife. His. Shedding his clothes as he stared down at her, he could not help but wonder if the tenderness he felt for her was becoming something deeper. It was as if his admiration for her had found his desire for her and twisted together so hopelessly that he could not pull one thread from the other. A very real fear had gripped him today when he had considered that Jarl Eirik might find a way to take her from him. Rurik had been prepared to battle for her, to the death if need be. He didn't know how she had captivated him so completely in such a short time.

Placing the knives at his hips on the chest at the end of the bed, he stepped out of his clothing and climbed under the blankets beside her. His hands encountered smooth, silky skin as he touched her. Sending up a silent plea of thanks, he drew the blanket back from her to look his fill of her naked body. There was not a part of her that he did not think was perfect.

The candlelight painted her skin gold as his fingertips followed the line of her spine down to the twin globes of her bottom. He paused as his gaze caught on an odd scar at her lower back. It was difficult to tell in the uneven light, but it looked like two jagged marks that crossed each other. They had almost certainly been made by a blade. How would she have been scarred in such a way? Surely, Cedric's training would not have led to that.

Before he could come up with any likely scenario, she sighed and rolled over on to her back. His fingers followed the movement of her hips, coming to rest on the smooth skin above the russet patch of hair between her thighs. His manhood twitched in response to the memory of how good it had felt to be inside her.

'Annis,' he whispered, pressing his palm to her belly.

Had his seed taken root in her the night before? A flare of hope sprang to life in him, surprising him with how pleasing he found the idea of sharing a child with her. Children had always been something far in his future. Now he could so easily see them. However, he also liked the idea of selfishly having her to himself for a while. Perhaps it would take months of ploughing before the seeds would find roots.

She shifted, her breathing changing as she turned towards him and came awake. 'Is it morning already?' she whispered.

'Far from it.'

She smiled, though her eyes were still closed as he pressed his mouth to the hollow of her throat. 'Jarl Eirik has not banished you?'

'If he has, it only means that I have come to take you with me.' He lapped at the salt of her skin with the tip of his tongue, marvelling at how he was ready for her so quickly. He was infatuated.

'Like a true marauder,' she whispered.

He grinned at their play. How easily he was coming to enjoy this sparring with her. 'It has been too long since I last pillaged. You may find me all the rougher for it.' He took her nipple into his mouth, drawing it deep and pulling a gasp from her at the same time. Her fingers curled in his hair as she held him tight. He did not allow her to stay him, however, and continued on his path down her body.

'What are you doing?' A faint thread of panic entered her voice when he passed her belly.

Instead of answering right away, he settled himself between her thighs, moving down until his shoulders had pushed them apart. Shifting his arms beneath her thighs, he held her open for him. The shadows of the night kept her mostly hidden from him, but he was able to see a slight tinge of pink through the dark red curls.

'Rurik...' She sat up on her elbows, staring down at him, her brows together in confusion.

The scent of her longing made his blood thicken in his veins as his need for her pulsed through him. 'I want to taste your desire for me, Annis. I want all of you.'

It was true. After the trying day, there was some part of him that he did not completely understand pushing him to claim every part of her as his. Because she did belong to him now. Whatever the Jarl ultimately decided, she would belong to Rurik for the rest of their lives.

Taking in another deep breath of her, he touched her with his tongue. She made a low sound in the back of her throat and her thighs tensed around him. He stroked her from the silken channel that had held him so tightly the night before to the tiny nub of swollen flesh peeking out from between her folds. Putting her knee over his shoulder, he let it go so that he could spread her with his fingers and ease the way for himself. She cried out when he covered her with his mouth.

He savoured every gasp and cry as he sucked her lightly. Only when she fell back, her hips bucking a bit with the rhythm he set, did he let a finger slip inside her. She clamped around him and he pulled it almost all the way free, only to gently work a second one into her. He loved having her under his power like this, his name falling from her lips as he controlled her pleasure. In some small and dark corner of his mind, he gloried in the fact that this at least was new to her. No one had ever given her pleasure like this.

It made him feel more powerful than he had any right to feel, like a god come to earth to pleasure this woman who was his. And he did pleasure her with a single-minded purpose that felt as irresistible as the potion she had laced into his ale on that first night in the tavern.

'Rurik!' she cried out and grabbed his hair in a twist that might have been painful were he not beyond all thought except for bringing her to completion. He wanted to hear her cry out as she came for him and then he wanted to fill her and take her until she cried out beneath him again.

In the next moment her body trembled and her cry filled the air. She clenched around his fingers as he tasted her release on his tongue. Only when she began to come down did he move over her. Her eyes were dazed and unfocused, but her arms went around his shoulders as he fell over her, taking her mouth in a deep kiss. He found a nipple with his fingers and plucked it gently but insistently. She groaned against his lips and raised her hips, grinding against him.

'Do you want me inside you?' he whispered between kisses.

'Hurry,' she said on a breathless gasp.

It was all the encouragement he needed. Lining himself up with her, he pushed inside in one deep stroke that had them both crying out. The way he fit her felt so right, as if he had been made for her. He tried to keep his thrusts slow and measured, wanting to prolong the pleasure for both of them. But having her beneath him like this was too much and, when she wrapped her legs around his hips, opening herself up to him even more, he was lost. It wasn't long before he was taking her with hard, deep thrusts of his hips while sweat rolled down his temple. Having this woman spread out beneath him, begging him for more, was too much. The very moment she began to shake beneath him, her body clenching tight around him, he came with a roar pulled from deep in his chest.

'Annis,' he whispered her name over and over into her hair as he fell over her, his lips finding her neck. Her arms held him tight as if unwilling to let him go, so he collapsed on to her, still buried deep inside her. He had never felt this almost complete obsession with a woman before. His hands still fisted in her hair as he spread kisses over her neck and cheek on his way to her mouth. There was no getting enough of her.

When strength came back to him, he raised up on

his forearms just enough to look down at her. She smiled up a him, a small tentative smile that reflected his own bewildered wonder. How was it possible that he had travelled all this way with vengeance spurring him on, only to find this woman who was dangerously close to stealing his heart? Had the gods brought him to her?

Her fingers caressed his cheek, so he turned his head to place a kiss in her palm. 'I never thought I would find anyone like you,' he whispered.

She let out a sigh that sounded suspiciously like a sob, but she pulled him down for a kiss before he could comment. One kiss led to another and he was lost for the rest of the night.

Annis's heart gave a small but pleasant start the next morning when Rurik took her hand. Tiny feathers of awareness tickled up from her hand to her wrist as he tightened his fingers around hers. He did not smile at her, but his eyes seemed to say so much more than words ever could as they made their way outside.

He had brought her to pleasure twice more last night and once again this morning before they left their bed. He had been slow and lazy—thorough was the only way she could think to describe how he had taken his time in waking her up. It had not mattered that a servant had knocked, or discreetly left a meal for them inside the door. He had not stopped until they were both limp and satiated. Then he had helped her dress, an endeavour that promised far more pleasure to be had later in the day.

Iron clanged outside as they made their way from their home, evidence that Jarl Eirik was already awake and running his men through their paces. No doubt he was impatient for them, but Rurik did not hurry his pace. As two of her men swung open the doors to the courtyard for them, he only gave her fingers a reassuring squeeze and held them. She liked that they had progressed from a supporting hand on her lower back. How quickly they could progress to so much more if they only had the chance.

She pushed back the weight of guilt that threatened to rise within her at the thought. She would tell Rurik everything very soon, as soon as the Jarl left them in peace. He would be hurt—she despised that his pain was necessary—but she hoped with time he could forgive her for the part she had played in Maerr. She did not fool herself that it would be an easy thing to overcome, but she did believe there could be a good life for them eventually. If he would only give them a chance.

Smiling up at him, she tightened her hand on his, making the barest hint of a smile turn up his lips. He would not let himself be so free before the Jarl, so the hint was enough to reassure her. There was the scantest ache between her thighs, a reminder of how recently he had been there. She was amazed to realise she was already wondering how soon they could sneak off for a private moment. The day was meant to be filled with a tour of Glannoventa and the surroundings, but surely there would be something—a copse, a nook—where she could at least kiss him again.

Rurik's face changed right before her eyes. His roar of outrage barely registered as his brows drove together and he lunged before her, driving her behind him with a forearm. The dagger on his hip came out as he got into a battle crouch before her. Distantly, she was aware of a sword striking stone—only after she heard the sound did she realise that it had narrowly missed Rurik, striking where he had been standing only to crash into the wall instead. She had been too much in her thoughts to anticipate danger.

Drawing the dagger kept in her boot, she rose to her full height and went to step around him. 'Stay behind me,' he said, his left arm coming out to keep her back as his right wielded his dagger.

Angry and uncomprehending, she glared out at Jarl Eirik and the men who stood near him. There were ten while the rest continued to spar farther off. 'What is the meaning of this?' she yelled.

The Jarl's brow was fierce and his gaze was calculating as it roved over Rurik, assessing him. 'If he is to take Wilfrid's place, he must prove his ability to protect himself and you.'

'That was unfair. You had no right to do that. What if you had hurt one of us?' Outrage filled her voice. Her gaze found the Jarl's warrior who had swung the sword. She had not noticed him the night before; she was quite certain she would have remembered. His wild mane of hair was pulled back from a face that was all angles, as if it had been chiselled from the side of a cliff, and he was taller than any man she had ever seen. His arms alone were nearly the width of her midriff.

Still the Jarl stared only at Rurik. 'You were never in danger, Lady Annis. The sword was aimed for Rurik. If the sword had found him, he would not deserve his place as your husband.'

'That is for me to decide.' She bit the words out, but, seeing that there was no immediate danger to her, Rurik put a hand on her shoulder.

'He is right. I must prove myself,' said Rurik.

Once more taking in the giant, she turned to her husband and lowered her voice. 'You do not. I chose you. That will be enough.'

'Perhaps for you, but not for them.' He gestured over his shoulder and she saw her own warriors spread out farther past the courtyard, between the stone outbuildings and homes farther out. 'Our own men need to know that I am capable of leading them. It would have come to this eventually.' The backs of his fingers stroked her chin before he turned back to the Jarl. 'I will fight any man you choose.'

A cheer went up through the Danes while her own men looked on in silence, but their eyes were gleaming with anticipation. The prospect of any sport seemed to be too much of a temptation to resist. It did not matter that her own heart seemed to have swallowed itself whole. Perhaps Rurik was right and the warriors needed to see this demonstration of brawn to begin to respect him.

'Valgautr!' Jarl Eirik's voice carried to every warrior.

The one who had nearly decapitated Rurik, the near giant, turned to face the Jarl and her stomach plummeted. He could not mean for Rurik to battle that beast. Even as Valgautr raised his sword high above his head to gain a roar of support from the Danes, she did not want to bring herself to believe that this was happening. With one blow of his fist, she feared that he would shatter Rurik's skull and she said as much in private after she had made her way to the Jarl.

He actually *laughed*, throwing back his head in a way she had never seen him behave before. She tightened her fingers around her dagger's hilt, itching to drive it into him. Not to kill him, but simply to stop him laughing. It wasn't worth it. She had learned her lesson about vengeance, but it did not stop the fantasy from playing through her mind.

'Why do you laugh?' she asked, her gaze on Rurik who had moved farther away from the house to a more open space.

'Because you are likely correct in your assessment.' He stood with his arms crossed and his legs wide as he watched on with obvious pride. Catching her rage-filled gaze on him from the corner of his eyes, he softened his stance. 'I won't allow it to progress that far. Valgautr needs a bit of sport or he becomes ill-tempered.' When that still did not placate her, he sighed and dropped his arms, turning towards her. 'If you truly wish for Rurik to stay as your husband, then he must overcome some obstacles to prove himself before your men as well as mine, or no one will accept him and you'll have a revolt on your hands.'

She took in a frustrated breath and watched as Cedric, who had disappeared briefly, returned from the house, sword in hand. The exhale stopped in her throat when she recognised it as Wilfrid's battle sword. It had been hiding in the armoury these last few years. Rurik sheathed his dagger, murmuring something to Cedric as he took the sword in hand and gave it a few practice swings.

'What do you mean if I wish him to stay? He is my husband. It is done.'

He gave her a dubious glance and looked back over to where the men were about to face off. The giant swung his sword around and around in a big arc over his head, gaining the approval of the Danes. 'He does not have to keep being your husband if you do not wish it. There are ways to do away with it if he has forced you or coerced you in some way.'

His voice lowered and had become almost gentle, as if he were attempting to determine if those things were true. Touched by his concern, she hurried to reassure him. 'He has not forced me.'

'What of Wilfrid or Cedric? I know they can be...' he paused as if seeking the right description '...bullheaded in their hatred of Danes.'

Shocked by this concern from him, she said, 'They distrust and resent your high-handedness. Can you say that you were not here to force me to wed one of your own men?'

'You must wed, Lady Annis. There is no question of the need for that. Glannoventa's future must be secured. I do not wish to see you suffer needlessly for that, however. The man I selected would have treated you well, not only because he is a kind and honourable man, but because he would have had to answer to me. We know nothing of this Norseman.'

She had never quite thought of that particular benefit to marrying one of the Jarl's men. 'I did not know that you cared,' she said, keeping her voice light.

'I have known you as a child and now as a woman. I would see you content.' When he looked down at her, his eyes betrayed his concern.

'Rurik is like no man I have met. He is both fierce and kind. I feel that I could be very content with him as my husband.' Content did not begin to describe the happiness that welled inside her this morning when she had awakened next to him. Given time, she knew that seed of bliss could grow roots that would wind themselves deep into her heart. She did not believe that she was mistaken in thinking Rurik felt the same.

The Jarl grunted and turned back to the men who had begun to circle one another. The giant was the first to move, his sword swinging down in a death blow that whistled through the cold morning air. Every muscle in her body tensed and her heart paused, only resuming when Rurik deftly shifted out of the way, his own sword coming up to block the attack with a loud clang.

Valgautr heaved a grunt, pushing Rurik back with his greater weight. Rurik feinted one way, but spun the other, bringing his sword down in a move that should have been a devastating blow across the giant's shoulders. Except he twisted almost as fast as Rurik, so he was able to block in the last moment. She wanted to cover her face to keep from watching the spectacle, but she knew it would be folly to show such weakness. Instead, she watched with her hands clenched into fists at her side, barely breathing.

As if aware of her distress, Jarl Eirik put a hand on her back. 'Calm yourself. Valgautr will not disobey my wishes. Loyalty is his greatest strength.'

In a man so accomplished, it was saying a lot. Annis nodded, but barely drew another breath as she watched the battle unfold over the next few moments. The only sounds were those of the swords knocking together, and the heavy breathing and occasional grunts from the two men fighting. Even the Danes had settled in, watching with fascinated interest rather than cheering their own to victory. The men seemed well matched, despite the fact that the giant greatly outweighed Rurik. What the larger man gained in brawn,

Rurik gained in grace and speed. They feinted and swung their swords, crossing the courtyard and moving down the hill, requiring the observing warriors to part, like the prow of a ship cutting through the sea.

Finally, they both heaved for breath, sweat trickling down their brows despite the cold. They had progressed to the stone road cut into the hillside that would lead to Glannoventa and warriors had moved to fill in the space overlooking both sides. Annis could imagine that if no one put a stop to it, their fight could take them into the village and perhaps even into the sea. Neither was willing to give so it seemed they could go on for ever. She stood on the retaining wall above the curve in the road that lead to a steeper decline. If they made it past this point, the battle could turn deadly if one should lose his footing and take a tumble.

'Enough!' Jarl Eirik's voice rang out beside her. The swords clanged together two more times before the men were able to register the command.

The giant was the first to pause, his brows drawing together as he searched for the Jarl's place on the ridge above them. Rurik never took his eyes from the giant, not trusting that this wasn't a ploy to catch him off balance. Annis's chest swelled with pride for how well he had handled himself in the fight. When only days ago she had hoped his skill was not nearly that which he claimed, now she was glad to see that it was far more than she had imagined.

'You have proven yourself in this, Norseman,' said Jarl Eirik. The giant hung his head. 'You have done well, Valgautr. We only wanted to test the man. We shall not kill him yet.'

The giant nodded and raised his hand to Rurik who clasped the man's shoulder. They congratulated each other as the warriors became animated around them, showering them with praise and taunts in equal measure. She could see in that moment how Rurik had been able to gain the respect of the Glannoventa warriors. The fight had been a necessary step in gaining his place among them.

In the midst of the commotion, Rurik looked up, his eyes finding her on the ridge. His gaze was heavy with meaning as the corner of his mouth tipped up in the hint of a smile. There was a flutter in her stomach as she realised he was seeking her approval. Warmth spread throughout her chest as she watched him make his way over to her, stopping every few steps to accept a congratulations. Finally, he was standing at the base of the retaining wall where she and the Jarl had looked out over the men. In one swift and unexpected move, he vaulted up, his muscles straining as he climbed to where she was and stood beside her.

'Well done,' she said, smiling.

His grin widened and he took her hand for all to see. It was a sort of claiming, but it was also a show of solidarity. He was hers as she was his. They were together.

# Chapter Twenty

Jarl Eirik ended up staying for the better part of a month, leaving only when the weather broke. The weeks had been filled with tests and obstacles, all meant to prove to Annis that Rurik was not a good choice for her or Glannoventa. There had been physical trials during the days—could Rurik wrestle whichever man the Jarl put forth that day? Could he swim in the freezing sea faster than the Jarl's best swimmer?—while the evenings had tested his intelligence. Was he capable of strategy and scheming to win at all sorts of games from board to dice? Could he match wits with the Jarl's men or even the Jarl himself?

Every night in the hall he was forced to hold his own as he was plied with drink. Frequently, he was goaded into composing a lyric of poetry cleverer than the man next to him. Afterwards he would often stumble to their chamber with Annis at his side. Sometimes they would undress each other and fall into bed in a haze of pleasure. Other times he was so exhausted from the day's trials that he was asleep before she pulled the blanket over him, but he would always make it up to her in the morning. He delighted in waking her in different ways, his hands and mouth finding all the parts of her body that made her sigh and moan.

As the days passed, Rurik had found himself anticipating when the Jarl would leave and he would have her to himself. He could scarcely believe that he had found a woman who matched him in every way. He was looking forward to starting their lives together and figuring out what it would mean to govern Glannoventa together, a challenge he had never anticipated but was firmly embracing.

However, as the time grew close for Jarl Eirik to leave, Rurik would find Annis more and more withdrawn. It would happen at odd moments, such as when he would come upon her unexpectedly alone. She would tense, her eyes far away as if thinking of the past. After a moment, she would come back to him. The pain in her eyes would slowly give way to joy as he kissed her or whispered to her.

He thought that perhaps she missed her old life, her husband and the babe that had never truly lived. But then she would seek him out among the warriors, her eyes shining with love, and he would think that he was wrong. She did feel affection for him and it was a connection that deepened every day. He had resolved to give her a babe to love as soon as possible, his own selfishness to have her to himself be damned.

Now, several days after the Jarl had left, he led the men through their paces. He had been surprised at how skilled the warriors were with their weapons, but he should not have been. Cedric was a diligent leader and had taught them well. Rurik had been focusing on training them in grappling techniques, the most recent one a simple move that would allow them to take down an opponent who outweighed them. As he called out a correction, his eye was caught by flaming red hair as his wife turned the corner of the barracks. Cedric followed her, his face thunderous. She walked with the single-minded determination of someone bent on leaving a tense encounter.

Wondering what they had fought about, he indicated that the warrior next to him should take over and followed her towards the house.

'Annis,' he called as he approached her from behind.

She wiped at the corner of her eye as she paused and turned towards him. 'Rurik.' Her eyes were troubled, but she did genuinely smile at him.

Something had been wrong for days, but he had hoped it would pass over like a summer storm. Instead, it seemed to be one of those storms that came in deep winter and settled, never happy to leave until the whole world had been very nearly blighted out. Instead of questioning her there in the open, he put a hand to her waist and guided her around the corner of a building to afford them a bit of privacy.

Instead of speaking immediately, he engaged in one of his favourite pastimes of late and kissed her, allowing his lips to nibble at the corner of her mouth. 'You are unwell?' he whispered, gratified when she opened to him without coaxing, seeking more of his kiss.

'I'm not unwell,' she said, drawing back only to answer before kissing him again. Then she put her arms around his waist and buried her face in his chest. 'How is this possible? How are you mine?'

He smiled and ran his palms up and down her back, holding her closer. 'It is fate. Our lives have been threaded together from the beginning. We simply didn't know it.'

She jerked back at that, her brows pushed together as she stared up at him. Not understanding what about that bothered her, he gently stroked her brow line with the pad of his thumb. Inexplicably, her eyes glistened.

There was the look again. The one that told him deep down that something was amiss. It had scared him every time he saw it, because it made him think that their time together could be at risk. It was a feeling he could not explain. More than fear.

'What is it?' he asked, taking a deep breath, suddenly certain that whatever she would say would change everything. 'What did Cedric say to upset you?' He resolved then and there to take the matter up with Cedric if she wouldn't confide in him.

'Do you remember on the night of our wedding that I wanted to tell you something?' Her bottom lip trembled.

His gut knotted and he touched her face, needing to feel her skin against his. Nodding, he said, 'I do.'

'I wanted to tell you before…but then Jarl Eirik came and it seemed that there was too much facing us.'

'You can tell me anything, Wife.' A flash of pain crossed her face and he tightened his hold on her. 'Is it about the assassins?'

Rurik had intentionally not mentioned them again. It wasn't that he had given up on revenge or hunting them down. It was simply that they had found peace and a sort of happiness in the few days since the Jarl had left and now he was reluctant to let in the outside world. There would be time to find the men later when winter had left and the risk of hunting them down wasn't as great.

She nodded. 'In a way, but it's even more than that.' Her gold eyes were shining up at him, asking for forgiveness, but he didn't understand why that could be.

'What is it, Annis?' he asked, hoping to relieve her of the burden she obviously carried.

She took a deep breath and opened her mouth, but no words came out. Making a sound he didn't recognise, he brushed his lips to her brow, soothing her. Her palm flattened against his chest as if savouring the beat of his heart.

'Lady Annis!' a woman called, her voice shrill with alarm. 'Lady Annis!'

Annis pushed away from him and hurried around the corner of the building. The healer from the village stood there. She was an old crone with a kindly face who came up once a week to check Wilfrid.

'I am here,' Annis said.

'Lord Wilfrid calls for you. He seems rather agitated.'

'How is he? Is it another attack?'

The woman shook her head. 'Not an attack, but he seems more confused than usual. Please come.'

Annis gave him a worried glance and Rurik smoothed a hand down her back. Leaning forward, he whispered in her ear, 'Go now. I'll find you soon.'

She touched her fingertips to his cheek before hurrying away with the woman. He watched her go, tense uncertainty roiling in his belly. He turned to find Cedric, who had disappeared somewhere, probably inside to attend Wilfrid, when Alder rushed up to him, catching his eye.

'You must come, Lord. There is a man here. He says he is your brother.'

'My brother?' The words fell rather stiffly from his lips. Before he could even contemplate which one it could be, Alder solved the mystery for him.

'A man named Sandulf.'

# Chapter Twenty-One

Rurik hurried to the hall where his brother awaited him, hardly daring to believe that he would find Sandulf there. A hundred thoughts ran around in his head, colliding with each other before settling on one. Something had to be wrong to bring Sandulf all this way The last time he had seen his youngest brother had been after the massacre when he had boarded a ship bound for Constantinople. The harsh words Rurik had said to him rang in his ears. Part of him had thought he would never see Sandulf again and he could hardly believe that he had the chance to take them back.

How had he even found Rurik here? Or had he somehow traced Wilfrid's involvement?

Two men guarded the door, reminiscent of the guards that had constantly lingered in the passages before his marriage. Rurik was only glad they hadn't left Sandulf in the underground cell to await him. Giving them a brief nod, he opened the door to find a man standing near the hearth, warming himself at the fire. He recognised the set of Sandulf's shoulders a moment before the boy turned his face to him.

Only, it was not the face of the half-boy, half-man that Rurik remembered. Gone was any lingering softness of childhood to be replaced by the battle-chiselled features of a warrior.

'Sandulf?' he asked, still not believing, although the man's eyes were the same. He still had the cleft in his chin, but his jaw seemed harder.

Sandulf gave him a slow almost-grin, as if he had forgotten how to use the muscles required for the act. 'Brother,' he said in a voice more solemn than the one Rurik had known.

Despite the fact that the last time they had seen each other had been just after the massacre and Rurik had spoken harsh words to him, his chest lightened with joy at the sight of him, at this small bit of home that had found him in this near-forgotten corner of the world.

Walking over to him, they clasped arms and Rurik pulled him in until their shoulders touched. 'Welcome, Brother,' said Rurik, pounding his back. 'I can hardly believe you are here.'

Sandulf's smile came a bit easier this time, though it was by no means warm, and his eyes were troubled when he pulled back. 'I cannot believe *you* are here.' In response to Rurik's furrowed brow, he said, 'I didn't know you would be here when I came. It wasn't until I heard your name mentioned in the village that I knew.'

'You found out about Wilfrid, then? Is that what brought you here?'

Sandulf nodded, leading him over to the table. He scouted the chamber with his eyes as if making certain they were alone.

'No one is here. There are only my men outside the door,' Rurik reassured him. 'How was your journey?'

'Long,' said Sandulf as he settled himself and partook of the ale Rurik had poured for him. He grimaced near the end. 'I miss the mead of home.'

There were many things Rurik missed of home, too, but he was finding that with every day he spent here with Annis, he was coming to think of Mulcasterhas as his home. 'There is much work here for me to do.' He gave a wry smile.

The quirk of his lips seemed to catch Sandulf's attention and provoke a frown. 'How have you come to be here?'

A grumble of unease returned to his belly. He had only barely reconciled himself to the affection he felt for his enemy's daughter-in-law. If the truth was known, his initial hatred of Wilfrid had begun to wear thin as well. But how would he explain that to Sandulf?

He spent the next few moments telling his brother about his time in Éireann with Alarr. About King Feann and how he had learned the truth of his mother. Finally, he spoke of what he had learned of Wilfrid of Glannoventa and how it had brought him here.

Now it was Sandulf's turn to look puzzled. 'Am I to understand that you married his daughter, Lady Annis?'

'It happens that Wilfrid is very ill and he despises Danes.' Another smile curved his lips and Sandulf noticed, the groove between his brows deepening.

'I've never seen you smile so much. You're smitten with her.' Sandulf said it as an admonishment.

Taking in a slow, steady breath, Rurik searched

for a way to explain. It turned out there was no way other than the truth. 'I have affection for my wife, yes. Wilfrid had not plotted the murders at home as I had thought. He hired assassins to go and only to target our father. I never knew this, but several years ago Sigurd came here to this area. There was a…disagreement and Wilfrid's son was killed, apparently brutally.'

'That is all well and good, but have you forgotten what happened at home? That was brutal murder.'

'If there is one thing I understand, it's the need for vengeance.' It was all he had thought about since. Until Annis. 'But Wilfrid is all but bedridden. Killing him will not avenge anyone.' Hoping to turn the conversation, he asked, 'What happened to you when you left us? Did you reach Constantinople?'

Sandulf nodded. 'It's where I've been all this time. Do you remember that I fought the ones who killed Ingrid?' Despite the fact that some time had passed, the wound was still raw for them both. A slash of pain crossed Sandulf's face and Rurik nodded in encouragement.

'I will never forget,' said Rurik.

'There were four of them. Two of them fled to Constantinople. I found them and killed them, but not before one of them told me where the others could be found.'

'In Glannoventa,' Rurik responded, wondering if they had been here all this time.

Sandulf nodded. 'Yes, one of them. The other seems lost, but I have hope I will learn his name.'

'But there were only three of them. Wilfrid admitted to hiring the three assassins and he says that he did not make the trip to Maerr. I believe him, because his health is very poor and was poor even then.'

Sandulf shook his head and his brows came together over his eyes, creating a deep groove, making him appear fierce. Rurik had never seen him look like that before.

'I didn't come here for Wilfrid,' said Sandulf. 'There were four there, Rurik. Two of them were fighting Father's warriors. The third is the one who murdered Ingrid.'

'And the fourth?' Rurik asked.

'She went with the man who attacked Ingrid. I tried to fight them off, but the man was vicious. I wasn't able to stop him, but I marked the girl.'

'The girl?' Rurik echoed the words as blood roared in his head. There was a girl among the assassins Wilfrid had hired to kill their father. Why had he not known that before? Somewhere deep down, he knew where Sandulf was leading, but he couldn't bring himself to accept it. Shaking his head, he said, 'No, you're mistaken.'

'Before I killed him, the assassin told me she could be found here.'

Rurik shook his head. 'But I was told one of them was called Wilfrid and that wasn't true. The assassin lied to you.' Each statement was a grasp at some plausible explanation. 'You think it's Annis.'

Sandulf nodded, as if only just realising that he was dealing with an animal on the very edge of becoming wild. He raised his hands, palms extended outward. 'It is possible.'

*His Annis.* Rurik thought of her as she had been

that morning, naked and panting, soft and yielding beneath him. *His*.

'Annis is not the one you seek. She had no part of that.' He closed his eyes, but his brother's next words penetrated anyway.

'The girl I remember from that day had auburn hair and pale skin. I marked her here with my blade. Two marks that cross.' He stood and indicated his back above his hip.

'No!' The word roared out of Rurik as he came to his feet. He brought his hands to his forehead, his fingers grasping handfuls of his hair as if he could pull out the knowledge Sandulf had given him. As if there was some hope of going back to how things had been before.

Is this what had been worrying her these past weeks? She had started to tell him something outside, but it hadn't been the first time. On their wedding night she had mentioned something and he hadn't let her talk for fear of losing what he had only just found.

He thought back further, back to the night she had confessed her family's involvement with Sigurd and Maerr. She had mentioned having blood on her hands, but he had dismissed the remark as guilt from her desire for revenge and condoning the hiring of the assassins.

Could the woman he was coming to love—no, the woman he was quite certain that he did love—participate in such a ruthless act? An image of Ingrid as she had been in death came to him before he could stop it, bloodied and disfigured, her face a mask of the obvious suffering she had felt before her death. Her unborn child... What person could do that to an innocent woman? No matter Sigurd's guilt in his alleged crimes against Glannoventa, Ingrid had not deserved her fate.

Rurik did not realise that tears blurred his vision until one of the warriors guarding the door had opened it, calling to him. He must have tried to get Rurik's attention several times, having been summoned by Rurik's cry of denial, because he came into the chamber reaching for the sword at his waist.

'Stay!' Rurik stopped his progress with the one word.

Sandulf would not lie to him about this. The description was too clear for the unknown assassin to be anyone but Annis, from her hair to the scar on her back. The very scar Rurik had noticed, wondering how she had come by such a thing. He had asked her once and she had responded that it was an accident, but he'd been too lost in his lust and affection for her to demand an answer.

He could not imagine the woman he knew participating in a brutal murder, not after what she had been forced to endure with Grim and her unborn child. But the evidence seemed overwhelming. Had she lied to him all these days? There was only one way to find out.

Blinking to clear his eyes, he said, 'Bring Annis to me.'

Annis stared down at Wilfrid's dear face. With his wrinkled hand in hers, she had finally managed to calm him into a deep sleep. He had not slept the night before and as a result he'd been disorientated most of the day. Wulfwyn, the healer, who was usually so calm could not keep the concern from her face.

'He is not long for this world, I fear.' Never one to mince words or make things appear better than they were, the healer had looked kindly on them both one last time before taking her leave.

Annis had stayed by his side long after his fitful breathing had lengthened and settled as he'd found his rest. Whether he had known her, Annis could not say, but her presence seemed to soothe him. Cedric had approached her this morning with the news of Wilfrid's fitful night. The two were closer than brothers and he hadn't been able to hide the sorrow from his face. Even he knew that Wilfrid's end was coming. Only a handful of years separated the two, but Wilfrid appeared decades older.

Annis had tried to comfort Cedric, but there was nothing she could say to take away his pain. In the end she feared that she had made things even worse. Instead of waiting for a better time, her thoughts had gone to Rurik and the terrible thing she was hiding from him. With Wilfrid near death, she had suggested that now was the time to tell Rurik everything. Jarl Eirik was gone and it appeared that their marriage would stand, but Cedric had not wanted to hear of it. He wanted to wait even longer, until after Wilfrid's death when Glannoventa's fate had been settled.

She had argued. 'It is only fair that Rurik know while Wilfrid is alive to answer his questions.'

Cedric waved away her concern. 'What questions could he have? You were there.' The words came out between his teeth, almost like an accusation. 'You can answer his questions.'

'True, but what if he has questions about the earlier confrontation between Wilfrid and Sigurd? What if there is something he must know?'

'What would he need to know?'

'I don't know. There could be anything.' She had shrugged, aware that she was making this worse for Cedric, but unable to stop herself from arguing on Rurik's behalf. 'The point is that this has been kept from him for too long. He must be told the truth.'

Cedric had come to stand over her then. 'And you are certain that when you tell him the truth, he will stay? He won't leave you, or worse…?'

Her stomach tumbling over herself, she had asked, 'Worse?'

'He came here for vengeance.' His tone had gentled, but it did not soften the harsh words. 'What is to stop him from taking his vengeance out on you? He could drag you back to Maerr and turn you over to the King or even his family.'

The flicker of unease those words brought had been in her belly ever since. She was certain now that Rurik would not physically harm her. It wasn't in his nature. But would he take his vengeance out on her in some other way? Would he hate her, or would he give her a chance to explain her part? Would he believe her and accept it when she told him that she had made a horrible mistake? She wanted to believe that the man who held her so tenderly every night would understand and accept her, but she couldn't be certain.

She had almost told him several times since Jarl Eirik's departure, most recently when he had seen her arguing with Cedric earlier that day. Perhaps it was time to stop wondering about his reaction and let him know the truth. Whatever he decided, she would have to be strong enough to accept. She could not keep lying to the man she loved.

Placing a kiss on the back of Wilfrid's hand, she laid it gently on his chest and let herself out of his chamber. To her surprise, one of the warriors stood there. 'Good afternoon, Ealdred. Have you seen my husband? I would have a word with him.'

He appeared hesitant, his mouth opening and closing before he finally said, 'He has sent me to bring you to him.'

She paused at the odd phrasing. 'Where is he?'

'The hall, my lady.' He stepped back to let her pass, but then he fell into step behind her and she had the oddest sensation that he was escorting her like a guard would a prisoner.

Glancing back at him, she asked, 'Is something the matter?'

'I...' He hesitated again, his gaze darting to the closed doorway that led to the hall. 'I could not say, my lady.'

A shiver of unease ran down her spine. Something had happened while she sat with Wilfrid and it seemed as if everyone knew it but her. The other warrior guarding the door would not meet her gaze.

'Let me in.' Her voice came out a whisper.

The door opened and she stepped inside, fixing a smile on her face to greet her husband. Nothing could have prepared her for what she found inside. Rurik was standing near the hearth, his face ragged and filled with a pain she had never seen there. At his side stood a man who appeared vaguely familiar. From his hair to his clothing, she immediately judged him to be Norse.

He knew her, too. He stared at her with a look of recognition tinged with loathing. It wasn't until she stepped closer, the doors closing behind her, that she remembered. He was the Norseman from the longhouse in Maerr. The one who had tried to fight Lugh when he attacked and killed the pregnant woman. The one who had fought her and marked her.

A quick glance at Rurik confirmed that he knew everything.

# *Chapter Twenty-Two*

A cold heat travelled down her spine and prickled over her skin. In an instant, she knew how things would go. Rurik would never understand. How could he? Her decision to keep her presence in Maerr from him was unforgivable. Nevertheless, the sudden pain that settled deep in her heart at the thought of losing him meant that she had to try to talk to him.

The look the younger Norseman gave her was so full of loathing that it was very nearly palpable where it touched her. Rurik's was hardly any better. A pressure held her chest tight.

'Rurik, please allow me to explain.'

'Yes, explain to me how all this time you have not told me about going to Maerr.' His voice was bitter and cold like she had never heard it. Even in the cell below, there had been a heat present as he had used his words to spar with her.

The frigidness caught her breath, as if she had jumped into a mountain lake soon after the spring thaw. 'I wanted to tell you, but—' She broke off. She would not use Cedric as an excuse. It was true that he had told her not to mention it, but it had been her decision to heed his warning. 'In the beginning, I was afraid that you might harm me.'

That only made his brow crease with contempt, so she raised her hands. 'Only in the beginning. I know now that you would never harm me… Not physically. I wanted to tell you on our wedding night, but you bid me to be silent.' When he jerked his head away, she was afraid he would think she was blaming him. She dropped her hands and clasped them together in front of her to keep from reaching for him. He would not welcome her touch now, maybe not ever again. The sense of loss welling inside her would soon become unbearable.

'Perhaps I should have forced the issue. But then Jarl Eirik came and there was so much to overcome that the timing didn't seem to be right. Glannoventa needed you and I could not risk you leaving. Please believe that I planned to tell you…' Her voice trailed off as she realised how pitiful her excuses sounded. To him there was no reason that would justify her continued silence. Not one that he would accept. Her silence on the matter had wounded him deeply. She could see that now.

He did not look at her when he spoke next. His furious gaze stared into the fire. 'You plotted to kill my family, Annis.'

Her palms itched to touch him and soothe his hurt. She wanted to curl her fingers in his hair and stroke down his back the way she knew he liked. 'It is true that I wanted revenge for Grim's death.' And that she had been in deep mourning for both him and her son.

'But I only wanted Sigurd to pay for his crimes. I never wanted anyone else to get hurt.'

It seemed foolishly innocent now that she could have believed there would be no danger to anyone but Sigurd. In hindsight she could see that her grief had not allowed her to think rationally, but even that was no excuse. She had picked her path and she had no choice but to accept the consequences.

'Lie.' This was from the younger Norseman.

'Sandulf?' she asked.

He gave a curt nod. 'You remember me. You remember that I was there when you and your assassin butchered Ingrid.'

Nausea roiled in her stomach. She had tried so hard to forget that day, that poor woman's scream of pain when Lugh had descended upon her. '*I* did no such thing.'

She looked back at Rurik to find him watching her with interest, so she directed her explanation to him. Whether Sandulf believed her or not, she did not care. She only needed Rurik to believe that she would not have slaughtered an innocent.

'It is true we were at the wedding. I thought the plan was to wait until after, to find Sigurd in seclusion and confront him. The battle started outside and then someone closed the doors to the hall and the whole place erupted in fury. We were not the only ones there that day who wanted Sigurd's death. But the assassin I was with, Lugh, had another target in mind. I lost sight of him in the chaos, but when I saw him again, he went straight for the woman. I swear to you that I did not know who she was before that day. I had no vengeance in my heart for her. Lugh was paid only for

Sigurd. It was as if a demon had come to life within him and spurred him towards her. As soon as I saw, I went after him and tried to stop him.'

'But you didn't stop him,' Sandulf said, stepping closer.

Facing him, she said, 'I tried. You have to believe that I did not want her death.' Stepping towards Rurik, she continued, 'Or the death of her child. Rurik, you must know how the pain of my own loss haunted me. I would never have agreed to do harm to a mother and her unborn.'

Rurik merely stared at her, the coldness in his eyes chilling her to her bones.

'You attacked me.' Sandulf's voice rose, refusing to give up his accusations.

'Only to defend myself when you came for me. I tried to stop Lugh and you attacked me, then you attacked Lugh.' In her memory, the next several moments of the battle were a blur. She knew that Lugh had pushed her away roughly, knocking her into a wall so hard that she had become disorientated. Sandulf had attacked Lugh, but the assassin had been bigger and stronger. She had run towards them both and somehow had ended up on the floor with Sandulf above her, carving her wound, before she had twisted away and Lugh had pulled her along as they fled the longhouse.

Sandulf's brow twisted in confusion as he considered her words.

'Is it as she says?' Rurik asked and she held her breath for Sandulf's answer.

'Perhaps. I did not see her attack Ingrid, but she

was there beside the assassin,' he answered, latent anger in his voice.

'To pull him off her!' Annis argued. 'She was never part of the plan.'

Rurik looked away again, not listening, and she could hardly blame him. What did her intention matter when the result was that innocents had been killed? She closed her eyes briefly against the pain that lanced through her. Her chest squeezed so tight that she could hardly draw breath. This was how it felt to lose him. It was like losing Grim all over again, only worse. Fresher, and this time like a double-edged blade, because she had caused this all on her own.

'Where is this Lugh?' Rurik asked, drawing her gaze to him. 'Where can we find him?'

She paused, hesitating because she had hoped to put this behind her. She did not want to be the cause of more death and pain.

'Tell me.' Rurik stepped closer to her. Fury vibrated off him, the force of it very nearly tangible.

'I do not want to cause more death. Please let this be the end of it, Rurik.' She touched his forearm and he jerked it away as if her touch had burned him or was too abhorrent to bear. A fresh wave of agony rolled over her, nearly taking her to the ground.

'Tell me, Annis.' He spoke through clenched teeth. 'Tell me or I will have you committed to the cell below instead of your chamber.'

Whether he would follow through with that or not, she could not say. She knew that she deserved his fury, but that did not help her accept it any easier. The shard of pain his words brought drew a gasp from her as she took a step back. 'He has chosen to take his vows and repent his sins.'

'Where has he gone to repent these sins?' Sandulf spoke with a thread of mockery lacing his voice.

Rurik did not speak, but his cold eyes were frozen on her, letting her know that he would not accept anything less than the man's location.

Swallowing past the ache in her throat, she said, 'A monastery in Nrurim. It's in the Strathallen Valley.'

Rurik and Sandulf exchanged a dubious look.

'What more can you tell us of what happened in Maerr? If you did not plan to kill Ingrid, then why would Lugh go after her?' asked Sandulf. He still looked as if he would prefer to mete out physical punishment rather than talk to her.

Rurik seemed finished talking to her. He had crossed his arms over his chest and his face was impassive. Tears burned the backs of her eyes, but she refused to let them fall.

'I have asked myself that many times. The way he went for her…it seemed intentional. It was almost as if he knew her. The only thing I remember is that he disappeared from our camp the night before the wedding. I slept poorly that night and woke up to see that he was gone. He had returned by morning.'

'So he could have met with someone,' Sandulf concluded.

'It is possible.'

Sandulf nodded, but his thoughts had turned inwards, probably working through what might have happened. She looked to Rurik. It frightened her that the pain she had seen on his face earlier had gone to be replaced by this impassive stranger she did not recognise.

Hoping that this time he might accept her touch, she raised her hand to his cheek. 'Please give me a chance to—'

'Leave us.' He jerked his face away from her fingers.

The pain in her heart turned to a sort of panic. She feared that if she walked out the door, she would never see the man she loved again. That he would be replaced by this stranger. 'Rurik, I love you. We can—'

'Go.' He did not raise his voice, but the word brooked no argument. 'Do not attempt to leave Mulcasterhas. I haven't decided what to do with you yet.'

Despite her best attempt, a hot tear escaped to run down her cheek. He despised her. She loved him beyond reason and he hated her. If there was a worse punishment, she could not imagine it.

The next several days passed in a haze for Rurik. He tried to turn his attention to planning with Sandulf. They would go north to find Lugh as soon as the weather allowed. He could not bring himself to think of Annis or even contemplate how to deal with her. He had not confined her to her chamber, but he should have. The few times he passed her in the corridor had nearly crushed him, leaving his chest hot and tight. The pain of her betrayal was still fresh and nearly too much to bear; to deal with it he threw himself into training his warriors and plotting.

So he had thought that he loved her and she had betrayed him. What of it? Hadn't he learned that betrayal was the way of the world? He should have learned it well before Annis.

'Here. I found them.' Cedric's voice rang through the hall as he walked through the open doorway, several rolled parchments in his hands. 'I had to search many chests, but I believe these are what you need.'

Rurik rose from his place at the end of the table, deftly avoiding looking towards Annis's empty bench. She took her meals in Wilfrid's chamber and he told himself that he preferred it that way. It was easier not to see her than to see her and still want her despite her lies.

'Why would maps of the north be so difficult to find?' he asked as Cedric laid them on the table which had recently been cleared from the evening meal. A meal that he had barely touched. Everything sat heavy in his stomach lately, so he had taken to sipping on mead and water.

Cedric shrugged. 'Our troubles have been from the south and to the east. Alba and the Picts have been too absorbed with their own troubles to bother us.'

Sandulf stood on his other side, rolling out the first one. 'You're certain these are accurate?'

Cedric shrugged again. 'They are decades old. No one from Glannoventa has been there in ages. I am certain there are villages not contained here.'

Rurik searched the map whose ink had faded with time. His fingers ran over the smooth vellum as he searched the writings trying to make out the names. 'Where is Nrurim? I do not see it marked.'

Cedric leaned over it, frowning before unrolling the other two only to find similar results. 'This is the Strathallan Valley.' He pointed to an area inland, dragging the pad of his finger in a slow sweep. 'I believe it to be here.'

They spoke for a long while about its potential location and the best direction from which to approach given the landscape. He hoped the weather would clear enough in a matter of weeks. Rurik told no one this, but he did not know if he would return after finding Lugh. The pain of being near Annis and not having her was more than he was willing to bear. But he could not have her knowing that she had lied to him. He had allowed himself to believe that she might be coming to love him and it had nearly made him crumble to hear her say it the last time they had spoken. However, he could not imagine her keeping such a secret from him if her love was true. His own parents' affair had been built on the lie of love and look where it had got them. Saorla had died bitter and heartsick.

He realised that he had allowed himself to become absorbed in his own thoughts when Sandulf stood to seek his bed. Bidding him goodnight, he moved to follow, but Cedric stayed him with a hand on his shoulder.

'A moment?' asked Cedric.

'What do you need?'

'Annis,' he said, offering no further explanation.

Rurik tensed, unwilling to have a conversation about her. 'Sandulf knew of her guilt. She had no way of keeping it secret any longer.'

The man looked down at his hand where it had fallen to rest on the table. 'I want to confess to you that I knew of her involvement. She told me the night she took you prisoner from the village. I advised her not to tell you.'

Rurik gritted his teeth. 'I assumed that you had.' It was no surprise that Cedric knew.

'Then why are you not angry with me?'

'Because Annis is my wife. She spoke vows to me and then continued to lie to me. That was her choice. I know her well enough to know that she would have done what she wanted had she disagreed with you. It was her choice not to tell me.'

Cedric surprised him by smiling. 'That much is true. She makes up her own mind, which is how she ended up in Maerr to begin with. Had I known that she planned to go there, I would have stopped her.'

Rurik was surprised at the intensity of the surge of anger that pulsed through him. Yes, he was angry at her betrayal, but he thought he had come to a sort of unwilling acceptance of it. Yet speaking of it only raked across the raw wound, like pulling clothing on over sunburned skin. 'What have you come to say? If you have come to ask me to forgive her then you waste your breath.' Rurik ground his molars together.

Cedric's expression sobered. 'I have not come to seek your forgiveness, only your understanding. Annis has cared for Glannoventa since she was a young girl. Having always known that she would be lady here one day, she came to see the people as her responsibility from the beginning.'

'Yes?' Rurik was inclined to leave, not wanting to subject himself to the torture of talking about her, but something made him stay. Likely it was the same thing that made him pause to take an extra breath when he passed through an area where she had recently walked. A part of him that he was coming to despise had a deep hunger for her, no matter how she had betrayed him.

'In the summer we have a fair in the village. There are warrior contests and games for children. Merchants come from far places to sell their trinkets.'

'What is your meaning, Cedric? The hour is late.' Rurik was not inclined to sit and listen to the man ruminate any longer than necessary.

The lines around Cedric's mouth deepened, but he continued. 'The first time Annis went, she was eight winters, perhaps nine, and Wilfrid promised that he would buy her one trinket of her choosing. She walked from stall to stall, taking her time. I know because I was tasked with following her. Finally, she decided on something… I cannot remember what it was. I handed over a coin and she promptly ran to deliver it into the arms of a village child who stood there bedraggled and obviously unkempt.'

Rurik stood. 'I do not have time for this.'

Cedric came to his feet and followed when Rurik walked towards the door. 'There are many more examples of her sense of responsibility to them. Several years ago, before Grim's death, the village was struck by a sickness. At risk to her own health, she kept the fires working day and night to provide broth and pottage to the sickly, taking it herself in cases where the matron of the family had been struck down. I could also tell you of the times she stood in Wilfrid's stead, successfully mitigating disputes between families that go back decades—'

Finally having had enough, Rurik interrupted him. 'Yes, I am aware of her loyalty to the people of Glannoventa. What does that have to do with her betrayal?'

'It is because of her loyalty that she withheld the truth. We were all afraid of what might happen if the Danes installed their man here. Jarl Eirik can be fair—in his own way—but Dane interests are not our interests. He would be an outsider.'

'I am an outsider,' Rurik was fast to point out.

'But you are not under Jarl Eirik's thumb. You are your own man. From what I have learned, you are beholden to no one but yourself.'

'And my family.' He did not know whether to be insulted by Cedric's words or gratified by them.

'Your family is scattered. You have no home but Glannoventa now. Whether you accept it or not, Glannoventa's interest is your interest.'

'Is that why you were so quick to choose me for Annis, because you thought I would so easily put myself under *your* thumb?' And hadn't he put himself under Annis's thumb? A new surge of anger at how easily he had been deceived by her threatened to make him drive his fist into the next man who dared to cross his path.

Cedric backed down, shaking his head. 'Not under my thumb. Because you were your own man and I knew that you would be fair to our people. Also, because Annis chose you. I had not seen her come to life in years. But she was alive with you.'

'It did not stop her from betraying me.'

Cedric glared at him. 'She argued with me many times about that. You can blame me if you want.'

'I'll blame the person responsible. Annis,' he put in before Cedric continued as if he hadn't spoken.

'But she did not tell you because of her loyalty to them.' He gestured towards the village below the walls of Mulcasterhas. 'We even argued about it the morning your brother arrived.'

So that had been the argument Rurik had witnessed between them. It was good to know, but it hardly changed anything.

'I say this so that you understand her motive. Give it time before you harden yourself to her. She does not deserve your hatred.'

'I will decide that,' said Rurik, walking around Cedric and out of the hall. He was surprised to find Sandulf there waiting for him and stopped short. From his brother's expression, it was obvious he had heard the exchange.

'If you want her, you can still have her, Brother. Know that I will not see it as a betrayal,' said Sandulf, his voice low and solemn.

'How could you not? She brought those killers to our door.' It was the one thing Rurik kept coming back to when he felt himself wanting to soften towards her.

'Wilfrid paid them. They were coming regardless of her presence.'

'You spoke with Cedric?'

Sandulf nodded. 'Yesterday. I wanted the details, to try to understand. I am not saying that I forgive her, or that I can ever forgive her, but I understand her side of it. Things can quickly go beyond our control. I have seen it happen more than once and I believe her when she says she did not intend Ingrid harm.'

Rurik ran a hand through his hair, the familiar tug on his scalp grounding him when anger and heartache wanted to take over. 'I already believe that she didn't intend harm to Ingrid, but that hardly changes the result.' Or that she had lied to him.

'I've been thinking more about that day. When I confronted the assassin… Lugh, Annis came between us briefly. He pushed her down, but the distraction was enough to give me time.'

'Are you saying that she might have saved you?'

'She helped.' Sandulf shrugged one shoulder. 'I will leave her fate to you. Forgive her or punish her — whatever you decide, it is obvious to me that you care for her.'

Rurik felt as if a great, depthless pit opened in his stomach, threatening to swallow him whole. He truly did not know if he could forgive her. The need for vengeance had existed inside him for so long that he could not see his way forward without it. There had been a time with her when he had thought it might be possible.

But not now. Not knowing that she had been involved and had chosen not to tell him. He didn't know if he was capable of forgiving her.

## Chapter Twenty-Three

Wilfrid died in the small hours of the morning a few weeks later. Annis and Cedric were at his side. Annis had felt helpless in her bedside vigil, watching the man who had become a father to her struggle to draw air or even know where he was. He had been labouring to breathe for a while, so his passing came as no surprise and even as a relief. In the days that followed, the household and all of Glannoventa went into mourning.

Whatever Rurik felt at Wilfrid's passing, she did not know. He had come to Wilfrid's chamber the morning of his death to express his sorrow to Cedric and Annis for their loss, but no other words had been spoken. He had not spoken to her since. She longed for him to take her in his arms and help ease the pain of Wilfrid's loss, but she knew now that it was impossible. She had been given a chance at happiness and had lost it. The affection her husband had felt for her was well and truly gone. It was this certainty that gave her the strength after Wilfrid's death to make the decision she knew would be best for them all.

Sandulf was leaving to go north in the morning.

While Rurik had initially planned to go with him, Wilfrid's death had changed everything. Although Wilfrid had been interred, a more formal ceremony was planned in a few weeks when the Jarl and other lords could attend to pay their respects. Rurik would officially be named Lord of Glannoventa at that time, so leaving was impossible.

It was late in the evening as she made her way to the hall where Rurik had closed himself up with his brother to make final preparations. She gave a brisk knock and let herself inside without waiting for their summons. The men stopped talking and looked up at her from their places at the table. A quick glance confirmed that they were alone.

'A word, if you please.' She made certain to keep her shoulders back and her chin up, but she had to clear her throat to control the tremor in her voice. Both men stood and Sandulf made as if to leave. 'Please stay. I brought this for you.'

Walking to the table, she handed him a rolled vellum she had prepared. His brows drew together in confusion as he took it from her. 'It is an accounting of the events in Maerr as I remember them, including Lugh's involvement. I've signed my name and affixed our seal on the chance that it might prove useful to you.'

His eyes widened in surprise as his fingers closed around it. 'Thank you,' he mumbled, glancing down at the vellum. When he met her gaze again, his eyes were not filled with disgust. It was progress.

'Please be careful when you approach him,' she said. 'He was a dangerous man when I knew him.

If he is insincere in his repenting, then you cannot trust him.'

Sandulf gave her a nod of agreement, seemingly at a loss for words. The vellum wasn't much, but it had been the only thing she could think to do to help him in his journey. It didn't absolve her of her guilt, but she hoped it would help him.

Turning her attention to Rurik, his stony expression nearly made the wobble in her voice come back. 'I have come to a decision and would like to discuss it with you.'

'*You* have come to a decision? Isn't it I who am weighing how to deal with you?' asked Rurik.

The comment smarted, so she ignored it. From the corner of her eye, she could see Sandulf making his way around the table to leave them alone and this time she did not try to stop him. If she was to receive a chastisement, she would rather it happen in private. With nothing left to hold on to, her fingers fumbled with the hem of her sleeve.

'If you have a punishment in mind, then I'd like to hear it, but I doubt that you do since you haven't come forward with it yet.'

'Perhaps I am biding my time.' His voice was flat, as if she meant nothing to him, and her heart clenched with the knowledge. This is exactly why she had avoided him.

'I have a solution in mind if you would hear me out,' she said.

He paused a few heartbeats before inclining his head.

'I think it best that one of us leave. Since you are now Lord, it obviously should be me. I do not want to put Glannoventa in jeopardy and any strife between us could do just that. Not only could it make us appear weaker to any enemies who may seek to prey on us, but I believe it will lead to confusion for everyone. I have already heard rumours that there is talk in the village about our discontent.' Not to mention the fact that she could not survive being this near to him and having him hate her. Every day that passed was like another twist of the dagger in her heart.

'Where will you go?' His voice was nearly quiet.

'I have an older sister near Wexborough where I was born. I can go there.' She had seven brothers and sisters of all different ages. She had not seen most of them since coming to Wilfrid as a child, but she had no doubt that this was the best way forward. Anything was better than facing Rurik's indifference. She would float from household to household if she had to.

He seemed to be weighing her words, before he spoke. 'Cedric told me at some length how much you value your position here. You would leave that behind?'

Unable to withstand the blandness of his gaze, she feigned interest in the map laid open on the table. 'I cannot pretend my reasons are unselfish… I do want what's best for Glannoventa and, barring any sort of reconciliation, I believe this is it.'

'And how is that selfish?'

Was it her imagining it or did his voice sound closer? Treacherous tears burned her eyes, so she did not dare look back at him to check. Swallowing several times against the lump in her throat, she said, 'That part isn't.' Damn tears. She would *not* cry before him.

'Then which part is?' His voice was too low to make out any sort of intonation.

'The part that cannot bear staying here knowing that I lost you.' A strangled gasp tore out of her as she tried and failed to hold back her tears. She turned to run, but he was standing in front of her. *Right there* in front of her with scarcely a breath between them. She sucked in a gulp of air, her fingernails biting into her palms to distract her and stop more tears from falling.

'You lied to me.' His voice shook from emotion, but she did not know if it was anger or something else. His eyes burned with it.

'I am sorry I didn't tell you.' The way he was looking at her…it was as if he wanted to devour her. A tender ache bloomed inside her, but she didn't know if the change in his eyes was her imagining his change in sentiment towards her. 'I don't know how to make it right, but you should not suffer any longer. Take Glannoventa. Take Mulcasterhas. Take everything and know that I will live my life being sorry for how I hurt you. I have already arranged an escort with Cedric. I leave in the morning.'

His eyes widened in shock and she used his moment of stunned silence to dart past him. Praying that she would reach the privacy of her chamber before she dissolved into a mass of tears, she ran as fast as she could.

Annis was leaving. She was giving up the only thing that mattered to her to atone for her lie. To help the people she loved so much. Sigurd had lied more times than Rurik could count, but he had lied only for his selfish gain. To gain Saorla. To gain wealth. To gain power. Never, to Rurik's knowledge, had he lied to protect anyone but himself. Annis had been willing to tell the truth, but not if that truth would bring potential harm to her people.

Their lies were not created equal. Rurik could not consider them with an equal level of contempt. Perhaps by treating them the same, he was being unfair. The realisation left him momentarily dazed. It only took a few heartbeats to come to his senses, but it was enough time for Annis to slip by him and out the door.

'Annis!' he called to her as he followed behind her, but the sound of his voice only seemed to make her run faster. The knowledge that she intended to lock him out spurred him on, his strides eating up the distance so that he reached her door as she was shutting it behind her.

'Let me in, Annis.' He shoved his foot between the door and frame just in time to keep it from shutting him out, but he couldn't quite hold in a grunt as pain shot across his foot and up his ankle.

'Go away!' she cried, putting all her weight against the door. It was no use, because he had managed to wedge his shoulder into the opening and make it wider. She stumbled away in dismay, her eyes wet and miserable.

He forced the door closed behind him harder than he had intended. The harsh slam reverberated in the still room. 'You will not leave in the morning or any other morning.' By the gods, the very thought of her gone away from him for ever made him grow cold.

'I cannot stay.' She brought the back of her hand to her mouth as she sucked in a trembling breath, her chest heaving as she struggled to contain her obvious pain. 'Rurik, please do not force that on me.'

Watching her and the physical manifestation of her hurt and sorrow play across her face made the nearly unbearable pressure that had been building inside him every day they were apart break open. It splintered inside him, leaving him shaken and weak. He walked towards her, but it became more of a stalking because she backed up with every step until she came up against the wall and could move no farther.

'Consider it your punishment,' he said, hardly recognising his own voice.

Anguish slashed across her features, but she was able to hold back more tears as she drew her chin up. 'Think of the people who count on us. This is not in their best interest. I cannot stay here and cause conflict. I will not.'

Rurik put his hands to the wall on either side of her, leaning close. 'You do not have a choice, Wife. You will stay here and let me love you every day for the rest of our lives.' He did not realise how much he meant those words until they were hanging in the space between them.

Her eyes widened with hope which she quickly suppressed, sending a pang shooting through him. He cupped her jaw, his thumb tracing the ridge of her lower lip. 'You see, I find that I cannot live without you.'

'Rurik...do you mean...?' Her voice trailed off as if afraid to hope.

'I know now you didn't mean for that to happen in Maerr. Not at first... I let my anger decide, but after the anger wore off, I knew. And still I couldn't get past the betrayal that you had lied to me.'

'I shouldn't—'

He pressed his thumb to her lips to quiet her. 'I understand why you did. If I'm being honest, I don't know how I would have reacted had you told me before the wedding. I know that I wouldn't have gone through with it. At least not right away.'

Against the pad of his thumb, she said, 'If Jarl Eirik hadn't been on his way…'

The corner of his mouth pulled upwards. 'If he hadn't been on his way, there would have been no need for us to wed in such haste. I can't forget that, or how glad I am that we wed.'

'Do you mean that?'

'Yes, only I didn't let myself admit it until tonight. Until you were willing to give up everything important to you for me.' His hands slid into her hair so he held her precious face between his palms.

'I love you, Rurik.' A tear slipped out of the corner of her eye and he caught it with his lips. 'I don't want to hurt you and I don't want Glannoventa to suffer. If you want me to go—'

'Shh…' His heart filled up at her words. 'Stay. In my bed. In my life. In my heart. Stay with me.' His lips brushed kisses across the crest of her cheekbone and down to her mouth, light touches that had him craving more of her.

She let out a sob and he covered her mouth with his. She kissed him back until they were both breathless and her fingers were tangled in the hair at the nape of his neck. 'Are you certain you can forgive me?' she whispered.

A hand ran down her back to pull her soft body close to him, needing to feel every part of her against him like a starving man. He took in her earnest gaze, golden in the soft candlelight. 'These past weeks have been torture. I don't want to live without you, Annis. From this day forward, nothing comes between us again. Swear it to me.'

Giving him a slow smile full of the hope she had tried to suppress until now, she rose up and kissed him again. 'I swear it.' Her fingers tightened in his hair almost painfully, but he wanted the pain if it meant that she was touching him again. 'Every moment of every day you will know exactly what I feel and what I am thinking because I won't stop talking about how much I love you.'

He laughed at that as she had meant him to and twirled around with her in his arms. They landed on the bed. She giggled in a way that he had never heard from her before as she pushed herself back so that he could crawl over her. He stared down at her in awe, wondering what else this woman he had married had in store for him. But he didn't get to wonder for long, because she wrapped her arms around him and pulled him over her, her mouth taking his in a plundering kiss that left him breathless and craving more.

His hands went between them. First to her breasts, skating over her rigid nipples, and then down to the skirt of her gown, tugging the fabric upwards in a suddenly desperate bid to feel her bare flesh against his. Her touches became frenzied as she roughly pulled his tunic up. He was forced to let her go to tug it off over his head. By then her fingers had found the fastenings of his trousers and slipped inside to grasp him. He was already so hard with his need for her that her touch drew the breath from his lungs. Gasping for air, he tugged at her skirts, not bothering to take off the rest of his clothing. His need to make them one, to make them whole again, overrode any thoughts of prolonging their pleasure.

'Hurry,' she whispered as she guided his length to her.

'Annis,' he groaned when he felt how slippery and hot she was for him. Easing inside her bit by bit, he laughed when she arched her hips, desperate for the same thing he wanted. Taking her hands, he laced his fingers with hers and held them pressed to the bed above her head as he entered her in one long and deep stroke, until their hips were pressed together. Her ragged sigh of gratification filled his ears. He stared down into her golden eyes, slightly unfocused now with pleasure.

'I love you, Wife,' he whispered, knowing with certainty that she would hold his heart until the end of time.

He moved in a soft rhythm, filling her up and then drawing away, loving the way he fit inside her. Her inner muscles gripped him as if she was made for him, as if she never wanted to let him go. He loved her with his body until they both came, shattering into a thousand tiny pieces that slowly came back together, creating something that was both stronger and more resilient than either of them had ever been separately.

# *Epilogue*

*Several months later*

Rurik pushed open the shutters to allow the warm morning sunlight into Wilfrid's bedchamber. The man had been gone for months, but Annis had only recently shown an interest in going through his personal things. Rurik hadn't pressed the issue, wanting to give her time to mourn. As a result, the chamber had been closed up ever since Rurik had ordered the various parchments and implements removed that would prove important to him in an official capacity.

She knelt on the floor beside a small chest she had just pulled out from beneath Wilfrid's bed. Leaning against the wall, he revelled in watching her. Her auburn hair shimmered like flames in the sunlight where it cascaded down her back. He had convinced her to leave it down as they worked, loving the ability to reach over and lose his fingers in it as he wanted.

Becoming aware of him, she glanced up and blushed at the look he was giving her. 'You don't have to stay. I know you have things to do.'

'Nothing more important than you.'

She gave a knowing smile and resumed riffling through the chest, metal clinking as she lifted items out and sorted them on the floor beside her. 'I'm certain you mentioned going into the village with Danr this morning to assess the storm's damage to the port.'

Danr had surprised them by arriving some time ago after having heard of Rurik's marriage. Rurik had been gratified at how his twin had accepted Annis, not questioning Rurik's desire to stay with her despite their past. The last several months had been some of the best of his entire life. He finally felt as if he had a place to belong. A home.

'He's only just returned from his morning ride and is breaking his fast. We'll leave after, which means we have time to retire to our chamber for a bit,' he said suggestively.

She wasn't paying him any attention, having unwrapped a trinket that had been tied with a leather thong and bundled in heavy wool. He frowned at how she ignored him and made his way to her to press his case. Twin lines marred the skin between her brows as she turned what looked to be an arrow-shaped trinket over in her hands to examine it.

Curious, he came down on to his haunches beside her and asked, 'What have you found?'

'I confess I have no idea.' She turned it over again. 'I've never seen it, but it seems foreign. Could it be from the Danes?'

A shock of recognition shot through him as she presented it to him. It was an arrowhead pendant made of gold with notches cut into the sides. A simple enough trinket, except the ridged line down the middle was made of silver. Hilda, his father's wife, had possessed one very similar. Sigurd had gifted it to her with the birth of one of her sons. If the idea wasn't so impossible, Rurik would have said this was it. It looked just like it, however. He knew because he had looked upon all the pendants, one for each son, with hatred for many years after his mother's death. He realised now that jealousy and resentment that Sigurd hadn't presented his own mother with such fine trinkets upon the birth of the twins had been behind the hatred.

'You know what it is?' she asked.

He shook his head, still not daring to believe, but unable to deny that it was an exact replica if it wasn't the same one. 'How long would he have possessed this?'

Her hand touched his shoulder in silent support, sensing that something was very wrong. 'I am not certain. At least several years. He hasn't left Glannoventa since Grim's death. You recognise it?'

'Yes, but it can't be.' Propelled to his feet, Annis followed him as he made his way to the hall to find Danr. He had to show him so his brother could tell him he was mistaken. That he was wrong in his memory.

Since Wilfrid's death, more tables had been brought in and the hall had been opened up to Rurik's warriors so that at any given time of day there were always several men partaking of mead and food. He found Danr easily at the main table in deep discussion with Alder. The two had formed a friendship since he'd arrived.

Leofe stood, refilling his tankard of mead, which had barely been touched, with a look of longing on her face that might have been comical had Rurik not felt very badly for her repeated and thwarted efforts to seduce Danr. Like all the brothers, Danr had changed in the years since the murders, in his case becoming more serious and seemingly less inclined to indulge himself where women were concerned. To Rurik's knowledge he had gone to bed alone every night since coming to Glannoventa.

Taking a seat beside Danr, he waited for the girl to make her way to another table before holding out the pendant. 'What do you make of this?'

Danr stared at the arrow resting on Rurik's palm for the space of a heartbeat before his eyes widened in recognition. His fingertip came up to float over the silver ridge. 'It looks like one of Hilda's.' Brows drawing together, he said, 'You don't think it is?'

They both stared at it, momentarily dumbstruck.

'How could it come to be in Wilfrid's possession?' Rurik asked.

Annis again put her hand on his shoulder, drawing his gaze to her. 'Wilfrid said that someone approached him about Sigurd…back when the Norse were here, before Grim's death.' She took a breath as if hesitant to voice what he knew she would say. 'I assumed he meant Lugh, but perhaps someone…whomever approached him about Sigurd…gave it to him then.'

Rurik looked from Annis to his brother. Danr stared back at him, both of them knowing that if anyone had access to Hilda's jewellery it would be someone close to the family.

Could that person have helped plot the massacre?

Danr picked up the arrowhead, staring at it for a moment more before closing his hand around it. 'I need to take this to Sandulf. He can verify if it is the one that belonged to Hilda.'

If anyone would know, it would be Sandulf. 'Let me know what you need and I'll have supplies packed to go with you.'

The quest to avenge their family was now in Sandulf's hands.

* * * * *

*If you enjoyed this story, be sure to read the*
*first book in the Sons of Sigurd miniseries*

Stolen by the Viking
*by Michelle Willingham*

*Don't miss the next stories in the*
*Sons of Sigurd miniseries, coming soon!*

Conveniently Wed to the Viking
*by Michelle Styles*
Redeeming Her Viking Warrior
*by Jenni Fletcher*
Tempted by Her Viking Enemy
*by Terri Brisbin*